(2002)

P9-EGK-581

ANDERSON PUBLIC LIBRARY
ANDERSON, INDIANA
WITHDRAWN

NECTAR

David C. Fickett

A Tom Doherty Associates Book
New York

This is a work of fiction. All the characters and events portrayed in this novel are either fictitious or are used fictitiously.

NECTAR

Copyright © 2002 by David C. Fickett

Quotations from *First Lessons in Beekeeping* by C. P. Dadant are reprinted by permission of Dadant & Son, Inc., Hamilton, Illinois.

All rights reserved, including the right to reproduce this book, or portions thereof, in any form.

This book is printed on acid-free paper.

A Forge Book
Published by Tom Doherty Associates, LLC
175 Fifth Avenue
New York, NY 10010

www.tor.com

Forge® is a registered trademark of Tom Doherty Associates, LLC.

ISBN 0-765-30174-1

First Edition: May 2002

Printed in the United States of America

0 9 8 7 6 5 4 3 2 1

For Liz

&
to the memory
of my father
Stanley W. Fickett
1925–1981

Acknowledgments

First and foremost, I'd like to thank Cindy Thayer for her years of support, encouragement, and friendship. If not for her, I never would have put one word down on paper, let alone enjoy the satisfaction of seeing it in print.

I'd also like to thank the past and present members of the Peninsula Writing Group, especially Thelma White, Joyce Varney, Peggy Bryant, Bettina Dudley, Annaliese Hood, Robert Taylor, Paul Markosian, and Chris Barstow, all of whom are great writers and expert critics.

Thanks to my sisters and brother, who have supported my creative endeavors for years, and special thanks to my mother, Janet Fickett; she always believed in me.

And without the help of my aunt, Shirley Chase, I would still be struggling with horrible first drafts. Her editor's eye is sharp and on target. She has been willing to read anything I've put down on paper, no matter how bad it was. Thank you.

I expressly want to thank Jill Grosjean, who has proven to be a writer's dream agent. Her faith and excitement in my work has kept me going, and without her I truly believe my work would be only a pile of papers on my desk.

Thank you, Stephanie Lane, for wanting my work at Forge, for your editing skills and astute observations and suggestions with this manuscript.

I thank the Powers That Be for my wife, Liz, and my children, Caroline, Samuel, and Israel, who are always patient with me through my many ups and downs.

It is true that until the middle of the last century bees were kept only in a rudimentary fashion, little being known of the natural history of the bee or what went on in the interior of the beehive.

—from FIRST LESSONS IN BEEKEEPING
by C. P. Dadant, c. 1957

PART ONE

Establishing the Colony

The hive is composed of a queen, the mother of all her people; of thousands of workers ... and lastly of some hundreds of males, from whom one shall be chosen as the sole and unfortunate consort of the queen....
                                —from THE LIFE OF THE BEE
                                by Maurice Maeterlinck, c. 1901

One runs chances in buying bees in full colonies . . . the bees are not likely to be of pure stock. . . .
—*from* FIRST LESSONS IN BEEKEEPING
by C. P. Dadant, c. 1957

CHAPTER ONE

Caleb Gilley

1956

The man I believe to have been my father has died. It's a cool Autumn day and my mother and I sit together on the porch, both of us still hearing his last breath, made only hours ago. Ma's in her rocker and I'm in Duffy's. Duffy lived with us all of my life, guiding me as a father guides a son, and loving my mother when no one else could. His heart has stopped. My mother turns to me, dry eyed, puts her hand on mine and says, "I'll cry when I'm sure I have enough tears to make it worth the effort," and then she takes her hand back from mine. "He was more to you and me than you'll ever know," she says. "We have to git him downstair." She stands and goes into the house.

Ma says things like this to me at times, leaving a little mystery behind her as she walks away. I don't know how to take most of what she says. There have always been unspoken words hanging between my mother, Duffy, and me like red apples, too high to reach, and too tempting to forget. Those *un-words* still swing above my head in gusty winds making me wonder. It seems my mother, a nervous little woman, always sweeping, always fussing, always moving away from me before I can reach her, has been moving to avoid something that follows her, or maybe it's only me she moves away from.

Maybe it was her age. She was close to forty when I was born. My sisters and brother were quite a bit older than me. Maybe she'd lost any interest she might have had in raising kids, or my brother's death, when I was still young, ruined her. I don't think I've ever impressed her much. I was never any good at games in school. I was an average student. I couldn't dribble a basketball with any sort of grace. I couldn't bat a ball to save my life. I've been told I have nice eyes, healthy hair, and at about the age of thirteen I started to grow taller than other boys my age, so that I was the tallest in my class. Hair, eyes, height. Those are the few things that make me Caleb, yet they don't make me into anything special.

I work on our farm, cut wood, tend to her bees (if she'll allow it) and take other odd jobs to make ends meet. I like collecting insects, and I know there are men out in the world who make a living studying insects, but Ma has told me there's no future in it. I like to think my father, who left us before I was born, would have pushed me to get an education, would have seen to it that I left these desolate Maine woods to be among the living. Ma always said I was foolish to think of going to college, we couldn't afford it.

Once, Duffy and I were working on cutting up a spruce that stood out back for more than seventy years. It had come down in a winter ice storm. That spring as we cut and piled up the broken, splintered wood, we noticed the rings inside the tree, a thin ring of a dry summer, a thick one from a wet season, a tough knot of stubbornness. And wedged deep into the core of the tree was a ten-inch spike where once someone had driven it. We had just missed it with our saw. It was lying horizontally through the cross section of the wood. The tree had healed over the wound and swallowed the spike completely until it was a part of it. The hidden history of an old tree.

When Ma looks at me during one of our long evenings together, just stares at me, looking for something, I think she looks for the spike that's been wedged into me. Those long looks, and then the shy smile at being caught, have been the only hints that maybe there is a story about me, one she can't tell.

I get up from the rocker and follow Ma into the house. Walter, an old friend of Ma's, is coming through the back door. She puts out her hand to him. "Will you help Caleb bring Duffy down here?" she asks. He nods. I go into the parlor and spread an old dark green bedspread over a sheet of plywood on two saw horses. This is where we will lay Duffy out. I go up the stairs with Walter following me. We go into the bedroom and look at Duff. Ma wouldn't let me cover his face, but she closed his eyes.

"He was a good man," Walter says, close to tears.

"Yes." I swallow hard.

"And you know he and your Ma loved each other since grade school," he whispers. I have heard this before. Where Duffy's wife and my father fit into the story I don't know. Ma will never say.

Walter puts his hands under Duffy's shoulders as I remove the blankets and take Duffy's white, dry feet in my hands. I can't lift him. I can't move. I can't move.

"I don't wanna hear no belly-achin," I can hear my mother saying to me when I was only seven and my brother died. Teddy wasn't right, simple-minded, retarded, but Ma had special feelings for him. He loved her without rules. Still she kept a stiff upper lip as I sat on the hard-packed ground of the drive and cried as the casket was being carried away. She wouldn't go down to the cemetery to see him buried. She blamed herself for his death. He'd died of beestings.

"Come on boy, lift him," Walter says.

I nod and try again. I try not to think about this old man's feet in my hands.

I never knew a dead body could weigh so much. We struggle to keep ahold of Duffy, his body constricted in places like cement. His eyelids open as we near the bottom of the steps. His green eyes, that somehow I seem to have as well. People around Josiahville think Duffy was my father but Duffy said no. I know I should believe him. He was an honest man. Why would he lie?

We manage to get Duffy to the green bedspread, the makeshift altar. We close his eyes again, and struggle to remove his nightshirt.

Ma wanted to lay him out the way she had laid out her mother, the old-fashioned way. She won't have him go to the funeral home in Milbridge. She covers him with a sheet up to his neck. She won't cover his face. I fetch the basin of warm, soapy water from the kitchen and bring it to her. I set it on the table next to where she stands.

"You go on now. I'll do this," she says. She looks at me, parting her lips, about to say something, about to reach into me, pull from me that rusted spike of who I am, but then she stops herself and looks down at Duffy. I back out of the parlor and partially close the door. I watch her slowly fold back the sheet to expose his chest. Her hands shake, but she doesn't cry. Even at the end, when we knew that it would only be hours, she didn't cry.

She looks old. I don't think I ever noticed before. Her dark hair is coiled tight in curls, no gray, but her face is old, with the lines she claims she earned, trudging through a hard life that she's only hinted about. I don't know what roads she's taken to bring her here, bathing the silent body of the man she loved.

Walter waits behind me. I close the parlor door and turn to him. "Was he my dad?" I ask.

"That's somethin' to ask her, not me," Walter says, his face red. He leaves, going out through the kitchen door like he did for years as our hired help.

I hear a truck coming toward the house. I go out onto the porch.

The sun is setting as the truck comes up the winding dirt road to the farm. The road is pink and the trees beyond are outlined with orange. The old pickup is rusted, and in places, a faded blue color. The passenger door is tied closed with wire. Letters that once spelled out Sorensen's Farm, are only a mottled puzzle of white paint and rust. There are corroding pits on the cab where the boys have shot at it when they were drunk. I see Gunnar, the old man, looking like a bulldog with his face twisted into a frown. One black eyebrow spreads across his forehead and the shadow of his nose hangs over his sunken, toothless mouth.

I turn behind me and see my mother's face, expressionless, as she steps out onto the porch and then she goes back into the house. The screen door slaps back against the door frame.

The three Sorensen boys are sitting on the truck bed glaring at me. I know what it is they've come for. They stop the truck in front of the porch in a cloud of dry dust.

"We just heard. When's the funeral?" the old man asks me, slurring his words. I can't speak. My throat is dry.

"Damn fool," the oldest of Gunnar's sons yells and they all laugh. I can see a woman sitting next to the old man. The side of her face is bruised. It plainly brands her as Gunnar's. She's watching the field on the far side of the road. She is pretty and far too young to be Gunnar's woman. His boys were raised without a mother. Noelle died not long after Olaf was born. Gunnar has never remarried but he's somehow always managed to keep a woman around to do the housework, feed the boys, and share his bed.

"It's only a graveside service. Just us," I say as Gunnar raises a bottle to his mouth. He and his boys live on a farm down the road. They're mostly drunkards and vandals. Olaf and I went through school together until he dropped out in the ninth grade.

Erik and Sven are the older brothers, always in trouble with the law.

"We ain't good enough? My dad and Duffy was friends all their lives," Sven, the middle son says. Then Erik, the oldest, laughs and stands up in the truck bed. He points his rifle into the sky and shoots at a bird overhead, missing. The flock of swallows on the roof of the porch swoop up together, startled, they flap and dart in different directions.

"Shit," Erik says and lowers his rifle.

Gunnar gets out of the truck, slaps at Erik's leg and tells him to put the gun down.

"We ain't wanted?" Gunnar asks me. "Duffy and me grew up together. I wanna pay my respects."

"I'll tell Ma. But she's not planning a funeral," I say as Gunnar approaches. There are pieces of food in the corners of his mouth. Stains on his torn T-shirt.

"Tell that old bitch she can go to hell." He points to the house.

"I'll talk to her. Wait out here," I say as I open the door and go inside.

"You git rid of them. I won't have them here," Ma says as I come toward her through the hall into the kitchen.

"Who's going to help me with Duffy?" I ask.

"I will, or ask Abel, git Walter," she says as she turns from me and leans on the sink. Her arms are ropy with veins and coiled hatred for the Sorensens. They aren't the sort of people I like to be with either, but Gunnar was friends with Duffy. Our families have been neighbors for generations. She's indifferent to most of our neighbors, but her feelings are much stronger concerning the Sorensens.

"Walter's old, Ma. I won't ask him for more help. I'll ask Olaf to come back later. Just Olaf. He'll help me dig the grave."

She turns to face me. She shakes her head slowly, looks at the floor. She understands me less than I understand her. She passes by me and heads into the parlor, closing the door.

I go outside.

"Olaf, would you be able to help me tomorrow, with the casket and all?"

"You won't let us come to the service, but you want my boy's help?" Gunnar's face looms in front of me.

"I'll talk to Ma tonight."

"Yeah, I can help ya," Olaf says as he dodges a swing from his father. He jumps up onto the truck bed.

Gunnar spits on the ground, turns, and gets in his truck. As they drive away I see Ma's face behind the lace curtain in the parlor.

She cooks our supper. We eat at the kitchen table and try not to look at the empty chair where Duffy always sat. I look out the kitchen door. Through the screen I can hear the bees coming back to the hives after working all day. They sound softer tonight. They're keeping the excitement of their work to themselves, out of respect to Ma. She has not been to visit them for over a week, but they continue on.

I try to think about my new collections of bugs I've been cataloging during Duffy's illness. I've been labeling the stages of a bee's growth in my journal and pinning perfect specimens of workers, drones, and queen, to one of the boards I've covered with burlap. I don't want to think about Duffy's death, or how Ma will cope without him.

"What do we do now?" she asks, making me focus on her.

She is just finishing up her squash and potato, wiping her plate with a thick slab of bread. She is angry and worried about her days ahead. I've always thought that she has too hard a shell to get hurt by much. Now I'm not so sure. She looks up at me when I don't jump to answer her question.

"I don't know," I finally say and quickly look down at my plate. I can't eat. "I'll work harder, get the place in shape."

"I've built it up and watched it fall again. There ain't no point," she says.

I don't remember this farm ever looking well kept. The barns are dilapidated, and the fields, where the horses and cows had wandered in my mother's day, are choking with poplar and birch. We had a few pigs once but Duffy hated to kill them when the time came, so he sold them and never got any more. Hens were a nuisance, always clucking, squabbling, and shitting. Always burnt-out bulbs in the coops, faulty wiring, fox or weasels raiding them. We rarely got many eggs. Duffy tried his best to take up where my mother's father left off but he'd finally given up. I don't think my mother's disposition helped matters much. It seems like she is always mad about something.

"Any bright ideas?" She stands up, with her plate in her hand, and stomps across the kitchen floor.

"I can plant," is all I say.

"And hire the help and keep them in line? Christ, you ain't even twenty-one yet, still a boy. You don't know nothin' about farmin', or beekeepin', neither." She whirls around at me with a bright glare in her eyes.

"I don't know then."

"You're right you don't know. If you'd taken more than five minutes away from studyin' them worms and flies, so Duffy could teach you somethin', you might know about hard work. You and your goddamned bugs. Well, mister, you better start looking up the ass of something else, 'stead of those bugs."

"I've been reading a lot lately about the bees. I could keep them," I say softly. "We could try to sell honey again, like you used to."

She shakes her head, disappointed, and turns to run water in the sink. I wish that my sisters lived at home, or that we still employed Walter and Royce, or Lois, who watched out for my brother. When I was very small we had several farmhands around and they would dote on Ma, knowing how difficult their life could be when she was mad. Some of them were men Ma had grown up with. When she had to let them go, she bawled like a baby and wouldn't speak to Duffy or me for weeks.

I'm mad at Henry Gilley. Mad at someone I never knew. The man who is supposed to have been my father. He abandoned us before I was born. Ma did the best she could. When he left, she had three other children to take care of, and me on the way. She built up the honey business, ran her own diner. That was before my brother died, before her arthritis got so bad. Now, with Duffy gone, she must be thinking her life is over.

After I help with the dishes, I go into the little room off the hallway at the foot of the stairs, passing by the closed doors of the parlor. This room had once been my grandfather's. It was also where Duffy would come each night to look over the books. It still smells of cherry-cured tobacco. His pipe, carved from bone, still rests on the desk.

I open an old cigar box where I keep my latest finds. Earlier today I found a bright red dragonfly. I work, until I hear Ma go upstairs, pinning the insect into a shadowbox.

At first it was ants, then butterflies, beetles and dragonflies. I kept them in jars when I was young. They'd last a long time but eventually they would crumble, wings falling away from bodies, legs coming off just by breathing on them. I had a whole bookcase, floor to ceiling filled with jars of bugs. I find them in the gardens, in the fields, in spider's webs. I won't kill them just to have them. I wait to find one. Finding them is the fun, the surprise.

I would sit in the schoolroom watching a fly bang and butt its head against a window until I was driven to jump up and open the window to free it. Whenever I saw a fly or a moth trapped in the schoolroom with dull-witted students and a boring teacher I felt letting it free was somehow letting myself free.

I've learned I can preserve the bugs by soaking them in glycerin and water, and drying them on screens laid flat. Duffy taught me how to build shadowboxes where I pin the insects to burlap, under glass. I put the boxes on the walls of my bedroom, write down information about the bug, and put the description next to the box, labeling them like in museums.

When I'm sure that Ma is in bed for the night, I open the cardboard box where she and Duffy kept the farm accounts. I sort through them, not understanding some of the bills, not sure which are paid and which aren't. In the bottom of the box is a plain, unmarked envelope. It's yellowed and shows signs of being handled many times. I open it. It's my grandfather's will, some of it I don't understand, but the most important part I do. It states that all the land, the house, and the farm are to be left in trust for Eugene Gilley's grandson. Why hasn't my mother ever told me this?

I put the document back in the envelope and go out into the hallway. I can think only of the things she has taken from me.

She has always lost her patience with me. She criticizes my insect collection, calls me lazy because I'm not as interested in the farm as she thinks I should be, discourages me from seeing the girls I've dated. The bugs bother her the most. Her father also collected moths, bees, and dragonflies and she tells me he was worthless.

Once when I was eleven, she opened the window in the pantry and a swarm of wasps that had made a home between the screen and the window chased her out through the kitchen and across the lower field where she threw herself into the frog pond until they left her. She seemed to think I had something to do with them living there even though I never collected live insects.

"Caleb, I'm gonna teach you a lesson you'll never forget," she snarled at me after she dragged her soaking body back up the hill to the house. There were ten or more stings on her face. Her lower lip swelled up like a plum. Her black hair was wet, but drying springs were popping back up on her head.

"What'd I do?" I asked.

"Them bugs didn't get in that window by themselves." she said.

I wondered if possibly I was responsible somehow. I had so many things in mustard and peanut-butter jars upstairs that I couldn't be sure. Maybe I'd brought in a live wasp, not realizing. And there was no point in arguing about it, she'd never believe that the wasps had come in on their own.

"Goddamn them! They ain't like my bees. They're mean, can't be tamed," she screamed grabbing me by my collar.

"Now, what's goin' on?" Duffy asked as he came around the corner of the house. Duffy was the peacemaker in the house, a man I liked to think of as my father. But he wasn't. She'd taken my father too. I was sure she was responsible for him leaving us.

"Stay outa this. Caleb's got himself in trouble and he's gonna be punished." She led me into the house and up to my room.

"Get every last one of them little bastards and bring them downstair," she said, pointing to my jars. She slammed the door and I started collecting them. I wasn't sure what she was planning but I knew I wouldn't like it.

I carried down armloads of bottles, jars, and tins of perfect insects that I'd discovered in dusty corners of the barn or under the porch.

I lined them all up on the table.

"Why? What are you going to do to them?" I asked.

"I oughta turn my bees loose on you," she said as she slammed around the kitchen.

"I got a pot of oatmeal on the stove but it needs somethin' for flavorin'," she said. "You like them bugs so much I thought maybe they'd do the trick." She arched one eyebrow up, looking like a pirate. "One at a time, I want you to open each jar and put the little critters in the oatmeal. Stick them down in there good."

"But, why?"

"Better start. Lot of bugs there. You're gonna have to work slow and careful. You might not be done by sundown."

"Why do you want them in the oatmeal?" I asked.

"It tastes better that way." She smiled, leaned back in her chair, and opened a magazine.

I stood in front of the hot oatmeal trying to think how I could save my collection, at least some of them. I looked at her out of the corner of my eye. Her head was down, quickly I snatched a couple of butterflies and a beetle and slipped them into the neck of my shirt. I felt them crumbling their way down to my belly.

With each bug that I pushed into that great big pot of thick glop, I slipped more into my shirt, hoping some would stay intact. Every once in awhile she'd stand up and come to see my progress. When she did I couldn't save the one that was in my palm. Before I put them in I thought of where I'd found them. The large white moth from the chicken coop. The butterfly that Mrs. Gossler found and saved for me. The largest queen bee I'd ever seen. Ma, in one of her calmest moments had brought it to me, uncrushed. Usually, with an old queen, a useless egg-layer, Ma replaces it, killing the old one under her heel. This one, with only a slightly flattened head, had been on my nightstand for well over two years. I begged to keep it.

"Just this one?"

She shook her head.

"This one?" I held a jewel-green dragonfly that I'd found in the swamp. I tasted my salty lips, took my time so that she'd sit back down and I could save more.

When I was done she made me sit down at the table, and for a good half hour she kept me believing that I was going to have to eat the whole horrible mess, bowl by bowl. Before I started crying she held my shoulders and said, "I hope you learned a lesson." And I did. Never to show her what mattered to me most.

I tipped up the bowl and let it crash to the floor; she lifted her hand to strike me.

"Put down your hand, Ginny. No point in hittin' him. He's learned his lesson," Duffy said through the backdoor screen. Ma stomped out of the kitchen, mad at us both, and I got up to clean the mess on the floor.

"She didn't get them all," I said. "I still got some."

"Then you better hide them like they was gold," Duffy said and bent down to help pick up the broken glass.

It was awhile before I let her know I still kept insects. At first I hid them, then Duffy made a shadowbox for me. With him on my side, she held back from saying anything. Some battles she knew she couldn't win.

I can't go up the stairs without seeing Duff again. Ma has put out the candles that she'd lit earlier and placed around the room. It's completely dark. I stumble into the leg of a side table and wait to hear if Ma heard the noise. She must be sleeping, her first night in weeks. I thought she might sit by his body until it was in the ground but maybe she is at last at peace.

I put my hands out ahead of me, to feel my way across the room. I feel the cold in the air that once was Duffy. I touch his face, putting my hand to his cheek for a long time. Then, in the blackness, I can see his face, the deep lines around his eyes, his smile, his green eyes. I can hear him telling me the things he couldn't before. I can smell his pipe and know that this is the closest I will ever come to what I've been told is love.

The drone bee spends its life with only one purpose, to service the queen. New drones are produced in the spring in time to mature for mating with virgin queens. When queens fly to mate, a mandibular-gland pheromone attracts the drones.

—*from* GROLIERS ENCYCLOPEDIA,
c. 1993

CHAPTER TWO

Duff Pendleton

1907–1911

When I first notice Ginny, really notice her, I'm in grade school. She's leanin on the old tire swing me and Sorenson put up for the younger kids. She's smilin like a sunbeam and I know right there I'd like to give it to her but she ain't no more than ten or eleven and I'm just thirteen but I'm a devil. Always had the yearnin, always ready to shoot it off. Have to hide my rithmitic book over it when I watch the schoolteacher swishin her tail round.

Ginny comes from good stock. Her people got lots of land. They ain't stone broke like mine. They got some dairy cows and a house with two floors. After I look her all over I think up a plan and go out to her daddy's place to look for work. All the kids spill out from school and I head to Merritt's farm, ahead of Ginny.

David C. Fickett

I talk to Old Eugene. He hems and haws. Tells me the work's hard. Am I tough enough to do it? Tough as a ox, I say. He knows a big kid like me looks like someone good for workin. He takes me on at his farm. I watch Ginny, tell her I'm hired on now.

It ain't long into my workin when Ginny and me is in the barn.

When I see her milkin them cows I git all stiff. I rub my fly and laugh. She don't mind. I knew right off she got spirit. She's still a kid but knows what's in my trousers and bout the time she asks for it she's gonna git it. But I can wait til she's ready. Besides, we got a cow, too, and they's good for more than just milking. Specially the baby cows. They take hold like they's attached to their own mother's teat.

So I watch and do my work like her old man tell me to. He don't know I got motives at this job. Old Eugene's a mean ol' cuss to most, but he knows I do what he says, even though I slack off when he ain't watchin, and so he don't harangue me none. The old woman ain't so generous. She see me sittin down and fore I know it she got a slop pail or a hatchet in my hands and starts drivin me to work. Ginny see her doin that and she starts up her chirpin like a jay. She's havin her fun watchin me.

I work most on the wood pile. I take my shirt off when those ugly sisters of Ginny's, and the old woman, are somewhere else. I git all sweaty and my muscles tighten up. Ginny walks right up to me. She's just a baby now, only ten years old, she wipes her hand down my back and laps that sweat right off her own hand and then she does the same to my frontside. There's names for girls like to tease. I've heard enough talk about it and that's how I git my best education, listenin to men talk. I git all jittery inside and then up it goes, straining there against my trousers. She laughs, points to it.

She's like that, but I know I should wait on her. She needs to fill out a bit fore I can take any privileges.

You shouldn't be doin that to no man, I say.

You ain't no man, you're a goddamned boy, she says.

I'm thirteen years old and nearly full grown. Some of me is all grown. Don't be startin somethin you ain't ready to finish, I say.

Let me see you finish, she says and bout knocks me over.

You kiddin? I ask.

She shakes her head and them black eyes spark up like hot coals. She takes my hand and leads me behind the outhouse.

Ain't it like milkin? she asks, her pigtails hangin down over her shoulders as she as looks down.

You ever seen one? I ask with my throat all dried up like frog pond bout August time.

I seen Daddy's plenty, she says.

You won't tell no one? I ask.

I'd git a damn lickin if I did, she says.

I start to unhitch my buttons then we hear her Mama callin "Regina!", from the house so she runs around the outhouse and I try to git myself put back in.

Later I see her on the porch eatin a slice of bread. She puts a dollop of her Mama's fresh butter on her finger and rolls it around on lips and tongue and smiles right at me like nobody's business.

The old man keeps after me to git them stalls cleaned and the wood chopped and all the time, he says he wishes he had a boy of his own. I don't think he'd run his own like a nigger, like he does me. I keep on with him cause of Ginny. I think I know what causes him to be so mean, his old woman is about as sorry as a woman could look and I start to wonder if he ain't pokin some other, cause to git under the covers with that old blister would make any man go soft.

He don't usually catch my tricks of slackin off on the job. Sometimes I don't chop all the wood he wants, but I fix up the pile to look like some work's gone on and sometimes I don't milk all the cows. I tell the Missus that they ain't givin enough, or I say I dropped a pailful and she calls me a goddamned fool and slaps me upside the head, but I take it cause I know I've fooled the old hag.

Most afternoons Eugene goes up to the higher gardens, or to work with his bees. Other times he just disappears into thin air and I wonder where he goes. So, I watch him and follow him around the place when he thinks I'm scrubbin the dairy. He heads out to the pasture where he's got some turnip and beets. I stay behind him to be safe. I don't make no sound. Then I see him slappin around his oldest girl, Dora. She's bout as homely as a cartload of assholes, as my pa says. He tells her she's doin a shithole job of things and cuffs her one. I lay low behind the hives and try to listen to the old man above the hummin of the bees.

He hauls Dora's arm and they head toward the grass off to the side of the gardens. He holds her real tight, it looks like, and puts his head tween her tits and starts moving franticlike all over her. He goes down on top of her and pulls up her skirts. She's turnin her head away from his face and not sayin nothin. I git all sick, scared sick in my gut and don't dare move. He opens up her blouse and she's got some pretty bosoms. I hardly believe my own eyes to see them all round and soft but I don't even git myself stiff lookin cause I'm so sickly in my gut. I don't wait long and he's done his business and off her. He's cryin like some child and she's pattin his head and tellin him it's all right, she don't mind, she says. One of the bees has took notice of me and lands on my face. I feel like yelpin and runnin but I don't want to be seen so I just sit there quiet and let the bee look me over. It takes its time too. But Old Eugene has told me best way from gittin stung is to sit still.

Dora and her old man git up and go about like nothing happened, like it's just the same as though they've pulled some potatoes or mowed the hay but I can't stop the sick feelin inside me. I watch the old man head toward the barn, and as soon as the bee gits off me, I hightail it back to the dairy fore he sees me gone. I don't say nothin bout what I saw in the turnip field and so I don't lose my job.

Ginny and me don't meet behind the outhouse after that one day cause I start thinkin on it and know I'd be strung up if my ma or pa ever knew. I steer clear of her for awhile and she stops pesterin me. I only think about her when I'm all alone. I start to think that soon, after eighth grade, I can git done school and work real. I think I might want more time at Merritt's farm or learn my own trade, like farming. My pa is a boatbuilder, but he's about as lazy as can be and don't git much work, and I know I don't want to be no boatbuilder. Farming seems easy if you handle things just right.

Ginny gits on good with the boys at school but most of the girls think she's too mouthy and too much a flirt and I don't think that bothers her none. She don't seem to hold much by another female. She starts to fill out her jumpers by-and-by and I keep my eye on her. She knows I'm watchin her too and she winks or licks her fingers whenever she sees me.

I finish up my eighth grade of schoolin and ask to be kept on full time at the Merritt's farm. The old man says he'll use me as much as he sees fit. He has me work more with Dora, workin with the cows. I don't much like workin with them cows and Dora's got an ugly puss on her, but I keep busy. When I think about her and Old Eugene, I end up feelin sickly.

I'm workin so much Ginny gits jealous. She sits on the grass under the apple tree and then calls me over to the woodpile. Tells me she seen Sorensen's you-know-what at school, says it was better than mine. I git all mad and tell her she don't know nothing bout it. She laughs at me and swishes her dress up around her thighs.

She's just tryin to git my goat. I think that now she's fillin out and pretty near twelve she's bout ready to git serious. I make sure we can't be seen by her ma, the old crow in the kitchen, then I move real close to her and put my mouth over hers. She latches onto me like a barnacle, her mouth all hard, like she don't know what she's doin. I show her it can be done soft and she catches on real quick. She starts feelin for me and grabs right hold through my overalls. Dora calls my name from the dairy but I don't pay no attention. I tug on Ginny's arm and we slink out to a clearin near the brook. We start up kissin again.

You really seen Gunnar Sorensen's thing? I ask her as I pin her under me.

You got a good face, is all she says to me. She moves her hands over my hind end and I don't think I can hold out much longer. I stand up and peel off my overalls like a house afire.

I was just lyin, Gunnar ain't put together like you. He ain't got them muscles and none of that dark hair down there, she says as she fans her skirts up over her legs and underthings.

I don't mind, now, that she's fooled with Gunnar, cause she likes what she sees here, better. I start to undo her buttons and pull her jumper up over her head. I can't help but look her all over. She's all grown up once she's outa them girlie dresses with flowers on them.

She lays right down on our clothes, reaches up, and I feel all jittery. Then we start kissin.

I can't help but wonder, though, if her old man been here before.

If a bee flies about (the beekeeper's) head in quick and threatening circles, he can lose (the bee) if he will stoop quietly and walk slowly out of the way.
—*from* First Lessons in Beekeeping
by C. P. Dadant, c. 1957

CHAPTER THREE

~≋⊙ ⊙≋~

Caleb

1956

"Caleb, what are you doin'?" Ma asks. I raise my head from the desk. The office is lit up by the morning sun. I must have fallen asleep after leaving Duffy last evening, and working until early morning, cleaning this room.

"What are you doin' in here?" she asks. She steps into the room and stands with her hands on her hips.

"I fell asleep."

"You been goin' through things?" She looks around. She sees the box on the desk. My grandfather's will is in the box.

"Yeah, I was cleaning things up," I say.

After I left Duff alone in the parlor I came in here to make some changes. Words never spoken became louder in the night as I sat with him, so loud that I had to leave. But scenes of my life, unanswered questions, scurried under the door as I closed it. They followed me across the hall like dried flower petals, tiny seeds, and thick dust. When I was a little boy Duffy would lay his gentle hand on my head as we walked to the village. He made the words that my mother spoke simple for me, tried to make me understand her. He told me why the moon grew and shrank. And how the drone bee must serve the queen and then die, it being useless and a burden to the hive. He told me these things as though I was to be part of a secret only he knew. I thought of those things as I left him.

"What do you need in this office?" Ma is looking over the books and the desk. I can tell she is checking to see what things of her father's and Duffy's have been moved.

On the wall opposite the desk there are built-in bookshelves, running floor to ceiling. I've taken down some of the books, ones I'll never read: mostly gardening and dairy textbooks, books on milling lumber, raising fowl. My grandfather's and father's books. I've stored away the crumbling posters from state fairs and tractor salesmen. I've moved the faded red wing-chair at an angle in front of the tiny fireplace, taken down the frayed and dry-rotted drapes. Swept the threadbare carpets.

In the bookshelves and on the mantle, I've neatly arranged my shadowboxes. My prize possession is a cream-colored moth whose wingspan is over six inches. Duffy and I found it in the hayloft four years ago. It lies pinned in its shadowbox in the center of the mantle.

"Where's Daddy's letter opener?" Ma asks.

"In the drawer."

"Where's the seed catalogs?"

"In the filing cabinet where they should be."

"Your grandfather's mantle clock?"

"I took it down. It hasn't worked as long as I can remember."

"So, what's up? What are you cookin' up? Who put you in charge?" She squints at me with her fierce little eyes and puckers her lips, then she picks up a snow globe that had been her father's. "You ain't keepin' this." She grabs it and turns to the bookcase.

"And that was my mother's." She sees the glass box that houses a dried flower and a bee carcass made by her parents when they began their career in beekeeping, nearly seventy years ago. She lunges toward it, frantic to take it from me, but her hand knocks against it and it goes crashing to the floor.

"Ma, what are you doing?" I kneel down beside the shattered glass, the crumbled queen. She looks at what she's done, her eyes wide and her mouth open. "You're crazy! For God's sake, can't you ever be rational?" I yell at her. She looks at me, her eyes narrow, her face grows a deeper red and then she moves quickly to the mantle.

"Rational? Let me tell you 'bout that man in the next room, 'bout what he and I've been to each other. Let me tell you things you couldn't listen to. Then we'll see who's rational." She screams and before I can stop her, her arm sweeps across the mantle, knocking the shadowboxes to the floor. She raises her left foot and brings it down on one of them, splintering the glass and obliterating the insect. I can only look at her, wondering what rages inside her. I don't move. I'm afraid of what my hands could do to her.

She sinks into a chair and cries. She must have enough tears in her now to make it worth the effort.

I hear a knock at the front door and leave her. I can see a man in a black suit through the window and I watch as two more men lift Duffy's casket from a hearse and bring it toward the house.

I think about digging the grave and know that I can't bury him until I know who he is, who she is.

It takes all four of us to lift Duffy and anchor him within the soft, shiny, white lining. He looks safe. Warm. Ma watches with dry eyes behind us. One of the men starts to close the lid and Ma stops him, grabbing hold of his arm.

"We'll take care of that," I say. I write the check, have Ma sign it, and they leave. Ma looks down at Duffy. She straightens his lapel, touches his face with the back of her hand.

She turns; grief has spoiled any good there might have been in her. Her eyes are dead. She points to Duffy.

"I wanna git right in there and go with him," she says.

I can't help but shake my head. She is amazing in her selfishness. I curl up my lip, disgusted with her.

"There's a shovel out by that back door. Don't you have some work to do?" she asks, looking back at Duffy.

I walk away wanting to say something, but know it will be of no use. I think of all the broken things in my life that she has caused, and seemingly without regret.

I go down the hill to the graveyard. The air is warm and dry. The trees below me that spread into the swamp and beyond are bright with the anger I feel.

I lean on the shovel and stare down at the graves. My grandfather, Eugene, my grandmother, my brother.

My brother, Teddy.

She not only loved him more than me when he was alive, but also in his death. He was lovable. I remember that about him. I was seven when he was almost eighteen, yet it seemed as though I was the older brother. I showed him how easy it was to open the hives without the bees getting mad. That was when we all learned how beestings affected him. At first his reactions were mild, a bit of swelling, a headache. We were told to stay away from the hives. Ma took Teddy to a doctor and got pills for him in case he was stung badly. He had to let the pill dissolve under his tongue, but he fought it, was frightened by it. He was frightened of many things. And fearless of others. He nearly drowned several times in the pond. Loved the water. He would chase after the truck, laughing, when Duffy went into town, grabbing at the fenders, the door handles. We couldn't get him to stop doing it. Once he had his foot driven over by a salesman who'd come to the farm to sell us some seed.

And bees.

He wasn't frightened by them after I'd shown him how tame they could be.

I found his body, swollen with stings, purple face with tear stains, on the ground near two open hives. It was too late for a pill. Ma said he was the brightest angel, the only angel she'd ever seen. I think she blamed me, or maybe herself. I'm not sure which.

I sink the shovel into the grassy knoll and lift the turf. Olaf is walking toward me with a shovel. I have enough strength to dig a dozen graves.

"Mornin'," Olaf says.

"Hi. Thanks for coming."

We start digging. Stones and sod, black earth. I dig and dig down, looking into a hole of gravel and broken root. I don't know I'm crying until I feel Olaf's hand on my back and I remember another time like this.

Last winter when I went to McGrath's for a few beers and ended up getting drunk. Tommy McGrath was telling me how the bar used to be my ma's diner. How she could cook. I could remember going in there on hot days to get a scoop of ice cream. He told me how busy the place was before the war. I kept drinking, didn't want to think about how Ma and Duff struggled or what I should do to help them. Olaf came in, without his brothers, and we got to playing darts and drinking too much.

He told me he'd heard some story about my ma and his dad. I wanted to punch him, but he didn't say it to be mean and I didn't much like fighting, so I drank. He told me things he'd heard about Duffy and Ma too, and how my dad ran off because of it all. Olaf never had many friends. I was about it. He was just trying to share something with me, but I couldn't take it. I got up and left. I was too drunk to be driving. The road kept lifting toward the windshield like a sheet moving on a clothesline. I had to keep shaking my head to stay awake.

Before I reached the road to the farm I had to stop and get out. Needed the cold, fresh air. I slipped into the ditch a few times. The sky spun with stars. My stomach heaved up the cheap beer on my shirt and shoes. I collapsed on my knees and kept retching.

"You all right?" someone said behind me.

"Huh?" I looked around and saw someone in the darkness. I started heaving again. Olaf put his hand on my back, then tried to lift me.

"You stink," he said.

He dragged me out of the ditch. I heard the door open and for a second I could see the inside of my truck, then nothing.

When I woke up I saw a cracked ceiling above me. I was lying on a bed. My body felt heavy like a keg of nails.

"Olaf? Where am I?" I asked.

"At my house. Didn't think you'd want your ma to see you like this." Olaf sat on the edge of the bed. I looked around the room and felt sorry for him. His room was cluttered with junk, dirty clothes, magazines. The place smelled of must and earth. The sheets on the bed hadn't been washed in a long time. The walls were covered in an old paper of faded roses. They seemed to swell and deflate. The cracks in the ceiling split wider apart and then became thin again.

"I ought to get home," I said and tried to get up but couldn't.

"You sleep it off. I'm goin' to bed too." He took off his boots, pants, and workshirt, and turned off the glaring lamp on the table beside me. He leaned back against the headboard and lit a cigarette. Handed it to me and then lit one for himself.

He was quiet for awhile and then spoke, startling me.

"It must be somethin' to have a ma. All I ever had is Pa's women around. I'd like havin' a meal at suppertime, and clean sheets."

"I don't want to talk about my ma," I said.

"Sorry, want some whisky?"

"I'm still spinning."

"It might knock you out." He turned on the light and jumped

up, grabbed a bottle from his closet and a couple of dirty canning jars. Poured whisky in them both and held a jar out to me. I took it and he got back into bed. He pulled the sheet over himself before turning out the light.

"Did you ever hear about my ma?" he asked.

"No, only that she died when you were born."

"I guess she was pretty. Pa never got over her. I wish I'd known her. I always miss her even though I don't remember her." He slid down in the bed. I felt his bare leg against mine. I realized he must have taken off my jeans. My workshirt was gone too, but I still had on my underclothes.

"It must be rough," I said to him, knowing how his brothers and father bullied him. I started to drift off again, then I heard him crying.

"Olaf . . . ?"

"You got your ma, I ain't got nothin'," he whispered.

"Sorry," was the only dumb thing I could think to say. I thought myself lucky for what I had. Ma. Duffy. Clean sheets.

I waited in the darkness for him to stop crying and wondered how we'd face each other in the morning. I thought I could pretend to forget it all in the light of the day. Then he moved closer to me. I felt his hand move over my chest. His mouth came close to my neck and I could feel his wet cheeks on my skin.

"Just let me sleep here," he whispered.

I didn't speak. Didn't move. His one hand stayed on my shoulder all night. I noticed for the first time, a penny-sized mole on his skin, just below his neck. I have one like it on my back. And I wondered again what drove my father away from us? Gunnar? Duffy?

Eventually the rhythm of his breathing lulled me to sleep. When I woke up in the morning he was gone. Nora, Gunnar's woman, came into the room. She was dressed in a thin nightgown. She was as surprised at seeing me, as I was. She smiled and I could see her clear eyes and deep thoughts. She deserved more than the likes of Gunnar. Her yellow hair was shining and I could see the swell of her breasts. I thought of nothing to say, I just stayed in the bed, waiting for her to leave. She laughed and walked out.

I dressed quickly and left. Olaf and I never once talked about that night.

We've dug deep enough. I've stopped my useless crying, have shaken off Olaf's hand.

"Thanks for the help," I say to him, throw down the shovel, and walk up the hill to the house.

As I head up the steps of the porch I see my sister Edith's car coming down the lane. I don't want to see her now. I need to talk to Ma.

"Ain't you gonna ask that boy in for something to drink? He's been workin' hard," Ma says as I come into the parlor. I slam the door and push a chair against it.

"Thought you hated the Sorensens," I say.

"Well, he did come over to help. What's wrong? You're all red in the face."

"I just dug a grave," I say and take her arms, move her away from Duffy's casket. "Sit down," I tell her.

"What's got into you? You mad about them broken boxes?"

"I want to know whose grave I just dug."

"What in hell are you . . ."

"Tell me."

It is necessary to have a queen that is prolific and should she become barren from any cause, or become lost, or even decrease in her fertility during the breeding season, or die from old age or from accident, the worker bees immediately prepare to rear another to take her place.
—*from* First Lessons in Beekeeping
by C. P. Dadant, c. 1957

CHAPTER FOUR

Regina Merritt

1907

When I was only ten my daddy pulled me along by the hand and led me to the side of the barn where he kept his beehives. At first I was nervous, thinkin he might be takin me out to the woodshed for a lickin. But I couldn't think of nothin I'd done to get whipped for. Or was he leadin me off to the fields where Mama couldn't see, like he did with my sisters?

We stopped by the hives. He let go of my hand and went to one of them. It was new. He built them himself in his tool-buildin. He lifted the top off, slid one of the new frames out, and smiled when he saw clusters of bees hummin right around, workin to build cells.

"You ain't afraid of them, are ya?" he asked, but he knew I wasn't and he was proud of me.

"No."

He poked through the bees, real gentle. I walked closer. I knew if we was quiet and didn't move quick they wouldn't bother us. Daddy sometimes let me help him gettin the honey. He came close to a big bee in the center of the frame and pointed.

"The queen," I said.

He nodded.

"Regina means 'queen'," he said.

"You've told me."

"Your mama says she can't do this work no more."

Mama collected the honey when Daddy was workin with the cows or in the fields, but whenever he got the chance he worked with them. I think they was his favorite part of farmin. "Ginny, I want you to do what work Mama did here. I don't trust them sisters of yours, not with the bees." He slipped the frame back into the hive and turned to me. I didn't like to look at his eyes too much so I watched the few stray bees lookin how to get back in their hive.

I nodded.

"I just got this swarm to settle in here. In a few weeks they'll have the cells full. You keep watch. The best honey comes from them cells that are just sealed. Don't let it sit there too long." The corners of his mouth went up a bit. I guess that was a smile. He didn't never smile much. And hardly ever spoke to me, my sisters, or Mama, unless he was givin out orders. I didn't like him much and wanted to get away from him. He was more patient with me than my sisters, I don't know why for sure, except maybe he could see I cared about the farm, about the bees. But still I didn't like to be in his company for too long.

"I can do it," I said. "I'll take care of them."

He sat down on a bench against the barn wall.

"Come sit," he patted the space next to him. I went over and sat. I felt like somethin was jumpin in my stomach, like tree frogs was havin a party. Daddy never sat with me alone. I don't know if I was happy or hopin to get away from him.

"I know you're just a baby, but I've watched ya. I think you can do a good job, if you put your mind to it."

"I ain't a baby," I snapped at him. He treated Dora and Lucy like they was all grown, always took them off when he delivered milk, or was workin in the fields. They was a lot older than me, but I didn't like him callin me a baby. He'd never hardly looked my way, or so I thought til he gave me such a big responsibility. He must have seen how smart I was.

"Can you watch them bees like they was your own children?" he asked, soundin a little mean, like he didn't like me talkin back.

"Yes," I said I could. "I know most of what to do."

"I know. I'll teach you the rest." Then he put his thick arm across my lap and patted my legs. I looked up at his almost tooth-less mouth. He was grinning. I stood up quick, too quick and he grabbed my arm.

"What's got into you?" he asked me, lettin go of my arm, lookin mad. His big furry eyebrows nearly hid his eyes when he scowled. I didn't say nothin. I went beyond the hives to where Mama grew cosmos, cleome, and bachelor buttons. I thumbed the prickly stems of the cleome.

He stood for a minute behind me. I could feel him lookin at me. Then he walked across the yard and around the corner of the milkin barn. I turned, lookin at all the hives. We had about twelve then. I thought of myself as their queen, now. They was mine, and all their honey.

Mama stopped workin with the bees and the chickens cause she was gettin sicker. She had some trouble breathin, and complained of aches and pains, but we hardly ever had a doctor out to the house, unless someone was really sick, like when Dora had pneumonia once.

I went back to the house and watched Mama takin some fresh bread out of the oven. She was scowlin like always, movin her little self around the kitchen mutterin, complainin about somethin. I always wanted her to look at me, see me, but she didn't much. I went back out the door and crossed the field, headin for the store.

It was early summer, school just let out a week before and I had it in my mind to play. If I hung around home then Mama or Daddy would put me to work. As it was, I'd probably get a talkin to, or a lickin, when I got home.

I went into the store and bought a candy cinnamon stick. It felt tingly and secret on my tongue. I'd swiped the penny from Daddy's overall pockets the day before. I felt wicked and warm inside for doin it. I sat on the edge of the porch at Gossler's and swung my legs back and forth as I slurped on the candy.

"How'd you git outa workin'?" Gunnar Sorensen walked down the road and stood in front of me. His family had a farm too. Gettin out of work wasn't no easy thing for farm kids.

"I just took a walk down here. No one paid no attention," I said, feelin like somethin special, somethin important.

"Wanna go swimmin'?" he asked.

"Gunnar, I know your daddy won't let you outa work to go swimmin."

"As soon as I git the pound of corn seed, I can take off. He won't know," Gunnar reached out for my candy stick. I don't know why, but I let him have a taste. He licked it all over and smiled and handed it back.

"Yuck!" I didn't expect him to slobber all over it. But then I thought how we'd practiced kissin before and decided his spit didn't bother me none.

"Let me go in the store and then you come on back with me to home. We'll sneak off," Gunnar said. He had a lot of yellow in his hair and sort of a handsome face, but he always looked funny, always thinkin on somethin other than what was goin on right around him. He'd be laughin and then right in the middle of a deep breath, he'd get angry, sometimes breakin things. Once I see him slice the legs off a frog and let it sit in the sun on a hot rock til it died. He laughed. I could imagine that inside Gunnar there were hollows where his heart or some other parts of him were supposed to be. He scared me a little, but it made me more curious to know him better.

Gunnar and I had grown up together. Our daddys always shared farmin secrets and our mamas swapped recipes and complaints. Gunnar was sorta like a cousin, familiar to me as the bean fields, yet he was always teeterin on the edge of a rail fence, about to lose his footin.

I waited for Gunnar that day, instead of goin back to his house with him. He came back to the store about an hour later, just when I was about to take off somewhere. I was never good at waitin.

"Where you been?" I asked.

"Couldn't git away easy. Come on." He smirked at me and I saw that flat sheen show off the surface of his eyes like grease layin on a pond. You can't quite see beneath it. Stirrin it only pushes it around, but don't let you see under it.

Last time we'd gone swimmin together, Gunnar had taken off all his clothes. When we was little we always went bare-naked, but as we started to change, we kept covered up. Until that last time. He was feelin as proud as a rooster about the changes in himself and wanted to show off. I'd looked at him, hung my mouth open at what I saw. It wasn't like I'd never seen one before, but I couldn't believe that Gunnar had changed so. It made me dizzy, a little sick. It made me hope we'd go swimmin again soon.

And now here we was on our way to the pond.

"I ain't takin my clothes off," I said to him.

"You should. Feels good." Then he turned up the corners of his mouth in a devillike smile. He was wicked and I loved wicked.

When we got to the pond there was other kids there and I felt disappointed.

"Guess we better keep somethin on," he said as he stripped down to his undershorts and jumped in the pond. He started horsin around with other boys, havin fun, like it didn't make no difference if I was there at all. I felt all hot and angry and a little bit relieved. I knew nothin strange or excitin would happen that day.

I slumped down near a tree and leaned into it. I could see the heads of Abel Gossler and Duff Pendleton comin up for air. They were tryin to throw Gunnar off a log that he'd climbed onto. They all laughed. I noticed a few other boys from school in the water, too. I felt out of place. I waited til it was plain to see that Gunnar wasn't gonna pay no attention to me. He had others to impress. Our days of actin foolish, playin house, or swipin penny candy together were on the way out. I felt like I'd lost my favorite dog.

I got up and walked back home.

I stood outside the barn listenin to Daddy yellin at Dora. He was always yellin, or walkin around sulky. Sometimes I wished he'd drop dead like Maude McClellan's daddy had last year. He was mean like Daddy. Maude always wore bruises and broaches like bracelets. When she told the teacher that she wouldn't be comin to school no more, cause she had to help her mama, I felt a burnin jealousy. I wished my daddy would die. The thought of Maude's good luck got me mad. I went home that day tryin to think of somethin that would make Daddy mad, maybe cause him to have a fit and drop dead. All I could think was to throw his chewin tobacco down the hole of the outhouse. He blamed everyone, screamin and yellin, "Who stole my tobacco?" he kept rantin. I laughed when he couldn't see me and pretended to hunt for it. He never did know what happened to it.

I listened at the door for a minute and then went around back to the hives. I sat on the ground behind some honeysuckle bushes, but where I could watch the bees comin and goin. I could imagine myself as one of them, flyin about free. I didn't realize at the time how much those bees worked, how everythin they did was part of a plan. They were born with only work on their minds. Except the drones, they didn't do nothin.

As I watched the hives, I noticed a bunch of them comin out of their little doorway. Like loads of black pepper they covered their little front porch and the sides of the hive, then in one big swirl they lifted up into the sky. There was no noise like it, a hummin so loud it filled the yard. Thousands of them came rushin out of the hive. A new queen was escapin with half of her mother's workers. They were swarmin. Daddy had shown me it happen once before. There was no room for two queens in one hive.

I looked up at the black funnel in the sky, watched it move around like a twister and then form a ball. A big engine risin up. What I should've done was go tell Daddy so he could herd the bees into an empty hive, but I liked watchin them escape. They'd find a hollow tree, or maybe, some other farmer's empty hive.

I liked the way they lived. As long as they had a queen, they worked and worked to keep their place full of honey, well-stocked til someone would come along and rob them. I hoped no one would rob from the queen that had just escaped. Maybe no one would know where she'd gone to make her queendom. When they got settled the queen would begin her matin dance, all the drones would try to win her. Then she'd keep on givin birth til she died, increasin her family, never losin her power til the end.

Pretty near a perfect circle.

The safe handling of bees is not so difficult a performance as many people imagine who are not initiated to the bee-keeping.

—*from* FIRST LESSONS IN BEEKEEPING
by C. P. Dadant, c. 1957

CHAPTER FIVE

Caleb

1956

I watch my mother's face. Her eyes water, but she is so in check with herself, her cheeks stay dry, and my heart continues to harden against her as it has been for so long. It seems as though I am absorbing her story, Duffy's story, through the pores in my skin rather than hearing her words. I see her as a child, Duffy as a young boy, both of them allowing their fears, their loves, and their separate greeds form who they've become. It's as though I've known these stories all along, but have to hear them again so that I can clearly understand what parts of them are in me.

She fusses with Duffy's clothes, straightening his sleeves, tucking dried flowers into his pockets. She tucks slips of paper between him and the lining of the coffin.

"We should try to locate his sons," Ma says.

"I'll try. Why are you putting those flowers in his pockets? And what's on the paper?" I ask.

"Me bein' foolish. He liked the lavender blossoms. I was always bringin' him some in the summer. These was up in our room since summer. Lost most of their smell," she says as she turns to me. "And these," she holds up pieces of note paper. "These is little notes we wrote to each other over the years. I've saved them. No one else needs to see them."

A knock on the parlor door makes Ma jump. She looks at me.

"It's Edith. I saw her driving in," I said.

"Well, you can't keep her locked outa here. Let her in." Ma heads toward the door, but I jump up from the chair and take her arm. "Not yet. I want to hear it all."

"Caleb, you've gone crazy in the head. Let your sister in here."

Edith calls our names and I tell her we're talking. We'll be out in awhile. She tells us that Rose, my other sister, cannot come home for the service.

"Ma, you all right?" Edith asks.

"I'm broke up awful. Your brother's bein' mean. Mean as a hornet." Ma looks at me, folds her arms over her chest. "A time like this and you puttin' me through more hell. Ungrateful. All I've done for you."

"You two come out here and settle whatever's the trouble. I'll put on tea water," Edith says. As though tea can solve all problems.

"He's askin' a lot of questions. 'Bout Duff and 'bout his daddy. He's just tryin' to torture me," Ma says, her face pouting like a child.

Edith doesn't say a thing. Her silence implicates her. I hear her walk away from the door toward the kitchen.

"I can tell you things, mister. Things you don't want to know. He could too." She points to Duffy. I feel as though I need to hear their story, my story, before he's deep under the earth, before she can run down the hall, up the stairs, or to the hives, clutching her secret like sweet, stolen honey.

The room dims as the sun sets. She lights candles and moves into her world.

"None of us was saints. That, you might have guessed," she says coldly, then laughs as she settles into a chair beside Duffy.

PART TWO

The Nuptial Flight

Their entire destiny depends on the ensuing nuptial flight. . . . Of this the bees are so well aware that when the young queen sallies forth in quest of her lover, they often will abandon the labours they have begun . . . accompany her in a body, dreading to let her pass out of their sight.

—from THE LIFE OF THE BEE
by Maurice Maeterlinck, c. 1901

The queen has a smooth, curved sting without any barbs.
She can use this again and again without harm to herself.
—from THE WORLD BOOK ENCYCLOPEDIA,
c. 1955

CHAPTER SIX

Regina

1909–1913

There was two things I hated as a child, my mother's misery and my daddy's preoccupation with the farm. Mama's mean disposition was something I understood though. If I'd been married to some-one like Daddy I would've been just as mean. Why she didn't up and leave him I'll never know. They were as different as a hen and a horse. Mama was small and bony and Daddy was tall and round. Mama was quiet, but had a quick, sharp temper that would fuse up and die right out. Daddy was loud when he was mad, or dark and gloomy, and held a grudge for a lifetime. He hardly spoke a word to folks less he had to. People around town steered clear of both of them. You never knew when he'd back-hand you for some-thin you'd done, or if he was even listenin to what was goin on around him. He could surprise you with every turn.

He'd get up on the wagon to go deliverin eggs and milk, and yell for Dora to load the wagon, then he might slap her one if she didn't move fast enough. He made her do an awful lot of work on the place, and when Lucy got old enough, he did the same to her. Mama would see the way he treated them and sometimes, if she dared, she'd yell at him. If she did, she'd end up with a slap. Once he was just touchin my sister Dora's face, real soft, and Mama come out of the house and told him to leave Dora be. He turned on Mama and hit her hard so that her spectacles come right off and landed in the gravel. Then he ground them up under his heel. I guess Mama thought he was gonna hit Dora but that was one time he was being nice.

Daddy would go out into the gardens and stare up toward the hills for so long that we thought he'd turned to stone. And then he'd get all red in the face about some new idea to make money. He was up and down, but mostly just frownin.

I think the insides of Mama must've been just like the insides of Daddy's beehives. She was always buzzin around the kitchen or the herb beds then on up the stairs, mutterin to herself, movin quick and fierce, givin out orders, cannin jelly, doin the wash or makin the beds. When she'd take a minute to stop and drink her chamomile tea, I'd stroke her hand or read to her from my schoolbooks just tryin to find a way to be close to her. I caught her more than once cryin to herself at the kitchen table, so I knew she was hurtin inside her and I wanted to touch that hurt place. She never said nothin, but I knew it was Daddy's mean, dark ways.

For some reason I got away with more than my older sisters ever did. With Daddy, that is. He was tough on them but not with me. It might've been cause I was younger than them. When I was twelve, Dora was nearly twenty and Lucy was eighteen. Daddy looked at them as grown women and if they weren't gonna get married then he was gonna make them work hard for their keep. I thought, well, when I get to be their ages I ain't lettin him push me around.

I was smarter than my sisters in school, so my Mama said. I think she had hopes for me. Wanted me to get out of Washington County and make something of myself, but I didn't see it that way.

All I loved in the world was right there on that three hundred acres. I loved the blueberry barrens, the ledges, the mosses, the great big spruce trees, and I loved the house. I could see a day when I could run it my way without Daddy around to fight me.

When Duffy Pendleton come to work on the place I started gettin ideas about how I could get the place for myself. All I needed was a healthy strong husband. I guess I shouldn't've been thinkin about the days when Mama and Daddy were gone but I couldn't help it. Duffy was a good-lookin boy and he was smart. It wasn't til I got to know him better that I realized he was lazy and wouldn't do me no good in the future. But still, I had such eyes for him that I couldn't think of much else than bein alone with him.

I won't tell you the things I did to tease that boy but I was wicked. I waited til I was twelve to sneak him off in the woods and let him have what it was he wanted from me.

Then I really had him. He'd do anything for me after that. I had some fun too but mostly my fun come from this power I had over him, or any boy for that matter. I'd filled out and I could turn a man's head.

Duffy acted like most boys, tough and cocky at times, but when we was alone he was just as soft and sweet as a flower blossom. I loved that in him, and I thought I better be careful or I'd be foolish and get myself in a mess. I knew if I wanted anything in this world I had to find myself a man with money and I just didn't see Duffy as ever amountin to much.

When I was fourteen and thought I might be pregnant with his baby I started blubberin all over his shoulder. He thought we should get married right then and there.

"Ginny, it won't be so bad. If your folks won't let us live with them I know mine will. We don't have much but we'll be all right," he said as he ran his hand down the length of my hair. I wanted to believe him but I kept thinkin about the farm. If I got married that young my daddy would disown me and I'd lose my chances to have the farm for myself. I had some crazy notion in my head that if I took over the farm I could show my daddy what I was made of. I wanted him to sample some humble pie. I wanted him to see that I was gonna be one woman he couldn't own or toss around like he did Mama and my sisters. I imagined him sickly and old, beggin my mother's forgiveness and her turnin on him, knowin that I would take care of her.

"Duffy, we're too young to get married. I've heard there are doctors who can take care of trouble like this," I cried into his shirt collar.

"Don't you think your daddy would accept things if this baby turned out to be a boy?"

I stopped cryin and lifted my head. There was somethin to those words. My daddy made no secret of the fact that he'd wanted a boy. Maybe he'd want this child. Maybe he'd turn everything over to my baby once he got too old to work the farm and then I could manage things.

Duffy and me packed up my mother's old leather suitcase and drove all night trying to figure out where we could get married. Would I be able to convince a preacher that I was old enough to get married without my daddy's consent? Well as luck would have it, on the car ride, I was filled with that familiar warm sensation between my legs. I guess I wasn't gonna have no baby.

I told Duffy to turn around and head back down Route One. He acted as though the wind had been knocked out of him.

"I'm sorry . . ." I said.

"I was gettin excited about a baby. A boy," Duffy said. "I thought we might name him Earl, after my daddy."

"Well, don't bellyache about it. I thank the dear lord in heaven that I don't have to go through with any of this," I blurted out, not thinkin it might hurt Duff. We didn't talk much on the rest of the way home. When he left me off, at the road to the house, I went to kiss him and he turned away. It was nearly six weeks before he spoke to me again. That night I was so late gettin home that my daddy paddled my ass and later came to my room. Some nights he'd sit by my bed all night makin me so angry I'd go to sleep in a black cloud of hate. That night I didn't move, pretended to be asleep, and he finally let me be.

Duff and I were on and off over the next two years. He never really forgave me for admittin I didn't want to marry him. I dated some of the other boys around but I couldn't find the kind of man I wanted. Even Gunnar, who might get his daddy's couple of hundred acres, didn't come close to what I needed. I was lookin for someone with money. I know that sounds selfish but it wasn't. I was thinkin about the farm and how to help Mama.

Then Mama took sick. The doctor that come said it was a liver disease. She had to stay to bed most days and I ended up doin her work with the hens, the cookin, the wash, all of it. Dora worked in the dairy most of the time, and Lucy up and married Hollis Spinney. She hadn't even told us she was datin him and one day they disappeared across the county line. I bet she laughed all the way out of the state of Maine.

Daddy didn't have no patience for Mama's sickness. I fixed up a room downstair for her and tended to her most of the time. Dora helped a little but Daddy kept her busy outside. It was the dead of winter and the snow had nearly covered all the outbuildins and the house. I couldn't see out none of the windows. I was fixin Mama some hot coffee when Dora nearly fell into the kitchen. Her whole face was bristlin with white snowflakes and her breath was as thick as the snow. Daddy had put her to work shoveling out paths to the buildins and said she had to finish before dinnertime. Her hands were bluer than Mama's agateware. I tried to warm her up but she was froze to the heart. When I got her thawed out a bit she started to cry.

"Daddy . . . Daddy . . ." she kept stutterin.

"I know he drives you too hard," I said but I noticed her

blouse had been torn and then like a flash of lightnin I understood. It made sense to me now why Mama had been so upset when Daddy was touchin Dora's face. Dora shook her head and cried harder.

"What is it Dora?" I pleaded with her to say the words.

"It's Daddy . . ."

"What about him?"

"He . . . he . . ." and then she fell to cryin more. I knew she couldn't say it.

I grabbed my wool coat and headed out toward the barn. Partway to it I see the shovel laying on the path that Dora had just dug. There was some blood on the snow and on the end of the shovel. I ran to the barn. I had trouble getting the door open cause the snow had started to drift up against it. But when I got it open I see Daddy layin facedown on the floor. The back of his head was clotted with blood. I turned him over and he had one eye shut and one open. I thought he was a goner but he started to say something that I couldn't figure out.

I looked down at his face, all red and bloated. He was havin a hard time sayin anything. I gripped tight to the shovel handle, raised it in the air, and thought if I hit him once more he'd be dead, and the thrill of that moment, knowin the power I had in my hands, flushed through every one of my veins. But I didn't do nothin. I couldn't be as brave as Dora, or as crazy as she must've been just before she whacked him. I lowered the shovel.

"What's happened?"

I turned around to see Duffy standin there with wide eyes. He looked at me and that shovel in my hands and must've thought I'd hit Daddy. He moved close to me and lifted my chin so that our eyes met. I don't know what he was thinkin but I could see his love for me in his big green eyes. He bent down to Daddy and listened to see if he was breathin.

"Ginny, go in the house," he whispered. I just turned and walked back out the barn door, still holdin that shovel. I dipped the end of it in a drift and then took a fistful of snow and scoured the blood away. I walked toward the house, drove the shovel into a snowbank, and went back indoor.

"Dora, get yourself together. Go upstair and pack whatever it is you want of your clothes," I said to my sister as I took off my coat and stomped the snow from my boots.

"But . . . Daddy . . . ," she stuttered.

"He'll kill you if you don't get out of here. Dress warm. You're gonna have to walk to the store. You get Abel to drive you to Aunt Eula's. You're gonna have to stay with her," I said as I started to pack up some biscuits and bread in a tin.

"Ginny, I can't just show up there."

"I'll get Mama to write a note. Go pack."

I stood still in the kitchen listenin to my sister moving around upstair in her room. I kept expecting the kitchen door to fly open with Daddy standin there ready to go after Dora, but a stillness come over the house, and all around the yard. I looked out the window, the dooryard was all white with snow, the sky as black as a kettle. I imagined I could hear the tiny snowflakes landin on the drifts like chips of broken beach glass. I thought that silence was a sign that Daddy had died, or maybe just the most clear moment I'd ever known inside my head.

I sent Dora off with some food and her clothes. I bundled her up best I could and had to push her out the door. Her face was blank, like she'd lost her senses all together. I figured once she got to Aunt Eula's she'd come around and realize I did the best thing by sendin her away.

I was on my way back into the kitchen to wash up the dinner dishes when in come Duffy with Daddy leanin on his shoulder.

"How is he?" I asked but I didn't make no move to go near him.

"He's just talkin foolish stuff. Not makin sense." Duffy eased Daddy into the rocker by the stove.

"He never did make no sense," I said.

"Has he been at you?" Duffy said as he took both my hands. He thought I'd tried to kill Daddy to keep him from hurtin me like he had my sisters. I didn't ask how Duffy knew about that, all I could think was here is this handsome boy that I've tried to stop lovin, filled right up with such love for me that I wanted to cry. If it was possible, Duffy loved me even more for thinkin I'd slammed Daddy over the head. I could see he was proud of me, proud that I could be that brave.

I shook my head, looked back at the sink, then said I had to check on Mama. When I came back to the kitchen Duffy had Daddy drinkin some strong tea. I don't think Daddy was quite sure what happened to him.

That night Daddy slept so soundly that I thought he'd died. Duffy stayed right beside me as we watched him sleep. In the mornin I told Daddy that Dora had left for good. He turned his face away from me so I wouldn't see the long tears runnin down his cheeks.

*The drone has the male organs, but nothing else useful
to the cooperative life of the hive. . . . It is on the whole,
the life of the wastrel; a lazy buzzing-around in the sun,
no work, (and) a preoccupation with sex.*

—*from* THE WORLD OF BEES
by Murray Hoyt, c. 1965

CHAPTER SEVEN

Duffy

1913–1914

Ginny's what keeps me here. She got the prettiest black hair I ever
seen on a girl. Someday I'll git her to marry me. That would about
finish her old man. He likes me as a worker but I don't think he'd
want me as family. Treats me like I'm ignorant and from poor folk,
not good enough to think of marryin his daughter.

I watch the old man. Sour lookin face. Long mustaches down
his chin stained with chewin tobacco. Only got a few teeth left in
his head. Tall man, taller than me with hands and feet big and flat
as planks of wood. He ain't no one I want to mess with. So I try
to steer clear of Ginny, thinkin he'd kill me if he knew bout us.
Eugene ain't the same since he was hit over the head with that
shovel last winter. His lips droop more and he waits for Ginny to
tell him what work needs to be done around the place. He's still
mean but awful forgetful.

I work for him but I like best the times he ain't around when I can work splittin wood or pickin beans by myself. He still don't know how I cheat him by takin just what I want for food myself or takin wagonloads of wood home for Ma and Pa, when I work in one of the wood lots alone. I know I take risks stealin from him and layin with his youngest girl when I can't stand to stay away from her no more, but my family needs things too. And they don't care where the good fortune comes from neither.

Ginny went on to high school, but I didn't want to go on after eighth grade cause I got tired of them teachers whackin me with rulers and clubs of wood. Miss Alcott was my grade school teacher with big bosoms and pretty little lips. Her hair was the color of a mare that Ginny's family once had, all red-brown and shiny. I was fourteen in the eighth grade and stood almost six feet tall. I'd filled out quick like my daddy's people. I was shavin then. I knew Miss Alcott liked me, not as one of her pupils but as a man. More than once she kept me after school for some lame reason. She liked whackin me with a switch too.

One day she says I'd smart-mouthed her and I was to stay after school and stack the wood and wash the floors. It was a hot day too and I wanted to go swimmin with my buddies at Smith Pond. I was stackin the wood and was sweatin terrible. She came out on the steps and watched me. Now we didn't need no firewood at this time of year and I thought she was crazy. She just watched me while I worked.

Take your shirt off or you'll explode with the heat, she said.

So I done it. When I finished my work she told me to go in the schoolhouse, so I did. She said I still hadn't been punished enough. Told me to take down my pants, she'd had enough of my fresh talk. I said I wouldn't do that, I wasn't no baby for her to paddle. So she told me to wash the floors and when I was finished she said I had to shovel out under the outhouse. I started washin and she sat at her desk eyein me. I started to think, this woman's got somethin else ailin her besides a mouthy boy. She wants somethin else from me.

Good work, she said, when I finished washin the floors. I threw down the mop and said there wasn't no way I was shovelin shit on a hot day. I told her I'd take the lickin instead. Her face got all red and then she went and pulled down all the shades on the windows.

Take down your trousers, she said. She was standin there in her long dress buttoned right up to the throat and she looked awful hot. I said to her why don't she unbutton it a little. She did and then took a flat piece of kindlin and told me to pull down my pants again. I unbuttoned myself and let them fall to the floor. There I was for her to see.

You're a man, she said. I smiled. She took the kindlin wood and put it up to my thing. It was gittin hard but still a little soft. She lifted it with the wood and let it drop. She sat down in her chair and told me to lay across her lap. Now I was stiff. I laid down and she started slappin that board across me with all her strength. I didn't make a sound but slipped my hand up her skirt and reached right up tween her legs. She wasn't even wearin nothin underneath that dress. She started moanin and cryin out while I worked away on her, but she never stopped poundin me. My ass was some red and swollen when she was through. It happened like that with her a few more times but she wouldn't let me do no more to her than what I had with my hand under her skirts. I was glad when the school year was over so my hind end could heal and I could spend all my time at Ginny's.

Ginny and me take a walk out through the woods after she's been all mornin sittin with her ma. Her ma's been in bed since last winter and Ginny hopes the spring air will force some of its warmth into the old woman and make her better. But the doctor told Ginny that her ma ain't long for the world. Ginny says she got plans when her ma dies. Says she's gonna find some way to keep the farm even though they owe so much to the doctor and back pay to the farmhands. Since her daddy's become sorta soft in the head Ginny's had to take care of most things.

You can't do it on your own, I say to Ginny.

You don't know what I can do.

You're only fifteen. But she don't listen to me. Says she needs money and she's gonna find it somehow.

I kiss her and hold her to me cause I know her ways of findin money ain't gonna include me. She smiles up at me and we wander back through the woods to back of the barn where her daddy's beehives are.

Watch this, she says and I back away from the hives as she creeps closer. She opens the top of one of the hives and a bunch of them come up through and dart around her.

If you're real careful, she says, they won't pay no attention to you while you scrape out the honeycomb. She takes a putty knife off the windowsill of the barn and lifts one of the stores right out, real slow. The bees light all over her. She gits a hunk of honeycomb and sets it on the windowsill. The bees jump all over it and more of them buzz out of the hive. She moves slow, slips the frame back into place, and closes the lid.

Give me one of them jars over there, she says. Move over here slow and hand it to me. Don't run or jump or you'll git stung. I do what she says and some of the bees land on me. Her eyes go over me, she smiles like she's proud of me. She takes the honeycomb and puts it in the jar but one bee flies off it and sticks me right in my hand.

Don't jump, she says. She puts her hand over mine and squashes the bee. We walk away careful and then she starts to laugh.

See, they don't git mad if you move slow. We go out by the road and sit in the field. The honey tastes sweet on her tongue. I think how she handles me, like that, careful, easy, and I wish I could stay like that with her for always.

It's close to the end of July. I git to the farm about seven o'clock and find Ginny sittin in the kitchen rocker. She says, Mama's gone and hands me a cup of coffee.

Where's your daddy? I ask. She says he's gone to town to pick out a coffin. Says the old man sat on the edge of her bed all night in the dark. Ginny says, I just pretended to sleep. I couldn't think about Mama downstair all white and cold in her bed. I lean close to her and try to hold her hand but she pulls it away and stands up. I've got too much to do, she says and goes into her ma's room.

I go out to the barn thinkin the most help I can be is to git some of the chores done. I know tomorrow is Ginny's sixteenth birthday and I try to think of somethin to make it special. Later on I see Eugene comin home with the coffin on the wagon and a few fellas from town to help him. I don't want to touch no dead body so I stay out of their way.

After I've finished milkin and cleanin the stalls I walk past the outhouse and see Ginny workin with the bees like nothin happened.

Ginny, how you doin? I ask but she shakes her head slowly and waves her hand to tell me to go away. I walk past her and by the house and head right down the lane but Eugene sees me and puts a shovel in my hands.

You got some diggin to do, he says.

It's mornin. I show up with some wildflowers and a lunch I packed in a paper sack. I made us cheese sandwiches and cut up some cakes for us and had my ma boil me some eggs. I swiped some of Papa's whisky in a jar.

Mornin, Ginny, I say when she sees me at the screen door. She says her daddy is waitin for me to help him carry the coffin down under the hill. I tell Ginny I want her to have a special day, it bein her birthday. She just laughs and says she don't have no time for birthdays now. There's too much to be done. Go help Daddy.

I wait in the field behind some trees while Ginny and her old man and some folks from town say a few words over her ma's grave. My shoulders ache from diggin and luggin that coffin. They lower it and toss some dirt over it. Then some men start fillin in the grave. I'm glad I'm hidin.

Eugene and the others leave the grave. The sun's high in the sky. Ginny kneels down on the gravel mound and puts some daisies and devil's tail around a wooden cross. I watch her right though suppertime.

Her black hair turns red under the settin sun.

Various reports came in from time to time that females
of some strains of bees had developed from unfertilized
eggs. This seemed to account for the occasions when a
colony, hopelessly queenless, suddenly, against all the
rules, had a queen and were back in business.

—from THE WORLD OF BEES
by Murray Hoyt, c. 1965

CHAPTER EIGHT

Ginny

1914–1916

I ain't one who's big on sentimental stuff. The belongins of those
who've passed on are only things that get in the way and surprise
you with thoughts about the past. I never had the time to sit around
and mope about the dead. After Mama died I packed up most of
her things and give them to the church in town. I just couldn't see
holdin onto things I'd never use. Like her weddin dress. It was just
a plain gray dress with a lace collar that her mama made. I knew
I'd never wear it and it was just collectin dust and feedin the moths.
Or her corsets and her one pair of silk gloves. Things like that are
useless and should be handed on to someone who can use them,
just like any old thoughts about the dead. Pack them in a box. Sell
them off and bank the change.

I had too many things to keep my mind busy after I lost Mama. The one thing that kept me the busiest was my father. He needed to be looked after. He still wore the signs of my sister's revenge on his head. His hair never grew back where she struck him and it was always stained purple, like a brand of his sins. He seemed to age awful quick. He was only in his late fifties but overnight he looked closer to seventy. His hair turned as white as the snow that was fallin when Dora lashed out at him. His face dropped down and he was always droolin. I could get good work out of him though, as long as I watched over him. I wanted like Hell to put him in one of those homes I'd heard about where old people get taken care of, but we didn't have money for that. I started keepin the books for the farm and I was only sixteen. I didn't really have a head for figurin but I did the best I could. My biggest problem was gettin Daddy to sign checks and papers, cause I had no power to do that. Not til he was dead or too crazy for me to control.

"Daddy you just gotta put your name on that line and I can get the money from the bank to pay off the hands," I said to him more than once. It would take me at least two days to make him understand. He was scared to sign his name, afraid he couldn't trust the bank. He kept his money in the bank, though, and every week for as far back as I could remember, he'd go down to Milbridge and make sure they hadn't siphoned off any of his savins. Now that he didn't make that trip so often, he was edgy and nervous, wary of signin any papers.

Daddy had made some money with the farm, sellin his honey and vegetables, eggs and meats, but he'd put too much money back into the wrong things and I was left without much cash to keep things goin. I had to make sure Daddy paid the doctor's bills and sent a little to Dora for her keep at Aunt Eula's.

"Sell the place and we can build somethin small. I can work over at Pratt's Garage," Duffy said to me one evenin when I was lookin over the books. Daddy had fallen asleep at the supper table and Duffy and I had taken him to bed.

"Sell the place? You lost your mind? There's good money in

this place. I just need somethin to get it on its feet," I snapped at Duff. He just couldn't understand me wantin to be on the farm. But he didn't feel the same way I did about my hens, the cows, or the bees. I was drawn to creatures like that. Once I'd told Duffy how much I needed those animals and things around me and he said it was cause they didn't talk back to me. He always had some smart answer when his feelins was hurt. He was afraid I cared more about the livestock than I did him.

"Ginny, let's get married. We can . . ." he started, but I put up my hand to stop him.

"I ain't gettin married. Ever." I slammed the accounts book closed and stood up from the kitchen table. "I got too much work to do," I said as I walked out the back door. He followed me, and slipped his arms around me, from behind, and pulled me close. I wanted to rip his arms off and take off into the woods. I struggled a bit but then gave in when I knew I couldn't get out of those arms of his. He was a big man now and not so easy for me to control like I had a few years earlier. It got me madder to think I was trapped in a woman's body and not able to fight the likes of him.

He started kissin my neck and puttin his hands wherever he damned well pleased. And then I was lost to the feel of his rough cheeks and soft lips against my skin. I was just like a cat in heat when he'd bite on my neck. Cats always let the Toms have their way when they took hold of their necks.

The spring after Mama died we were sunk in debt. I knew I had to let most of the farmhands go. We'd had Royce and Walter work for us as long as I could remember and I hated to see them wander down the lane with heads low when I told them. But I couldn't let Duffy go, and they resented that.

"If you need me Ginny just call," Walter said after I told him he had to go and that I would try to pay him his back wages as soon as I could. He was about to go out the door when he turned and said, "Now Ginny, I know it ain't my business but just so you know . . ." and then he stammered and fumbled with his cap.

"What is it?" I asked.

"Well, it's just . . . I don't know what kind of work you're gonna get out of that boy. He ain't prone to much hard work," he said.

"Duffy?" I asked. "Oh, Walter I know how Duffy slacks off. He's never fooled me with his ways. I've found him more than once asleep in the loft when he's s'posed to be plowin or cuttin wood." I laughed.

"Then why keep him on? Royce and me work hard."

"I can't afford your wages, Walt. Duffy don't get paid as much as you two. He ain't been here as long."

"And once you two git married you won't have to pay him at all, is that it?" Walter asked. His eyes squinted up like he was afraid I'd tell him to go to Hell or somethin. He'd seen me often enough swearin and thrashin around the house when I was in a mood.

"You let me worry about my home, Walter. I don't hear no weddin bells ringin for me in the near future."

"Well, Ginny I hope things go good for you." He left with Royce and I felt just like I'd sent my own kin off into the world on their own. I thought the best way to keep my mind on practical things was to do somethin practical. I took out Mama's old iron-stone bowls and mixing spoons, lifted the lid on the flour crock, and started whippin up some bread. I knew if I baked enough goods I could make some easy cash by sellin stuff over at Gossler's store. All the women around did their bakin for themselves but there were a fair share of blueberry pickers, widowers, and loggers that would pay a lot for good home cookin.

I made some pocket change from my baked goods but over the followin winter we lost most of the bees and two of our best milkin cows. Daddy was gettin worse, gettin scared of everything like lightning storms and blizzards, and he was spendin hours alone talkin to himself. At dinner times I had to keep remindin him to pick up his fork or wipe his chin. If it hadn't been for my closeness with Duffy I'd've lost my mind.

One night Daddy come to my room and I told him to get out. But he kept comin night after night. It was so bad for awhile I slept with a chunk of stove wood under my bed. First time I hit him he realized, then and there, I wasn't gonna put up with him. I shook with fear to think what might've happened if he'd been stronger than me. Those nights left me with an icy feelin. I could remember him standin over my bed when I was just a little girl. I wondered how many nights he'd come in when I was too stupid to understand his ways. But like memories of Mama, I put his face and the touch of his hands in a safe trunk in my head and latched the lid for good.

Through the followin spring I petted and coddled my hens and got good eggs to sell. Daddy tried to tell me what to do about the bees, how to get the hives goin again but he never made sense. I felt pulled in too many directions, so I focused on what I knew, the hens and my bakin. I seemed to share some secret way of talkin with Bossy or the rooster or hens and I didn't even have to utter a sound for my bees to know what I was thinkin. Things weren't goin too bad but then one day at Gossler's store I saw a chance for things to be even better.

I could tell by the cut of Henry's coat and his new shoes that he might be just what I needed.

I listened while he and Abel chatted. He was from New Hampshire, told Abel he was finishing up his schoolin and plannin to find a place to stay and write a paper about farming. He called it agriculture, though no one around here ever did. He thought Josiahville was as good a place as any to do his work. He'd been up this way fishing as a boy and remembered how pretty it was, he said.

"I'm going to need a place to stay. Any hotels or rooms to rent around?" His voice was clear and deep and had a ring of confidence to it.

"Not much around here," Abel said from behind the counter.

Henry looked over the advertisements and posters on the wall.

I went right up to him and smiled and tossed back my hair in the way I'd seen the women do it in the one movin picture I'd seen.

"You need a place to stay?" I asked him. I didn't think he was too bad to look at either. He smiled at me. I think he liked what he saw.

"Yes."

"I've got extra rooms that I rent out," I bent down, lifted up the hem of my skirt and made a show of scratchin my leg just so he could get a good look. I knew how men liked to see a little higher up on a girl's leg.

"You're rentin rooms now, Ginny?" Abel asked.

"Hard times for me. I gotta do anythin to feed myself." I glared at him and he looked away.

"My name's Ginny. Regina really, but people call me Ginny." I think I blushed while I said that. I know I felt foolish but I didn't know what else to say.

"I'm Henry Gilley." He put out his hand to shake mine like a gentleman. He had soft yellow curls and skin like a baby. He wasn't really the sort of man that turned my head, but he'd do.

He came back with me to the farm to have a look around, see if he liked the room and such. He gave me a ride in his motor car and I talked the farm up. Prepared him for the sagging roofs and overgrown fields, but told him how the place had once looked, years ago. I wanted him to know there was money in that old, rocky, dark soil.

"These buildings need some repairin but I don't have a man around. My daddy, well, I do the best I can," I said as we drove down the lane, passing by the chicken yard. I had some healthy birds and like they knew what I was up to, they behaved themselves, strutted around, proud of themselves and clucking away.

"I can give you a comfortable place to stay and if you want to help out around here, we could work out a deal. A trade for your labor. You won't learn about farmin in books, you gotta work the earth. Clean bedclothes and three squares a day. You won't find any better deal."

I entertained him with cookies and iced tea out on the front porch. The peonies that Mama had planted years ago were noddin in the breeze on either side of the walk, tossin their pink and white petals like flower girls at a weddin. I could tell Henry liked what he saw, both on my land and in my eyes.

That evenin I fed him a good boiled dinner and put him to bed in Dora's old room. I cooked for him every chance I got in the next few days and kept myself busy with my chores, wanted him to understand I was a hard worker. He knew Daddy wasn't quite right but somehow made conversation with him and Daddy liked havin him there. And I guess I did too. He had his charms, he could talk about anythin, been to places I knew I'd never go. He was somethin different to come along and I wanted to hold onto him.

It didn't take long for him to see that I was the ticket to ownin three hundred acres without buyin it. And it didn't take me no time to find out he had the cash to get the place up and workin. I'd guessed from his good clothes he come from money but one afternoon when he was outside I sneaked a peak at his savings book. He had more in there than I'd see in ten years of farmin.

He helped me out by doin some repairs on the buildins and helped with my animals during the day. At night he'd work on his school paper about farmin. He settled in with us in no time. Said he'd always dreamed of ownin and runnin a farm but he had wanted to get his degree, too. What someone needed a degree in farmin for was beyond me but I started right off teachin him what it was really all about.

By that summer, with Henry boot-deep in cow shit with cal-loused hands, I had a promise from him. I knew Duff would be hurt but he was never in a position to support me or any woman. Henry and I planned to get married right on the farm. I thought in order for us to start out right I had to get Daddy out of the way. Besides wanting a chance to make our marriage work, I needed to have a way to control what was mine.

"Daddy, you're too much work for me. I've found a place in town for you to stay. A place where there's someone to look out for you." While I chatted on I dressed him in his good clothes and he stuttered and fought with me, but I got him out to the buggy and we headed to town.

"See, Daddy it's a nice place." It was. I'd got him a room with a retired nurse. I was gonna have to pay good money to keep him there but I figured as soon as I was Mrs. Gilley I'd have it.

"Daddy, Henry wants me to himself. You'll like bein here," I said to him as we sat in the buggy lookin at the pretty little white house that was to be Daddy's new home. He shook his head and kept slapping my arm, but he had little control of his movements. He had no choice but to stay. I got him down with a fight but I won. He was so much weaker than he once was. I handed him over to the nurse and turned on my heel. He wasn't gonna be my burden no more. Now she had to put up with his filthy mouth and cleanin his shitty bed.

Duff didn't say nothin when I told him I was going to marry Henry. He'd spent so many years sweet on me, even when I was that snot-nosed little brat, teasin him and followin him around. I guess I kinda ruined all of that for him. We was awful close growin up and now he knew he'd lost me forever. I couldn't look at him after I told him. I couldn't stand to see those eyes. All I could think about was how we was always runnin off somewhere in the woods when he was supposed to be workin for my daddy. We grew up teachin each other all the secrets we'd learned about our bodies. I don't know what was wrong with us, but we had only one thing on our minds. Now it was over. Between us, like a thick spruce forest, stood all our memories. I guess I thought I didn't have no special feelin's for him like he had for me. So I had to put those memories alongside those of Mama and Daddy, in the trunk I kept at the back of my mind.

He didn't come to the weddin. Didn't see him around for a few weeks but then he showed up. He stayed on at the farm but we didn't hardly exchange a word. I knew Duff was a lazy slacker but Henry kept him on cause he liked Duff. Everyone that met Duff liked him. Those damned eyes of his could swallow a person whole.

But then Duff went to war and I thought that was the last I'd ever see of him.

"I can't believe you've enlisted. You'll get yourself killed," I said to him after I learned the truth.

"I'm tired of farmin. No rewards."

Now I knew that wasn't true. He loved the farm as much as I did. We were standin in the kitchen. He kept his hazel eyes focused on the butter I was churnin. He wouldn't look at my face.

"Well, Duff . . . I'll miss you."

"You'll be too busy," he said and looked at me for a second.

"Now Duff . . ." I started to say somethin and he wrapped his arms around me and laid a kiss on me. The old fire sprang right up again between us. That night we met in the dairy and went at it like two kids who'd just discovered the biggest secret of nature.

The next mornin, I heard he'd left. He didn't even come by to say so long. I missed him bad, but he was right, I was pretty busy with the chickens, the housework, and with Henry.

. . . the drones leave the hive to take the air on a fine day, always on the lookout for a queen setting out on her marriage-flight. They often miss the way back to their own hive, entering instead at the first available colony, where they are given a hospitable reception as long as swarming goes on.

—*from* THE DANCING BEES
by Karl Von Firsch, c. 1953

CHAPTER NINE

Duffy

1916–1918

Things don't go like I'd hoped. Ginny is awful different now. Since Henry. No more stealin a few minutes with her in the kitchen havin coffee or some of her cakes and muffins. She says she ain't some schoolgirl no more and has to keep her mind on work.

Even before Henry I could see I was gettin nudged aside. Each mornin she and her daddy would get up on the wagon and head into town, or over to Milbridge, or Cherryfield to sell their eggs, honey, and milk. I had to work alone mostly. I started spendin more time with Hassie, a girl I met at a dance, thinkin Ginny'd get jealous. Hassie didn't have as much fire as Ginny. She just laid there while I was on her, just waited til I was done.

When Ginny and Henry decided to get hitched I said I wouldn't go to her weddin. She looked a little hurt but I was glad. I hid out back while people come to the house for the ceremony. I thought about quittin but didn't want to think about not seein her every day.

I tolerated Henry. He was a dull one though, all serious and thinkin his new ideas bout the farm was gonna make him rich. I thought about takin those little round spectacles off his hook nose and knockin that high education right out of his narrow head. But I just shrugged him off and tried to keep my eyes away from Ginny. She did her best and stayed out of my way for awhile. But it ain't easy to put out a brush fire when you're in the middle of the woods. When I told her I'd enlisted, I see the old Ginny behind her business eyes and before I knew it we was in each other's arms. Ginny and I made the mistake of foolin together in the barn fore I went off to war.

Now that I'm away I think less about Ginny and more about savin my sorry ass from the Germans. I'm sent to France and I think how far away I am from my home, don't understand what it is all us men are here for. I'm a good mechanic so they use me mostly for repairin truck engines. Then they train me to work on the planes too. I stay at the base camp mostly til nearly the end of the war, then I make it to the frontline.

My troop trudges through shit and dead bodies for weeks, eatin nothin but dried meat and mush. We get to a place where our commander tells us to start diggin. We dig a trench and then bank it with sand bags. We dig up some dead, sorry soldiers and have to move them around to other places. We cover the long gully with what branches we can find. In the trench we mostly wait for the Germans. My feet are shakin right out of my boots. It's all muddy in there and stinks like rotten horse meat.

You from Maine? a fella asks me in my camp.

Yeah, how'd you know?

The way you talk. I'm from Aroostock. Jasper LaPierre, he says and shakes my hand.

After talkin we learn his folks are blood to my mother's folk way back. We call each other cousin and make a big joke of it. The other fellows in our camp make a joke of it too, sayin everyone from Maine is cousins. Ask us if our granddaddys is our own brothers and stuff like that.

We're sleepin under a cloudy night sky and I hear some of the men whimperin cause we been told we're goin into battle. I think how Ginny will feel if I'm killed. Jasper tells me stories about home. Says he shot himself a bear last year. I think how I'd like to be huntin deer or bear and not Germans.

How you gonna feel if you have to shoot a man? I ask Jasper.

I'm gonna think bout shootin a bear and bringin home the skin for my ma. She likes bear skin. What about you? he asks.

I'll think bout one particular man and I'll shoot right between his eyes. Jasper starts laughin cause I've told him bout Ginny and how she married someone else.

The only time we get right into battle, me and my cousin Jasper are side by side in the trench in France and there's aeroplanes comin toward us. There's quite a bit of gunfire goin off down the line and I see soldiers fallin over with their heads landin right in the water. Jasper and I know those planes are comin our way so we both lay down in the water. It comes right up to our waist, in places, so we decide to go under.

One of them goddamned German fighters goes over us shootin right for the live men and the dead ones. Jasper and I lay right down in the water so they can't tell we're there.

Lay just as still as if you were trackin a deer, Jasper says and puts his head under the water. The Germans keep on shootin down the line makin sure we're all dead. I hold my breath as long as I can and come up slow. The whole surface of the muddy water is floatin with shreds of army-issue green and getting darker with blood. I hear the planes goin off to the east and I climb out of the water. I grab Jasper's arm and tell him it's OK to git up. I see a few other fellows standin up. Jasper don't git up, though I nearly pull his arm off tryin to git him out of the water. I turn him over and see he's been shot up, right up his middle, and his arm is nearly shot right off.

I sit awhile and try to believe what just happened. Some of the others do the same, then there's an explosion right in front of us. It must have been dropped from one of the fighters and didn't go off til now when we think the worst is over. I git my leg burned pretty bad and there's a lot of blood from some metal that's stuck in there, but it don't seem to bother me. I just think about Jasper and his mama at home thinkin about him and how she's gonna feel about him dyin. He don't look more than eighteen.

One fellow bandages my leg while I sit there cause I don't do nothin about it and he gits worried I'm gonna bleed to death. But I think, so what? One guy takes charge of the few of us that's left. He says we gotta move on, can't go back to our camp, afraid that it's been found out. But I say we can't just leave all these men. One guy says he'll help me bury Jasper if I'm so determined. So I forget my leg and we work to dig a shallow grave for him. I take off Jasper's ID tags and put them in my pocket. This guy has some whisky in a flask so we share it and then go on to meet up with the rest of our troop.

We get hooked up with another camp. They radio for a plane to take the ones that got cut up to a hospital. I sleep as best I can as we fly somewhere. They give me somethin for the pain. I wake up I'm in a makeshift hospital. More noise from wounded men here than on the battlefield. I sleep some more. Lay awake in the night smokin, pushin bad thoughts out of my head. Then I'm sent back to the States with my bum leg.

In the plane, lookin down at scabbed up land, I wonder how many dead boys are down there. All them soldiers in the hospital have the eyes of the dead. What God in heaven would want these boys to be lookin like that?

From New York I take a bus back to Maine but I don't go home; for some reason I feel like I don't want to see nothin that I used to like.

I go up to Aroostock and hunt up the LaPierre family. There's a lot of them but I ask around and I'm sent to a Germaine LaPierre. She's bout my mother's age. Tall woman, with grizzly black hair and a hatchet face. She opens the door to me and I ask if she's Jasper's mama. She starts cryin and shows me inside. Said when she got the telegram she broke up all her mama's dishes and went so crazy they had to take her to the hospital for awhile.

She says, Jasper was all I had and now I don't got nothin. I give her his dog tags and she throws her arms around me like I'm one of hers. She shows me all the photographs of her boy and we have some coffee. She shows me Jasper's bear skin layin out on her bedroom floor. When I tell her I buried her boy, I lie and tell her I had a stone made for his grave.

She says, someday she's got to go see it. When I tell her I got to leave she asks me to stay. After all, she says, we got some distant relatives.

I stay on with her. She has me call her Germaine and she treats me like her son. I git a little worried that she might start to think I am her son. She introduces me to her niece, a French-Indian girl. Dark skin and hair. Looks like a squaw. She's a pretty girl and I like her right off. Her name is Florence and she used to live in the woods with her kind but likes the town better. We start goin to dance halls and git along good. She can drink me under the table but I like that. All I really think about these days is drinkin and forgettin. And when I ain't tryin, I think about Ginny.

Florence and I move right into Germaine's and feel right at home. Florence wants to get married but I don't really seem to be able to think about more than today. I got it good here, nice room, clean sheets. Meals. Ain't like livin at home with Mama and Papa. But still I can't shake the dead feelin from me. I know these rooms is pretty but I'm needin a heavy dose of the Maine woods. Hunt myself a bear for Jasper.

Germaine says, it's time you made an honest girl of Florence. I'd be awful disappointed in you if you don't marry my niece.

I don't know, Germaine. You been awful good to me, but I don't know.

What're ya gonna do? Leave her? Is there someone else? she asks.

Ain't no one. No one, I say.

You're just still shook up. The war and all, she says. You need to come to church with me. Faith will clean out that doubt.

I don't say it, but I don't know if it's the war or Ginny marryin Henry that has loosened my belief. Mama always took me to church with her, but I never felt like I should.

I don't know, I say to Germaine. She goes into the kitchen and cleans. I know it's time to move on, she'd startin wedgin me in. Workin on my guilt. I can't be her boy though. Don't think I can be part of her family.

I've been been back in Maine for awhile now, so I think it's time I got goin home. I don't know's I'm ready to settle this far north. I want to go home, but still need the woods, the smells, the snappin twigs, the sunlight bakin the ledges, and the wind whippin the spruce trees. I pack up my gear, leave Germaine and Florence a nice note and I head off on foot. Take the long way home, through places no one hardly been before.

Home calls to me, but I head a little bit further north just the same. I'll go back downeast after awhile, when wishin for the faces I'd left behind gets too damned hard to forget.

One face in particular.

It used to be thought that a queen mated only once, with one male, but the opinion now inclines to believe that she may mate with two or three, even taking more than one mating flight before she settles down to egg laying.
—*from* BEEKEEPING: THE GENTLE CRAFT
by John F. Adams, c. 1972

Out of the bee's egg . . . a little white grub emerges which shows not the slightest resemblance to its mother, having neither head, eyes, wings, nor even legs.
—*from* THE DANCING BEES
by Karl Von Firsch, c. 1953

CHAPTER TEN

Ginny

1917–1918

Duffy hadn't been gone for more than a week when I found myself feelin funny bout the way things had happened between us. I know I hurt him and sometimes when I'd stand across the kitchen floor lookin at Henry, or wake up with him beside me, I wondered why I done it. I didn't love Henry but I thought I had the sense to know that love wasn't what made up a good partnership. I'd imagine Duffy comin through the screen door with an armful of cabbage and find myself smilin, or I'd look out the window over the sink and expect to see him against the sunlight that lights the hayfield. Henry caught me like that a few times and asked what I was thinkin about. I always said I was rememberin the taste of my grammie's rhubarb pie, or about a sleigh ride I took as a kid on Christmas Eve, but it was never those things. The lid wasn't stayin closed on my memory box.

I knew people in town wondered why Henry married me and they were probably expectin to see me swell up with a baby that had been made too soon. People liked Henry, accepted him even though he couldn't go to war cause of his bad eyesight and flat feet, and they thought I was awful moody compared to his good nature. Henry was always chattin with folks, tellin about some trip he'd taken to India or China. He told them enough to make them wonder why he'd settled for an uneducated girl who'd never been further than the state line. They knew my quick ways of talkin and my snappin judgments. They knew I'd taken the reins from my daddy and I'd set out on an uphill ride. They were wonderin if I still held the reins and if Henry was the horse.

Funny enough, though, it was love that made Henry stay here in Josiahville. Even after the first coals of his fire for me started to cool, I knew he was in love with me. And it was his love that drove him on, knocked him off his feet, and made him lose all direction he once had for himself. I had a way with those two men that loved me. I could turn them inside out til they had no idea what was what.

"Regina, I've been readin about dairy cows," Henry said to me one mornin after I'd fed him four eggs and some sausage. "I think it would be a good idea if we bought some more. That dairy of your father's is outdated and the four cows are too old." I cringed whenever he talked about the farm. But I smiled and opened my eyes a little wider to make him think I was amazed by his ideas. "I was thinking of getting new equipment, the best I can afford. I want to get at least ten cows. We've got to increase our productivity or we'll never get ahead." I stared at his shiny forehead where the hair was recedin. I looked at the image of myself in his glasses. I looked beyond him to the empty kitchen window.

"You know, Henry. I was thinkin more in the lines of beans. Maybe plant the three biggest gardens with nothin but dry beans. That'd be over five acres of them. They keep an awfully long time. I heard Abel say at the store that there's a demand for things that can keep and be shipped to the trainin camps and even overseas. We should help out any way we can durin war times." I looked back at my warped image in his glasses and waited to see his eyebrows furl up, or his mouth to turn down. But he smiled.

"Regina, you're right. I would never have thought of it," he said, and put his hand over mine. His hands were large and warm. I hadn't minded layin next to him every night like I thought I might. His face was handsome in a familiar way, like a favorite cousin or a preacher that you've known all your life. But he was strong and put together with just enough of that rugged, hard-worked sort of body that he could make me flush when I didn't want to. On our weddin night I expected to compare every inch of him to Duffy, but I didn't. Henry was a bit pink from lack of sun but his arms and hands moved with a sort of skill that Duffy lacked. Henry gave off the look of a thin, standoffish sort of man who'd never worked hard before, but he'd hunted and fished and had earned his letters from two or three team sports durin his school days. And he'd had practice with women. I never trusted his ideas about the farm but I learned somethin new with him. I learned to give someone their due credit. Like us all, he had good points and bad. I owed him a lot.

"We could grow more beans than just the three gardens. I'll find out how we can sell our vegetables to the government. Yes, that's a much better idea than the dairy. Milk can spoil too easily." He jumped up from the kitchen table and kissed me before headin out the door. I could've given him one more reason to kiss me, but

I didn't tell him the news. If I told him I was expectin, it would make it more real for me. I was nervous, hesitant to talk about the baby cause I couldn't be sure if it was Henry's or Duff's. When I wasn't mad at Henry I felt the guilt lay on me like a dead bull. Some days I couldn't get out from under it.

On Sunday afternoons Henry and me went to visit Daddy in town. His mind was about the same. Cracked in places and a clean, fine line in others. Daddy could run on with Henry about the farm for hours. I could tell he liked Henry and it worried me. My daddy, and most men around, didn't trust women to do much, and I was gettin afraid that Daddy might leave the farm to Henry and not to me. After all, I was only a wife. Henry was a man.

"Ginny and I are planning to grow food for the war effort. The government will pay us quite well," Henry said to Daddy. Daddy would look back and forth between the two of us like he was choosin. I got the narrowed eyes and Henry got the wide. Daddy had never forgiven me for sendin him away but the secret of Dora lay between us like a hidden blood stain. I would bring her name up from time to time when I thought he was gettin too close to Henry. He'd lay deeper down into his fluffy white pillows and rub his bloodshot eyes, tryin to wash his filthy soul clean.

"You got any money for these plans?" Daddy asked Henry. I don't know if he was hopin the money had run out or if he wanted the farm to work. He knew if the money was gone then he'd have to come home. I was hopin, if the money did run out, that Daddy would be long gone to his reward.

As they talked more about how to repair some of the farm equipment and what land was best to plant, I paced Daddy's bedroom and sometimes wandered through Mrs. Harding's parlor lookin over her knickknacks. I got to thinkin about the baby and remembered what Duffy had said once when we thought I was gonna have his baby. "If it's a boy, your Daddy will accept it," he'd said. Bells jangled in my head and I went back to Daddy's bedside.

"I got somethin to tell you two," I said.

"What?" Henry smiled at me. Daddy frowned and wiped some spittle off his chin.

"I thought I'd tell you two together," I said. "I'm gonna have a baby."

Henry hugged me and Daddy just said, "Good." I'd counted back the last three months and knew this child could be Henry's or Duffy's but it didn't really matter as long as I had a boy and Daddy left the farm to this child.

Before I left Daddy that day I decided to add a little more syrup to the kettle of fresh fruit I was boilin down in my head. "Daddy, if it's a boy I want to name him Eugene after you." I bent down to kiss his whiskered cheek and said in a low voice that I'd received another letter from Dora, and she still liked livin at Aunt Eula's, and then I said that she sent her love.

The months that followed brought a lot of excitement to life at the farm. Henry got plowin the fields with the help of our old hired hands, Walter and Royce. I'd been able to pay them all their back pay and now we could take them on again. Henry got some help from a few others too.

Gunnar Sorensen had a new wife and a couple of ornery boys, and though they had their own farm, once his mother passed on, he was lookin for some extra work. Henry took him on even though I told Henry that Gunnar was once sweet on me. I didn't mention the fact that Gunnar and I had gone a little too far out behind the raspberry bushes when we was kids. But Gunnar seemed happy with his wife and never came to the kitchen door for ice water and cookies like the others.

All the fields were bein planted with beans, Jacob's Cattle, Black Turtle, Yellow Eye, kidney, and red. I was fierce to work myself but I was swellin up with the baby, so I stayed close to the house and hens. Duff was gone, but at least I still had the good company of the farmhands. Royce and Walter weren't called to war like the younger men; they were on into their middle years. But they worked as hard as any young fella.

They loved me. There weren't too many days they weren't in the house for some tea or a pitcher of lemonade, sometimes four or five times. They fussed over me and took a pinch of me whenever they could sneak one in. I always fixed them up a good lunch. Besides Walter and Royce, who I'd known all my life, we had four or five other men workin for us. My kitchen or back porch was like a mess hall at dinner time. I always threw together potato salads and fried chicken, or a few pots of baked beans with steamin brown bread for them. I knew if they were fed well we'd get good work out of them.

"No one can put a better table of food together than Ginny," Walter would say, at least every other day. He'd slap my backside and laugh his head off. Those men would start throwin the compliments at me faster than they could get down their food. I loved every minute of it.

By fall I was feelin tired and couldn't even help with the harvest or the packin up of the beans. We'd had a good crop and dry enough so the beans didn't rot on the vine. When the baby was born, it was the middle of November and we'd just seen the first of our government checks come in. Henry went out and bought a used truck. We were one of the first townspeople around to own a vehicle. Mostly it was the summer people we saw with fancy Model A's, and even a Rolls Royce once in Milbridge.

The day Henry drove that rattlin thing down the lane to the house, I started with my first labor pains. Henry went and got Gunnar's wife to help me. Noelle had come from Sweden so I couldn't understand her talk and don't think she understood mine. We argued more than anythin else while she wiped my brow and rubbed my achin back, so I should've known things weren't gonna go the way I'd hoped. I was still feelin the rip of my worst and last pain when I saw the baby come out feet first. I hadn't even seen a face yet and already I was let down. I had no time to get my strength back, before Noelle started laughin, and said somethin in her gibberish. I looked at the squirmin thing and saw I'd given birth to a girl. And I could tell the way it was squawlin, it was gonna fight me every time she could.

Henry named her Edith after his mother. I didn't call her nothin.

While I was laid up Henry let the coops go all to hell. Shit everywhere, straw and mash look like he'd just flung it to them. He didn't know how you had to baby those stupid birds to get good eggs. As soon as I was up, I cleaned the coops up, we had three then, with about fifty birds in each. I got them happy again and felt like I'd done a good piece of work. Petted my cows, told them Mama was back. Brushed down the horse. My need to be with them was stronger than any feelin I had to that baby.

Edith made me awful nervous. I could tell she was greedy by the way she latched on to me when she nursed. And she cried all night it seemed. Henry picked up the slack for me with her. He walked her through the house at night hummin to her and I got some sleep. He waited on me too, bringin me trays of food and candies from Gossler's.

Edith was a month old when I got her all dressed up in a blue nightgown, blue booties, and wrapped her in a blanket I'd made out of some old clothes of mine. I covered her head with a blue knit bonnet I'd made when I was waitin for my boy to be born. I thought my daddy need never know.

Mrs. Harding was a foolish old woman, plump and powdery, corseted and curled, but she was stern with her nursin. She kept her patient on a strict schedule and she followed the rules Doc

Proudy had laid out. Daddy's mind was weaker and he'd lost control of his bowels, but his worst ailment was his want for whisky. I would usually sneak him in a bottle from time to time just to keep him quiet and drunk, but when Mrs. Harding found out she made me leave my pocketbook in the parlor while I visited him. Doc Proudy came to see Daddy about once a month and had decided that Daddy's liver was gonna erupt from any more liquor so I had stopped tryin to get any into him.

Until Edith was born.

I stuffed a pint jar beneath her blanket and went to show him his "grandson."

"Named him after you, Daddy." I propped Edith up on Daddy's chest and let him look at her while her face sucked in like a shrunken, rotten apple. He looked at her with about as much joy as I'd seen on his face when he looked at me or my sisters. None. When I produced the jar of whisky is when I seen the glimmer in his old gray eyes.

"Now Daddy, don't let that woman find this or she'll throw you out and you can't come back to the farm. Tomorrow I'm bringin Percy Luther over here so you can sign some papers," I said as I unscrewed the jar and gave it to him.

"What papers?" He took a big gulp and winced. I took Edith back up into my arms and let her suck on a rag I'd soaked with sugar-water.

"For this boy here. You're not gettin any better. You need to sign things over to me til he's old enough to take on his responsibilities."

"I ain't signin nothin. Damn bank will take it. Have you talked this over with your ma?" he asked, forgettin that Mama had died awhile back.

"Yes, and she wants you to sign." I stared at his cold eyes, saw those evil dark streaks fanned out within circles of ice.

"I still won't sign nothin," he said and then took another swallow of the whisky.

"You wanna get struck over the head again with a shovel?" I

asked. My voice was cold, low. I could bring it down to his depths if I had to. For a second it was as though we were both watchin the same silent picture. The snow around the house whippin against the barn door. The black branches of the trees. Dora movin toward him, slow. The bloody iron end of the shovel.

He put his hand up to his bald spot, looked for a second like he didn't know me.

"I'll keep you supplied with whisky and you sign the papers."

He moaned and swallowed again, lettin that warm liquor seep down into his black throat.

"You really name that boy after me?"

"And I don't know why. Henry thought it would be nice."

"I oughta sign it over to him. He seems like a worker."

"Sign it to me. I don't care that your liver's givin out on you but I bet you don't want it to dry up like old dishcloth. Ought to keep it full and wet."

I never brought Henry back to see Daddy. I told him that he was supposed to keep still. No visitors. The night he died I woke up with a cold feelin movin through me, didn't realize it was his ghost til the next mornin when Mrs. Harding sent a note to the farm. I figured Daddy'd go soon but it took me only three more quarts of whisky to finish him and I had my signed papers, statin that I was owner of the Merritt farm til my "boy" became twenty-one. Percy Luther had made out the papers the way I asked, not mentionin the child's name in the documents. The heir was listed simply as "son of Regina Merritt Gilley." Percy didn't know I'd given birth to a girl, and since his offices were twenty miles away from Josiah-ville, I knew he'd never be the wiser.

Henry saw the papers after Daddy died and I told him that Daddy had misunderstood that we'd had a girl. He said we better hope we have a boy someday, but I wasn't worried. All I thought about was I had my hands on the place for good.

Unless I had a son.

The social structure of the bee colony seems to challenge our present system of so-called civilization. Can we or can we not, even with our reason, survive as a political entity as well as have those social insects like the bees?
—from First Lessons in Beekeeping
by C. P. Dadant, c. 1957

CHAPTER ELEVEN

Caleb

1956

I remember my sister Edith carrying me through the pasture, then sitting with me on the stone wall between our property and the Sorensen's, I must have been somewhere around a year old. My first memory, and a bit blurry in my mind. But I still see her face as it was when she was young. She is only in her late thirties now, but seems to bear the face of an old woman. It is a simple face, a small nose and mouth. Her eyes are always tired and dry, encircled with many thin lines of a person who carries the weight of the world silently within her bosom. Her hair is streaked with gray and she keeps it pulled tightly away from her forehead and tied in a bun. The stoic schoolmarm who eats tiny meals, lives quietly with few possessions. In my memory she still has long brown hair and the smile of a girl.

I remember sitting on her knee as she sang. I don't know what the song was. And I think the memory has stayed with me, because, as she sang, she started to cry. It frightened me. Then I don't really remember much more, just the impact of her tears. She taught school in northern Maine then, coming home only for a few holidays and occasionally in the summer. Someone not particularly involved in my world.

My sister, Rose, is different. Her smile is wide and full of how she thinks. She grew from a plump, pink-cheeked girl into a heavy, happy, round woman. She somehow escaped the gloom of my mother, never really saw it, and went from Josiahville to a teaching school, like Edith, but never taught. She married when she was twenty and now lives over fifty miles from us with her five children and her husband. Rose must have been born to another woman, or maybe she is more like my father, Henry, than like Ma. Rose would hug me, pull me to her and laugh, read to me.

It's late. Ma wants to eat, so we leave the parlor and go to see what Edith has made for supper. Ma is worn out with my questions and her sadness. Tomorrow we put Duffy in the ground.

Ma won't speak to me while we eat. Edith has made a dry meal of overcooked deer steak and boiled potatoes. Ma hardly touches her food. Edith keeps looking at me and smiling. Ma goes upstairs and I help Edith with the dishes.

"Is she going to be all right?" Edith asks.

"She always pulls through."

"Are you angry with her?"

"I don't know if angry is the right word."

"What's going on? What are you two talking about?" Edith takes hold of my arm as I wipe the dishes. With one mean word I could send her to her room in tears. I feel like hurting her, hurting everyone and I don't know exactly why.

"I've got to go out," I say and move past her, out the door. I need to be away from the house for awhile. I get in the truck and start it.

I go to one bar in town. McGrath's. It's nearly falling apart now, with tarred paper and a few weathered shingles. A piece of curled cardboard is stuck up in the window that says "McGrath's." Inside, the ceilings are low, warped, and yellowed from smoke. There are four or five mismatched tables and chairs in the center of the place. Some of the chair-backs have been broken, missing their spools, looking like open, toothless mouths. The bar is a few sheets of plywood on crates. Beer and liquor boxes piled underneath. Behind the bar is a row of bottles and pictures of Dolores McGrath from the twenties when she won the Miss Washington County Beauty Contest. Her husband, Tommy, is sitting behind the bar, reading a newspaper. He looks up.

"Hey, Caleb. Sorry about Duff. He was good man," he says. "What'll you have?"

"Pabst." I hear voices coming from the back room where there is a pool table. Olaf comes toward the bar, carrying a beer.

"Hi, Caleb," he says to me and sits down at a table. I nod. I take my beer from Tommy. "Sit over here if you want," Olaf says.

"Sure." I go over and we sit in silence. I think about Ma. I can't focus on the here and now.

"You're quiet tonight," Olaf says.

"Nothing to say."

Olaf looks up as the door opens and two people come in. The man I don't recognize. The woman is Nora. I look at Olaf. He sneers at her and finishes his drink.

"I ain't stayin' here if that slut's going to." He stands up and drains his beer and goes out the door.

I watch the woman.

There is a Hank Williams song playing from a phonograph behind the bar. The man orders drinks. The record is skipping. I watch as Tommy and the man talk. They're laughing and laughing. Old friends. Nora is fidgeting with her hands. Now that I see her face up close, I can see she is pretty. Her face is oval and she has long, thin blond hair. Her face reminds me of Judy Garland's. She looks at me and smiles, looks down at her hands, and then back to me.

"Damn record," she says softly. "Why don't one of them fix it?"

I shrug my shoulders. She sighs and tries to look busy by searching her purse for something. She looks back at me. She looks toward the bar and shakes her head.

"I guess they don't hear it," she says.

I get up and walk to the bar. The two men are at the far end. I go behind the bar and take the needle off the record. They don't even see me. I sit back down and finish my beer.

"Thank you," she says.

We look at the bar just as the men go in the back room.

"You've been abandoned," I say. I don't go back to my table but stand in front of her. "Want me to get you a beer?" She nods and I get her one.

Her friend doesn't return. I hear him playing pool in the back room. We finish our beers and I offer her a ride home.

"Thank you. I don't see much point in waiting for him," she says.

In the truck she smiles at me and puts her hand on the seat, close to mine. I want to take it but don't quite dare. I'm not sure if she's still with Gunnar, or if something has happened between them. I smile back at her.

"Where do all of those wood's roads go?" she asks as we drive through the darkness.

"All through the woods. That one over there goes to Smith Pond. That one goes to the barrens."

I think I know why she asks me about the roads. She likes me and wants me to take her deeper into the woods. She's very pretty, and older than me, I figure she must be about thirty. The idea of being with a woman, not a girl, excites me, but I don't like the idea of getting my head bashed in by the Sorensens.

"It's a beautiful night. Look at all the fireflies," she says. "I'd love to go for a swim."

"Me too," I whisper. I turn onto Smith Road and the truck bucks and bounces over the ruts. "You still with Gunnar?"

"No, the bastard hit me the other day." She puts her hand on mine. "You got a girlfriend?" she asks.

"No."

"Handsome guy like you?" She takes hold of my arm and moves closer.

Before I reach the lake I stop the truck and we start kissing. She unbuttons my shirt, and though I know it's wrong to be this selfish so soon after Duffy's death, when my head should be busy with making plans for the future, I give in. I put my hand inside her blouse. I kiss her and then lead her out of the truck, toward the lake. We undress slowly in the blue light of the moon, and then hold each other as we slip into the water.

When I get home Edith is waiting for me. Ma is upstairs.

"It's late. Where have you been?" Edith asks.

"Just out."

Edith looks up from the book she is reading. "I was waiting to talk to you. About Henry. What do you want to know?"

All I want to do is to get into bed, but I may not get this chance again to hear about my father. I think of a question that has plagued me. My mother's eyes are dark brown. Mine are light green.

"What color were his eyes? Why did he leave us?"

"Oh, Caleb. It was so long ago."

"So you won't tell me anything, is that it?"

She clears her throat, takes off her glasses, folds the bows, and sets them on the end table.

"Blue. His eyes were blue."

I ask her other things that she answers reluctantly: Did Ma

love him? Did she hate him? Was he really my father? Edith gives one-word answers. No. Maybe. Don't.

"Don't? Don't what?" I ask.

"Don't ask me to tell you things that she should tell you," Edith says and then runs from the parlor. Secrets pile up faster than dirty dishes.

I go into the office and search for my father's gardening journals. I've never read them. On the covers of the few that he wrote I run my fingers over his handwriting, over "Henry Gilley" and the various dates.

He writes of seed, cleared timber, horses. There are no references about Ma, the girls, or me. Possibly all I can gather here is an understanding of how his mind worked.

No sooner has the union been accomplished than the male's abdomen opens, the organ detaches itself, dragging with it the mass of the entrails; the wings relax; and, as though struck by lightning, the emptied body turns and turns on itself and sinks down into the abyss.

—*from* THE LIFE OF THE BEE
by Maurice Maeterlinck, c. 1901

CHAPTER TWELVE

Henry Gilley

1911–1920

Henry had grown up in Concord, New Hampshire, in a tidy, white clapboard house with dark green shutters and vines framing the doorway. A hedge of arborvitae and his mother's half-moon gardens of peonies embraced the front lawn. His father was a partner in a shoe factory and provided quite well for his small family. Their home life was organized and quiet. Henry was an only child. He was not allowed to play in his bedroom. His toys were kept on the sunporch, neatly arranged on shelves. He often found that after playing with them that replacing them on the shelves was more work than it was worth. It was very difficult to put them back exactly the way his mother had left them. His father often told Henry that it was important to respect the things he was fortunate enough to own, thus causing the boy to feel indebted for every little book, marble, or toy train that Father brought him.

"You'll spoil him," Mother said when Father handed the boy a small box with a chrome whistle. "And you know my nerves couldn't take the noise. I'll put it on the shelves. You can use it when you're older. Maybe you'll have a child one day that would like it."

But Henry had wanted to hear the whistle, just once. Mother took her naps in the late afternoon while Henry was to sit quietly on his bed and read. He crept downstairs and pulled a stool over to the toy shelves. He listened for Mother. He opened the box. With a small puff of air he blew into the whistle making a tiny shrill. He smiled. He liked the way it sounded.

"I thought I made myself clear," Mother stood in the doorway. She walked toward him. She was almost eye to eye with him as he stood on the stool. She took the whistle. "If you don't understand how to behave now, how do you think you'll ever be a good student, or help Father in the factory when you're grown? You must learn restraint." She took the whistle and Henry never saw it again.

He knew she was right. He wanted to be good. He went outside and raked up the fallen leaves off the lawn and dumped them over the bank behind the shrubbery. She watched him and smiled. He could be good. She liked him when he was quiet and reading, or working on a puzzle. Not when he ran in the park with boys from down the street.

When he was good she would make him cookies and let him help. Or she would let him sit in the sewing room and read while she hemmed dresses. He liked to be with her. She had fewer headaches when he was good.

So, he realized that in order to accept gifts from his father he had to try harder to be on his best behavior. When Henry was ten, his father brought home a brand-new bicycle. Henry politely accepted the gift and spent the next few days cleaning out the barn, grooming the horse, and polishing the carriage. He worked away on trimming around the stone walls and helped his mother carry her many jars of strawberry jam to the cellar to be stored. He avoided his friends for over a week just helping around the house, thinking about the bright red bicycle. He was allowed to ride it in the park with Father on Saturdays.

When he came home, Mother may have made Henry his favorite pie, banana cream, or sometimes, lime squares, so Henry worked with Mother in the garden. He helped Father organize the nails and screws into jars, out in the barn. His grandfather gave him a new ball and glove, so Henry went to spend part of the summer with his grandparents. He worked with his grandfather in the garden, helped repapering his grandmother's kitchen shelves. They lived on a farm and Henry understood the immediate reward in seeing newly tilled soil, or holding a ripe tomato in his hand, or smelling the crisp smell of a fresh cucumber. He understood hard work. Knew that nothing should be free. Physical work brought rewards. There was a great amount of goodness in work.

He felt a nourishment in his bones, in his blood, when he accomplished each and every task he set out to do. The world was full of workers to keep it maintained and he seized every opportunity to participate. As he grew older this need to work moved him toward the idea of farming. His parents were appalled. They had hoped he would go into law or medicine. Henry himself saw those choices of a profession as redeeming and he contemplated the notion of saving people with delicate surgical procedures, or helping out the victims of crime and abuse. But it was having his hands deep in rich soil, or entwined around something green and fresh that convinced him to pursue agriculture.

Mother couldn't help her tears as Henry left for college in the dim morning light in 1911 on the train. His father shook his hand and Henry thought he saw respect in his father's eyes. Henry was thrilled to be going but apprehensive about leaving behind Muriel, his high-school sweetheart.

College was a swift tumult of years. Books and lessons, the drowning sense of learning too much, but he was strong enough to swim, to rise above the water he was thirsty for, so he prospered.

In his personal life he learned to understand women, or so he thought. He met a girl in New York named Anthea and fell in love. Muriel became a tinted memory of youth, like his bicycle. Anthea, all too willing to give herself up to him, caused him to feel guilt. That same old guilt of not taking what you've not earned. So he bartered for those weak-willed, desperate, secret nights in her dormitory room. He began by helping her with her trigonometry and then by doing all of it himself. He studied with her, made notes for her tests. He had no choice. He had to work for the love that Anthea gave him.

Anthea watched this boy reach for every opportunity to please her, to reward her, and so she began to hint for gifts, like the brooch she'd seen in a jeweler's window, and then a charm bracelet. It was finally an engagement ring that she sought. Henry was eager to please her; as her husband he would work even harder for her admiration. Rushing to her room, after deciding he'd get a job to buy the ring, he overheard a conversation through her opened doorway. Anthea was telling her girlfriend "how easy it was to get Henry to jump." Henry didn't understand. Was he too eager to please her? But, the harder he worked the more she loved him, or so he had believed.

He didn't buy the ring. He told Anthea that he was leaving college. He was nearly finished at any rate and he was earning his degree by visiting rural farms and working on a lengthy paper about the decline of agriculture. He left, broken hearted and disillusioned.

He was twenty-two when he traveled as far north as Josiahville, Maine, a place he had once gone as a boy to fish with his father. He sought out the bedsores of the land caused by the disuse of fertile soil and the villagers' lack of an agricultural education.

He met Regina Merritt, a hard-bitten girl, frosty around the eyes, obviously determined by the severe set of her mouth. She was a farm girl, pretty in a mature way, but surely not sophisticated enough in the world's ways to toy with him like Anthea had. He took a room at her house. Spent evenings talking to her father about the land, when the ailing father was feeling up to it. Henry saw the three hundred acres in all of their green glory, their lush forests, ripe blueberries, and apple trees. He saw this in Regina's eyes. He saw her love for it, too. He saw years stretching ahead of them surrounded by many children. He saw a new tin roof on the barn and outbuildings, the house freshly painted, and fields of green, green growth.

They married as soon as the war started.

Henry felt guilty about the war, wishing he could fight, wishing his bad eyesight hadn't kept him away from the battlefields. He was afraid of losing his wife's respect, and Mother's too. But he'd regain it with the farm. He would turn the place into profit. He'd work day and night.

Making love to someone as removed from the outside world as his wife was simple. It was enjoyable. What demands could she make on him? Certainly she had nothing to compare him to. He was warm and slow, gentle. She got used to lovemaking, like a good wife does, and he was free to devote himself to farming and the dairy. At first he was suspicious of the closeness he sensed between his wife and one of the farmhands, Duff Pendleton. Maybe they'd been childhood sweethearts, but nothing to worry about. Obviously she preferred her husband and was hungry to make the farm a success.

Regina's father got worse and needed constant care, so they sent him to live with a retired nurse in town. Together, husband and wife planted beets, carrots, cabbage, potatoes, and strawberries. Regina worked hard to keep up with the orders she got for her pies and cakes. She labored over her hens and beehives. She sold honey and eggs and Henry pondered the unused fields. With his trust fund and borrowed money, he had some land cleared, planted more. He thought of increasing the livestock, getting more milking cows, but his astute farm wife thought about dried beans to supply the soldiers. She was remarkable. He could plow, plant, weed, dry, and box up food for the war effort. He could do his part to ease his guilt of being denied by the service.

Henry only missed one thing from his former life: Mother.

She would not come to his wedding, but he didn't tell Regina that. He partly told the truth by saying that his father was ill, a bad heart, and that they couldn't travel. Henry ordered a sterling silver punch bowl with twelve matching cups and ladle and sent it to Regina with a card wishing them well. He signed the card from his parents.

When his first daughter was born he named her for his mother, Edith, and wrote another unanswered letter to her, begging her to come for a visit. He'd thought of taking his young family to New Hampshire for awhile, but the farm demanded too much of them, and would Regina really fit in? He could imagine his mother frowning in disgust at Regina's bad grammar, something he thought endearing.

When Regina's father died and she inherited the farm, Henry felt like he did the day his father brought home the bicycle. He cleared more land, he repaired the old plows, he bought a truck so he could take his wife to town without the smells of a horse. He made love to her frequently. He had a great debt to repay.

By the spring of 1919 Regina had given birth again, to a girl.

One summer afternoon as Henry rocked their newest daughter, Rose, on his knee, he looked through the mail on the porch of Gossler's store, and saw with amazement a letter from his mother.

He tore it open. It was a brief note stating that his father had dropped dead while at work at the shoe factory. She asked Henry to come home to be with her.

"I can't go. Who'll tend the bees? The chickens? The girls? I don't have nothin to wear." Regina moved through the kitchen grabbing at pot handles and dishes, scurrying about like a caged mouse. He took her in his arms and said they would buy what she needed, he wouldn't go alone.

"I don't like to travel," she said as she pulled out of his arms.

"I need you to be with me," Henry said, removing his spectacles and wiping his eyes.

That evening, as was her habit lately, Regina put together bowls of leftovers and walked into town, even though Henry offered to drive her. She'd go to see Duffy's father. Since Duffy's mother had died, Regina did what she could to keep the man fed. Henry applauded her noble gesture.

Henry took her to Ellsworth to browse in the dress shops and milliner's. She slapped at his hands, refused to look at the dresses he chose, laughed at the height of the heels on women's dress shoes. He took her to the first restaurant she'd ever been to. She thought the rolls were too dense, the fish too salty, she wouldn't touch her salad. Who'd ever heard of eating leaves and raw vegetables drenched in oil? she asked.

Passing by a hat shop she saw something that caught her eye. An elaborate straw hat with the top woven into something that looked like a bee skep, complete with silk bees and a cherry blossom.

"I suppose I could use that," she said.

It was easier after that for Henry to get her to buy a few simple dresses and even a pair of shoes with low heels.

The train trip to New Hampshire made Regina sick. Henry had to care for the girls. Edith would run back and forth down the aisles and Rose wanted fistfuls of soda crackers. Henry sat in a shower of crumbs meeting the stern, level eyes of annoyed passengers. Occasionally he'd tip his silver flask of whisky to his lips and regret his decision to bring the family.

Mother was an imposing figure of a woman. Henry himself felt somewhat insignificant in her presence and thoughts of cleaning her pantry or whitewashing the picket fences ran through his head. She was tall, severely dressed in long black skirts, a brooch at her throat, with white, neatly pinned hair. She viewed them all before speaking.

"I waited to bury your father until you arrived," she said, and moved inside the doorway so they could pass.

"Mother, this is Regina," Henry said with difficulty, well aware of what details of his wife's appearance Mother was scrutinizing. The awkward hat. The plain dress, with a hem that ended just below the calf of her legs. The practical shoes.

"This is Edith," Regina pushed the child forward.

"Doesn't she smile?" Mother asked.

"Of course she does," Henry said. Edith ran to his side, staring up at the white-haired woman who wore a frown.

"And this is Rose," Regina held tight to the chubby baby and glared at Mother.

"I've never liked the name Rose, so I'll have to think of something else to call her." Mother walked through the foyer and into the sitting room that Henry was never allowed to go into except when there was company.

"Don't put her on the carpet," Mother said to her daughter-in-law.

For a brief second Henry saw his mother as others must have, stiff and cold. With difficulty he tried to remember her as the woman who had coddled him, made his favorite foods, watched at the train station when he left for school.

The funeral was held inside a church the size of the whole farm. Henry hadn't realized before how big and sickeningly overdone things were outside of Washington County, a place he now felt was home. Regina had hardly spoken a word the evening before at the dinner table as he quickly showed her which fork, which spoon to use. The girls were unhappy in the care of Mother's housekeeper while they ate and he winced every time he heard Edith yell or her feet run across the upstairs rooms.

As the minister spoke on and on about Henry's father's attributes and accomplishment within the community, and then about the everlasting life, Regina twitched in her seat and sighed loudly. She would frown whenever Henry looked at her or shook his head silently.

"I won't stay here another minute with that . . . that . . ." Regina said after the guests had left the house. The worst was over, thought Henry. The funeral, the refreshments, the relatives, but now he wasn't so sure.

"We can't up and leave. I want Mother to get to know you and the girls. I want you to see her differently. She can be nice." Henry helped his wife out of her tightly buttoned dress that he'd bribed her into buying with the promise of new hives. She wanted six more and he thought it was a meager price to pay.

"Who does she think she is? She hasn't said a nice thing to me. She hasn't gone near the kids. Old bat, I'd like to give her a piece of my mind."

"It will be better now. The funeral is over. She might warm to you."

"Get me out of this damned thing."

Later when Regina came downstairs she was wearing one of her faded cotton dresses and canvas shoes. Her hair was out of its coiled braid and hung loose and crimped down her shoulders.

"My my, the farm girl," Mother said with arched eyebrows.

Henry's mouth hung open. The girls were sitting quietly at their father's feet, Edith was playing with a box of old toys that had been Henry's and Rose was crawling toward the stairs.

"That's right. I might as well dress in what I'm accustomed to." Regina walked into the parlor and plopped herself into a chair.

"But it's so unflattering to you. And after all the trouble I've gone through." As Mother said this, she took Regina's straw hat off a basket of sewing. It had been stripped of its silk bees and blossom. The top had been pushed down a bit, obliterating the bee skep. A wide black, grossgrain ribbon was around the circumference, with perfect tails hanging behind. "I thought this might be more in keeping with the styles. I noticed how out-of-date your things are."

Regina lunged forward and grabbed the hat from Mother. She ripped the ribbon off it and threw it to the floor.

"What in Hell did you do to it?" Her eyes flared, her face turned red.

"I've tried to . . . to . . . " Mother stood up and ran from the room. Henry started to follow but was met with his wife's angry glare.

"Now she's upset," he said.

"She should be, look what she'd done to that pretty hat," Regina said as she reached down to pull a wet, soggy, silk bee from Rose's mouth. "For Christ's sake, look. Rose could've choked to death on this."

Henry went to Mother's bedroom door and knocked but she wouldn't answer. He followed Regina to their bedroom and watched as she began to pack her bags.

"I can't leave her like this," Henry said. "You go back. I'll stay here with the girls."

"You stay here and you might as well forget ever comin home. I won't let them kids be treated like shit neither. They ain't stayin here."

Henry walked softly back down the hall to Mother's room.

"We're leaving, Mother," he said through the paneled door.

"I don't understand why you can't get along with my wife."

The door opened slowly and Mother looked at him with red eyes and wet cheeks. "I was only trying," she said and let him into the bedroom. He sat down on the edge of her bed.

"She might not be what you'd hoped for me, but I love her," Henry said.

"I don't know what to do with myself now that your father is gone," Mother wept into her white handkerchief.

"I know," Henry held out his hands for her and she sat down beside him on the bed.

"I'll be so lonely. Too much time to myself . . ." she muttered.

He was at a crossroads. He was familiar with this juncture. He'd passed by it in thought before when Mother wouldn't answer his letters and his feet sunk deeper into the soil of the farm. He'd made his choice by staying with Regina and giving her children, but now he felt as though he had to tell Mother his decision. Had she really wanted him to come home to help or had she hoped he'd stay, leaving behind his family?

"Mother, I love Regina. You can't expect me to give up my life."

"I can't stay in this house alone."

"I have two children and another on the way."

"Remember how I taught you to ride your bicycle?"

"I love the farm, the land . . ."

"Your father always expected you to take over at the factory."

"Regina and I will be leaving in the morning."

"And this house, what will I do with it? Your father wanted you to live here."

"I hope you'll apologize to Regina before we leave," he said and stood up. He left her there crying, wanting to go to her, wanting to be her little boy again, but it couldn't happen that way.

Even as they walked out the front door with their baggage he watched the staircase, still expecting Mother to give in and come after him. But no doors opened. He looked at Regina as she picked up Rose. He saw her dark hair knotted beneath her scarf, her gentle neck turning as she moved, her quick hands tying the ribbons of Edith's bonnet under the girl's sharp chin.

There had never been a choice for him to make between the two women who dominated his heart. His love for Regina was planted as deep as root. Mother's love was tough as bone.

As they sat together in the club car waiting for the train to leave the platform, he saw something change in his wife's face. As she looked out the window her eyes widened, as soldiers, businessmen, and mothers with small children passed by. Another train was unloading mostly homecoming soldiers. The war had been over for months but still they were arriving home. One man turned his back to them. He stood alone. No one was there to greet him. There was something familiar about him but Henry wasn't sure what it was. His dark hair? His broad shoulders? His height? This man was dressed in uniform. He lit a cigarette and blended into the crowd. Regina was looking too, but he wasn't sure if she was looking at the same person. Had it been someone she knew? He opened his mouth to speak but then noticed for the first time since he'd met Regina a pink softness to her face, a brightening around the rim of her eyes, a slight tremble of her jaw. A look she had never shown to him.

He didn't say a thing, he wanted nothing to change that expression. It was something he might never see again on her face.

It was utter helplessness.

He knew he'd made the right choices for his life in marrying her. She was capable of every emotion. He could see that now. Beneath her fierce, strong currents she was vulnerable and he longed to tap into that reservoir, drink from her.

What had caused this unmasking was irrelevant now. The only thing that was important was that he'd witnessed it.

Preparation for the winter naturally follows the harvest-
ing of the crop. Yet, the beekeeper who waits until fall
to think about the proper preparation of his bees for the
winter may not find it a simple matter to give his bees
all the prerequisites to a successful survival.
  —*from* FIRST LESSONS IN BEEKEEPING
      by C. P. Dadant, c. 1957

CHAPTER THIRTEEN

Caleb

1956

I close the gardening journals, leave the office, pass by the parlor door, notice the light from within. I linger in the kitchen for awhile watching the moonlight over the swamp, waiting for Ma to leave Duffy for the night, but she doesn't come out. Then I head out to the barn to look over the extractors. Ma has been negligent with the bees this past summer and so have I. I scrape the crusted honey and wax from inside the metal pails with my jackknife. Ma never would have left them like this in the past. I know the bees will be mine now. Ma has little hope, and less enthusiasm in her than she's ever had. I wish I'd been older when she ran the Queen Bee Diner, managed her hives, raised her hens. Even in her meanness I'd have respected her energy. Was it Teddy's death that wore her out? Or has she other miseries she's never shared?

Tomorrow we bury Duffy.

I wander through the beeyard. I know I must feed the bees soon, once the frosts come. Some of them will not make it through our cold New England winter, but the strongest will survive. They'll feed on the sugar and water I give them, they'll huddle around their queen, beating their wings to raise the temperature within the hive. So many of them will beat with such energy that they will work themselves to death. The black carcasses will be tossed out the opening and pile up on the snow, or feed hungry mice.

Tonight the air is colder than last night. I sit on the porch and swing my feet over the brittle branches of Ma's forgotten flowers. I see the candlelight in the front parlor. I go to the window without making a sound and listen to her muffled voice.

I know I shouldn't eavesdrop but I can't help it. I open the door to the house quietly and close it behind me. I pause by the parlor door. I hear her say, "I'm sorry 'bout Henry. He was my burden to bear, you shouldn't've done nothin to help." Then I hear her cry again. I start to move away. She speaks again and I wait to hear. "I don't know how I'm gonna close the lid of this thing."

I wonder how will I? How can I close Duffy in there? He still has so much to tell me.

His voice like fine sandpaper moving slowly over soft wood.

. . . it might be well to say a few words about the location
of the apiary. First, it ought to be some distance from the
highway. What that distance should be, depends upon
what there is between the bees and the street.
—from ADVANCED BEE CULTURE
by W. Z. Hutchinson, c. 1911

CHAPTER FOURTEEN

Duffy

1918–1922

When I left these parts to go to war, it came to me how much I like the country. After I got out of the war and left old Florence and Germaine up in Aroostock, I spent a good long time wanderin around Maine on foot. The reason I went into hidin was cause of Ginny. She seems to be the reason for most things I do. As I waited for the train to take me from New Hampshire to Maine, I think I see her inside a train, all dressed up in a hat. It couldn't have been Ginny, but enough like her to remind me.

So I went up through the parts of Maine that aren't even set-tled. Way up north I was campin out in woods so thick you needed lantern light durin the daytime just to see your hands in front of you. It was up there I met a strange gal, name of Aurora Swan. It turned out her people were from Evangeline, not far from my own town. She was up in the woods doin just what I was doin, tryin to stay away from people. She was around her mid-twenties, I'd guess. Not too good to look at and as fierce as an old black bear if she had a mind to git mad. I come upon her sleepin in an old canvas tent full of holes. She bout killed me when I got too close. Pulled a knife on me. I noticed she had a deer carcass strung up in a tree and over her campfire she was roastin some venison on a spit she'd made from sticks. I hadn't had any good meat for awhile and I thought if I was to get any of hers I better calm her down.

I don't mean no harm, just passin through, I said.

She didn't talk much. Looked sorta wild. I guessed she'd been up in those woods for awhile. Her yellowish hair was a mess of tangles and she had more dirt under her nails than I ever seen under mine.

What do you want? she asked.

I said I could do with a taste of that meat and then I'd be on my way.

She fed me and then she made some good strong tea from roots. She seemed to know all about what plants you could eat and such. I said I liked my tea sweetened and I missed the taste of sugar. She got a funny grin on her face and told me to follow her. We walked a ways through the woods and come out into a clearin. There was a big old tree with a hollow openin in it. There was at least a million bees swarmin around the hole. I shrunk back into the woods a little and she laughed.

She went right up to the tree and them bees startin lightin on her everywhere. Her whole head become a black, buzzin mass of them things. She stood real close to the tree and put her bare arm right into the hollow and fished around in there awhile. I thought, well this is it, this crazy coot is a goner. Fore I knew it she pulled out a thick chunk of honeycomb and walked right back to me. The bees just went about their business.

I knew I was headin home but this woman with the bees only showed me how close home had always been to me. Somewhere in the center of that hive was a queen. And not too many miles away was Ginny.

We went back to the campsite and she put some honey in my tea and didn't it taste some good. I've always taken my tea like that since.

Aurora and me become pretty good companions for awhile. Not in the way you might think. She didn't seem to have an inclination to be close with no one, but we shared some good times as we hunted and trudged around the woods, makin our way back downeast. I never met anyone could make home brew like her. She'd brung some with her and we shared it together after a long hike.

Now whenever I walk the woods, eat fresh venison, or go huntin, I think bout her, and how she steered me home.

Over two years after I got out of the service and trudged around, I go home. While I was gone my ma died and I didn't even know it til I walked in the house. Ma was the only one in my family that could write good so they didn't tell me. I never got a letter anyway, while I was gone. My brother and sister both married and moved away and my papa is livin alone like a junkyard dog, eatin whatever someone give him, or whatever he can kife off someone's back porch or out of their gardens. He says he bout froze in the winter til an old lady down the road let him stay in part of her house for the worst months. He tells me Ginny brings him some homemade dishes from time to time and Henry brings fresh vegetables and eggs and such. I think that sounds like Ginny, lookin out for my poor old daddy.

I replace some panes of glass and throw out the piles of trash Papa had let pile up and get things situated enough so we can use two rooms of the house. We each have a cot and I let Papa have the one dry mattress and I get our blankets washed out. I do some paintin, mostly to kill the stink.

I think about goin to Henry and askin for my old job but to see Ginny's somethin I still ain't ready for. So I take some cash and buy myself some clean clothes that aren't so threadbare. I git all slicked up and walk to a tavern on old Route One name of Sutter's Tavern. I think I'll walk in there and in no time get myself a woman for the night. All I see is an old bat we always called Spread-them-Edna. I'm not about to get in the sack with Edna Cheney. I take a stroll around town and then hitch a ride with a fella to Cherryfield.

I see a lot of vehicles parked in front of the Odd Fellows Hall so I walk right in and see what's goin on. It's the Baptist Church congregation havin a party of some sort, one fella tells me. Now, there's only one reason a fella like Duff Pendleton goes to a church function and I can tell ya. To look for women. I come home from the northern woods of Maine with a yearnin for a good downeast woman. Ginny was what I wanted but I had to forget her.

Standing to the back of the room at the Odd Fellows Hall is a girl in a light blue dress and a pretty white sweater with little buttons to look like pearls. I tell her my name and get her a glass of punch. She says her name is Coris. I can tell she's took a shinin to me by the way she blushes whenever my hand brushes up against hers.

Coris says her people are from up Bangor way originally, but her folks come down here to summer on Stanley's Point. Coris says she likes to stay here as long as she can keep warm in the camp. I figure she must come from some money. Coris is a pretty gal and smart on her feet. I get to thinkin bout the nice house she tells me she has on the point. I think about the look in Ginny's eyes if she gits wind that I'm home and datin someone upstandin like Coris.

I see Ginny one day at Gossler's store. Abel has told me she's been askin if I was around but he knows I don't want her to know where I am. If she brings Papa food I hide out and he just tells her I'm seein someone from over to Number Seven. I hide behind an old truck and watch her pushin a baby buggy along the dirt road. Her backside has filled out more now that she's been havin kids. She looks large with one now. I step out from behind the truck and sure enough she turns and sees me.

I head the other way but she don't give up. She comes after me and leaves that buggy right in the road. She says, You can't keep hidin from me Duffy Pendleton. I see ya. I know it's you. Turn around.

So I turn around. I don't quite dare myself to look directly at her eyes, but after a second I look up her big belly, to her chin, to her smile, to her eyes and I see she ain't changed none.

I can't believe you've been home so long and not come to see me, she says.

Why would I do that? You with your husband and your babies, why'd I come out there to see you? I pull a plug of my tobacco from my tin and start chewin. I tell her to git that buggy out of the road fore some fool drives it over. She hauls it back to where I'm standin at the truck.

Your daddy wouldn't tell me where you were. He says you're seein someone.

How I'm keepin my feet planted on the ground, not pickin Ginny up and lettin her hold on, is what's surprisin me. Her arms I never forgot.

You know my daddy died and I got the farm, she says.

You and Henry, I say.

I thought you might've got killed over there, she says.

Well, I didn't. Here I am.

Don't you need some work? she asks.

I'm gettin married, I say and then Ginny's baby starts to cry so she picks it up.

You got girls? I ask.

Two of them and probably this one comin is a girl.

You never much liked girls, I say.

This one's all right. She gives it a kiss and jiggles it. It smiles and I can see Ginny in her. Pretty thing. I wish it were mine. I think about that baby Ginny and me thought we was gonna have once.

How's your hens and them bees? I ask.

Good. Come see them. I got a lot more. And Henry put a new roof on the barn, even painted the house. It don't look like it did when we was kids, she says. She waits for me to smile at that but I can't.

I gotta go, I say and I turn right around to leave. As I walk down the road I keep lookin back and she don't move, just lets me stretch this thin rope that's always been between us, til it has to give way and snap.

Coris is waitin for me at my papa's house. She's all fixed up for us to go dancin at the Grange Hall tonight. She's got everything Ginny don't got. Yellow hair, blue eyes, sort of a light around her shinin cause of her smile and sweet nature. But bright light gits hard on the eyes.

I wonder what Coris sees when she looks at me. If I'm slicked up in new clothes and make myself talk more like her people, Coris must see someone I really ain't. She wants a husband and I guess she puts that picture of what she wants on me. I go clean up and then we head out to Cherryfield in one of her daddy's vehicles. With my hands gripped on the steerin wheel I feel like the fancy man that Coris wants.

It's at this Grange Hall dance that I drink too much whisky and hold Coris tight to me as we dance. Sometimes spinnin on the floor to the fiddles and piano I forgit there is a Ginny. The feel of Coris against me takes on a movement like the music, slow thumpin and soft, like the brush on the drum.

Coris it's time we set a date, I whisper into her sweet-smellin neck.

I think so too, she says and pulls away from me to look at my face. She's happy like nothin I ever seen and then the music sweeps over me and I feel the need to swallow the guilty notion that sticks in my throat. I don't know if it's whisky, music, or the way Ginny stood still watchin me walk away, that makes me kiss Coris. Like the kiss can wash out old feelins stainin my sorry soul.

Coris and me git married at her church. Her folks can see I ain't nothin much, just a country fella that looks good enough to a young girl whose lookin to be married. Her daddy offers me a job thinkin he'll find the son-in-law he hopes to have. But I don't take it; I like odd-jobbin better.

I ain't up to snuff with her people. I admit I don't think like they do and I don't have no problem just feelin and actin like I damn well please. For awhile, I think I can be just what it is her daddy and mama, and Coris herself want. But to Hell with that, I say to myself after goin to a few of them church socials and tryin like Hell to please her daddy.

I just ain't the type of man s'pose to sit behind a desk and her daddy, Roland Hancock, owns a gas company. He wants us to move to Bangor for a spell. He wants to teach me how to manage his accounts but I know I'd miss good ol' Sunrise County. I'd miss a lot of things like havin my head shoved under the hood of a truck, workin to beat the band on what I love. Engines.

I love motors and loggin and fishin and diggin in the ground and I love the things that those peoples' rules don't abide by, like a cold beer bout mid mornin, or a smoke, or talkin bout things the way they really are. I could never figure why folks have such a hard time talkin bout beddin and such. Like we don't all do it and like we don't all sit on the pot two or three times a day to lighten our loads. Foolish, that's all I can figure.

After we git married we go to Bangor to visit her folks and her daddy tries to talk me into goin into business with him, even though I know he thinks I'm just a fool. I tell Coris one night in bed I can't work for him, I have to git home.

She lifts her head off the pillow and I see nothin but a child in her eyes. I say, I can't work for your daddy and I can't live in this house. But I kiss her to let her know I want to be with her. I say, let's go back downeast, let's live in the house on the point.

Papa will be furious, she says.

I kiss her some more and then we git to it. She's gittin to like it as much as me.

Morning comes. I dress in the suit Coris got for me and I head down the stairs to have breakfast with her daddy. Coris looked long and hard at me before I left the bedroom, with those baby-doll eyes, beggin me to keep my mouth shut, to change my mind. I guess she don't know me too good.

Mr. Hancock, I say. I don't think this job would be for me. I don't know much about numbers or sellin. Coris and me was thinkin bout goin back home, to my home.

He puffs away on his cigar and I watch the sweat beads formin on his bald head. His fat lips grip his cigar like he's got lockjaw. I wait for his steam to rise and his sweat to pour and for him to tell me what he really thinks of me.

I knew it would come to this, he says, blowin smoke. If I could have stopped the wedding, I would have. But she loves you. Then he stares at me. Has his mouth turned down like he tasted pig swill.

I'm sorry but it ain't gonna work out, I say. Coris says we can live in your place on the point. I can git work. It's just a fox can't live in a trap for long without gnawin off a limb or his heart givin out.

What will you do? How will you provide for my daughter? he asks. Shoveling horse shit? Oiling tractors? he says real nasty to me.

Honest work, work that comes easy to me.

I won't let her move down there and live the life of a maid. The life of those women in Washington County isn't worth the shit you'll be shoveling, he says.

Sorry you feel that way, but she wants to go.

I can't see what she sees in you.

Maybe it's what you can't see that she likes, I say.

His face gets redder and he puts his cigar out in his eggs.

How much? How much do you want? he asks.

I don't want no money. I want to go home. I want my wife at my side, I tell him.

I won't have it. You'll break her heart.

You ain't got no choice, I say. Me and Coris want to live down-east.

I can see he's thinkin and I can see he don't like where I've put him. He ain't used to bein wedged into a corner.

He says, after thinkin on it awhile, It won't be more than five years and she'll be back.

I don't say nothin. I start to think how funny he is all puffed up like he's God or somethin, and I start to laugh and it takes me awhile to stop. He says he's convinced I'm a lunatic.

PART THREE

The Swarm

*But we are forgetting the hive wherein the swarming bees
have begun to lose patience, the hive whose black and
vibrating waves are bubbling and overflowing, like a bra-
zen cup beneath an ardent sun....*

—from THE LIFE OF THE BEE
by Maurice Maeterlinck, c. 1901

... the queen seems completely uninterested in the care of her young; her efforts in that department end strictly with the laying of the eggs in the cell. All the rest of the work that a mother usually does, and there is a fantastic amount of it, she leaves to the worker bees.

—*from* THE WORLD OF BEES
by Murray Hoyt, c. 1965

CHAPTER FIFTEEN

Ginny

1922

My life was a sack of spilled beans, loose pieces of myself were poppin every which way, teeterin off solid edges, rolling down cracks in the floorboards. There was a lot for me to separate out in my head, Duffy, the girls, Henry, my cookin, my hens, my bees. I wish I could've sat right in the center of a hive and had everyone buzzin around to take care of me. I think there must be some peace of mind for those bees, every one of em knowin what their work is, what makes up the beginnin of a day and the end.

I had the farm though. There was some peace in knowin that. But the work was hard, and motherin was hard, and forgettin was hard. I'd taken things for myself by workin my way around a lot of people. I was movin toward the things I thought I wanted, to make a success of the old place, to show people what I was by how hard I worked. But I didn't have the one thing I should've took years ago. He was gone. I didn't know the loss of him til two, three, five years had passed and I hadn't seen him but once. As the train rolled out of Concord I saw his face amongst all them soldiers and wives. The war was over and I thought he'd be back home but he stayed away. He wasn't runnin back to me like I thought.

When I looked out that train window and seen those green eyes, the dark stubble on his chin, the slower way he moved, I think it was the first time my insides wanted to let go. I felt like my stomach was stretchin out and about to burst. I felt the heat of a July day even though it was winter. And what was worse, I thought, was that the two of us passing each other like that in some out-of-state train station, had to be a sign. A message from God that he and me was meant for each other. Or maybe just some God rubbin my nose in what I could've had.

For a few weeks after seein him and not bein able to touch him, to even speak to him, I sunk low. I couldn't get up mornins to make breakfast. I let the wash go, I didn't clean the chunks of honey out of the hives. I just couldn't move myself. Henry thought I was sick, and he babied me, but I didn't feel sick. I felt dead.

After the war was over time dragged through my days, like that dead bull that once was guilt, only this time it wasn't the weight of guilt, it was the weight of lonesomeness. Duffy didn't come back to Josiahville for so long that I thought I might never want to get out of bed.

I thought about Duff and me as kids. I remembered that well of feelin that sometimes nearly drowned me, comin up on me slow and goin over my head. Every touch he gave me brought on water. Sweet water that any woman would love to drown in, cause all the time I was goin down his big arms was around me. I remembered the things that a sensible girl shouldn't. I remembered laughing. But did he stay away cause he loved me, or hated me? I wasn't sure. My mind was swirlin, things comin up, and things goin down the drain in a muddy, swirlin funnel. Things was muddied enough to get me mad at him, at who I was, at everything.

I waited for that anger. I had to be strong enough to lift the heavy top off my old trunk of memories and put away all that was useless to dwell on. Then I had to get up and do my work.

Besides missin Duffy, I had two little girls to contend with and had another on the way. Edith was mean-spirited, kept me jittery, my nerves would ball up and twist me so inside I'd start up screamin and rantin. I tried not to slap her around much but by God, what's a person supposed to do with somethin that wild?

It was a day when Edith and me had been fightin over a doll she'd found in the attic when I up and left the house with Rose, and saw Duffy at the store. That doll had been mine when I was a girl and I just wasn't ready to pass it on. Edith struck the doll's head against the table so hard that the bisque face cracked and split. If Henry hadn't happened along I think I would've throttled her. I took off to the store for some glue to fix my doll. Henry promised Edith he'd get her one just like it. I didn't think she deserved nothin.

And then after all that time there was Duffy tryin to hide on me behind an old truck at the store. I called out to him and he come from behind the cab of the truck with a long face. I couldn't read him, didn't know what he was thinkin, but he must've still loved me cause he'd tried so hard to stay away from me.

He told me he was gettin married. I tried not to show what I felt but as soon as I walked away from him I felt that same sinkin feelin in my gut like I had when I seen him from the train. I wanted to go home, pack up everything I had, and walk right out on Henry and Edith, but I knew I couldn't leave Rose. I even felt a twinge of missin Edith after I let my anger die down. No, I was stuck with my family. Duffy was someone else's.

After I got back to the house Henry hit me with some bad news.

"We got a letter from the government. They don't need our beans or anything, anymore. All those acres of beans . . . What'll we do?" Henry said as he sunk deeper into the easy chair in the front parlor. He still held the letter in his left hand and I took it up. We'd been afraid of losin our government contracts after the war but it hadn't happened yet and we'd had no warnin. The government was still responsible for a lot of wounded and maimed soldiers, and for their families too, so we'd hoped to be growin food for em for a long time still.

I got Edith and Rose to sit quiet with their books on the kitchen floor and went back to the parlor. I sat down in the chair across from Henry and waited for him to speak. I had ideas of my own but one thing a man doesn't like is for a woman to think faster than him, so I kept my mouth shut.

Eventually he took off his spectacles and leaned his head back. "I suppose we could try to sell the beans around here, either out of the back of the truck, or open a farm stand," he said.

I knew he wouldn't come up with anything better than that, so I thought I'd throw out a yard or two of rope for him to hang onto.

"The bags of dried bean down at the store are more money than most want to spend around here. We could undercut the prices. My daddy knew a man in Portland who owned a business. He used to come through here and try to sell split peas, beans, and lentils. I wonder if he's still in business," I looked at the frayed threads on the hem of my skirt as though they were all I was thinkin about.

"Regina . . . ," he said and sat up puttin his glasses back on. "Maybe we could sell to those big companies."

"You think we could?"

"It's worth trying. I could get the names of those places off some of Abel's boxes and bags and we'll write to them." He came over and kissed me and then he was out the door.

Over the next few weeks he contacted a few names he got hold of, and when only one wrote back he was pullin his long face again. Then the rains come, lastin through the month of August. Our dried bean crops was quickly sucked up in mold and mildew. Row after row there weren't nothin but brown and black, soggy leaves with swollen beans. Henry waited til it was dry enough to go into the fields before he tilled it all under.

Well, we were approachin some hard times but I knew we weren't gonna starve. We'd still been able to harvest some of the other vegetables and I canned or stored everything for the winter. Henry slaughtered our pigs and I had all my hens. It would be all right but Henry felt like he'd failed. He stopped eatin and filled his belly with whisky. When he was sober he was quiet and when he was drunk he was spendin time with the likes of Gunnar Sorensen. Gunnar was a sullen creature that I'd never quite understood. We'd always been friendly but he had a mean streak and I always thought he looked at me too long when I was wantin him to turn away.

It was a cold November night and I was about ready to give birth and my husband was nowhere to be found. I'd been readin to Rose just before her bedtime when I felt the first pain. I hadn't felt right all that day and what I feared was about to happen.

"Edith, you're gonna have to go find Walter or Royce, or Lois," I said as I struggled to stand up from the chair, settin Rose on the floor. Edith was just a little girl but I knew I could trust her to find help. "I think it's my time," I groaned out as my body clenched up like a fist.

"Mama, Lois has gone home for the day," Edith said. Lois was an Indian woman that worked the dairy for us. She was a strange bird and I didn't much like the idea of her helpin me through my pain anyway.

Edith ran out to the barn without her coat and then I saw her go over to the woodpile where the men had been workin. She came back quick and out of breath. "Everyone's gone," she said.

"You think you can run as far as Sorensen's place 'fore dark?" I asked.

"Yes!" Her eyes sparked up. I'd never let her go that far by herself. If you went through the woods you could get to Gunnar's place in ten minutes, but by road it was a good twenty, and right along the main road where I feared she might git hit by a truck or some other vehicle.

"You be careful and don't get in the road, stay to the side," I hollered to her after I got her bundled up in a coat and hat. For all our differences, I knew me and Edith was alike in our determination. She wanted a job that she could prove herself by.

I sat back down with Rose who had toddled all over the parlor pullin at things that had been my mama's, and I tried to forget the pains. I waited and waited til I could feel the child inside me buckin its head to get free. I managed to get Rose into bed and make myself some tea but time was runnin out and I felt swells of panic risin up in me. I could see the sun settin from the kitchen window and could only imagine the worst. If Edith had ever made it to Gunnar's then Henry would have been home totin Gunnar's wife to help me.

I paced the floors til I couldn't no more, sat by the parlor window waitin, driftin in and out of some darkness. It was well past nine o'clock when I heard a truck comin up the lane. I could barely walk to the door. The pains had been strong and constant but still nothin happened. I thought there had to be somethin wrong or I'd have had my baby in my arms by now.

I opened the door and Edith came runnin from the truck. Her hair was a mess and she didn't have her hat. Her face was scratched and muddy.

"What happened? Where've you been?" I asked her through clenched teeth.

"Lost!" she shrieked at me. She started to cry and threw herself at me. I held onto her and started cryin myself. I wanted to claw Henry's eyes out for stayin out so long at night, I wanted to kill him. I craned my head expectin to see him stagger out of the truck, but when I looked it wasn't Henry. It was Duffy.

"Poor little thing," he said as he came up on the porch. "If she hadn't wandered into my dooryard I don't know what would've happened." He smiled at me and I swear I saw the faint glow of a halo around his perfect head.

"Duffy, I'm havin trouble with this baby . . ." Then it was like a tree struck me, the pain was so bad. I crumpled to the floor and watched as the room was swallowed up by a blackness. I came to every now and then with his face above mine and his worried eyes tuggin me through every pain.

I thought I was gonna die. I looked through the blackness until I could see a pinpoint of light. I swam to it, and as I got closer it got bigger and there was Mama on the other side. I crossed the line and held onto her as she talked me through it. She patted my hair, wiped my brow, like she'd never done in life, and told me to give up that baby to her. She said she'd watch over it for me. Then I felt I was fallin into a empty quarry. The fallin wasn't scary though, it was a letup from the pain. I struck bottom, opened my eyes to see Duffy and I knew the baby was dead.

"It's dead isn't it?" I panted out, lookin around my bedroom for it.

"Not yet. But, well, Ginny I don't know . . ." He held it up to me. It was still wet and bloody. It's eyes were shaped funny. The back of its head was flat and it wasn't breathin right. I almost didn't want to take it, it sent such a chill up my back, but it whimpered and I felt that familiar twinge within my breasts. I couldn't deny the little thing, but when I put him to me, he wouldn't take nothin. I thought, maybe, he was just wore out from the birth.

Duffy sat close to the bed as I tried to nurse. We didn't say nothin, there wasn't nothin to say. He kept moppin my forehead and gave me some cold water. I couldn't ever remember feelin peace like that.

I slipped off to sleep and woke to the sound of voices comin up the stairs. The baby wasn't in the room with me and neither was Duffy. The sun was high in the sky. I heard Henry and Edith talkin a mile-a-minute. They both rushed into the room. Henry looked like he'd been on a drunk. He looked that way a lot them days.

"Where's Duff gone to?" I asked.

"He's with Rose and the baby," Henry said. He had tears in eyes. "It's a boy, Regina! A boy!"

"I know what it is. I've been sufferin through his birth while you was out drunk. Edith could've been killed tryin to find you!" I yelled at him feelin the pain all through me. "I want to sleep, leave me alone."

Both of them started to leave, I called for Edith. "Edith, go ask Duffy to come up to see me."

After a second or two Duffy knocked at my door. I told him to come in.

"What do you need, Ginny?" He sat down and took my hand.

"How's the baby?" I asked.

"I've got him wrapped up tight, right next to the stove. I think he's gonna have to be bullied into nursin, though. He don't seem to want to suck on my finger or nothin. He don't have no strength."

"Like that lamb. Remember that one born so queer lookin? Wouldn't eat. Daddy had to kill it."

"Somethin like that." Then Duffy pushed some wet strands of my hair away from my forehead and bent to kiss me. How many mistakes would I go on makin in my life? I wondered.

"How'd you learn to deliver babies?" I asked.

"Wasn't much different than the cows or sheep," he said.

Days slipped past as I let myself heal. Noelle Sorensen took care of my girls and I hoped everyday that Duffy would come back but he didn't. I waited for the child to die. Even after it finally took hold of my breast and suckled, I still kept waitin. I wouldn't name it. Henry started to call it Theodore, "Teddy" for short. He started struttin around the house like a rooster, actin like he'd fathered Christ Almighty. He never saw its slanted eyes or odd-shaped head, never felt the limp arms and legs, never wondered why it didn't cry.

Inexperienced beekeepers are sometimes tempted to extract too closely. They thus ruin the colony. . . . In the fall it is best to leave the hive body as full as possible.
—from FIRST LESSONS IN BEEKEEPING
by C. P. Dadant, c. 1957

CHAPTER SIXTEEN

Caleb

1956

I have loved my mother, though she makes it easy to forget that. From the kitchen I can see her defeated, shrunken body make its way slowly up the stairs, and I want to run to her, hold her, tell her I will make it right again. But I can't bring back the dead.

In time she will soften from the shock of Duffy's death, though I know she'll never really recover from it. It will be then that I can enjoy her company, she will listen to me, maybe take my advice. We will play cards at night and wait like an elderly couple for the return of our daughters. When Rose comes home the house is full of laughter, yes, even Ma laughs when Rose is here. And when Edith comes back there are cups of quiet tea and comforting walks down to Gossler's for penny candy.

To make Ma happy I will have to be patient. I will have to forget my own life. But isn't that what Duffy and I did all along?

Forget our own needs for the sake of Ma? But I must admit it wasn't that simple. I've had wants and desires, but somehow all the work it has taken to please my mother has been worth it. There is a certain satisfaction in pleasing her. Duffy felt the same way. Our needs were not as important. There is a part of me that wants to live on my own, find the right woman, go to school and get away from farming, but is it possible to leave her?

I follow her up the stairs, knock on her door and step inside.

"Ma, I need to talk," I say.

"It's late," she says from the darkness.

"Did you love Teddy more than me? Did you love Duffy more than Henry?" I ask. I sit on her bed in the dark. I hear her sit up, see her pale, milky form in the bit of moonlight that comes through the cracks in the shades.

"You ask too many questions. I ain't good with words, Caleb. You're askin' for more'n I can say." She sits quietly for awhile, probably hoping I will leave. But I don't. She breathes softly and then slowly reaches across the quilt and takes my hand.

"I done more for you than any of mine. Don't wonder if I love you. I just ain't one to show what I feel. If it weren't for this darkness I couldn't even say these words to you," she whispers, her voice cracking with the sobs that she's stifling.

"But tell me about Henry, tell me . . ."

"You want to take too much from me. Leave me something," she says and lies back down, turns away from me.

When the time draws near for the young queens to come out of their cocoons, the old queen grows nervous. She buzzes around, and edges toward their cells. The workers know she wants to sting her daughters to death so that none of them can take her place as queen.

—*from* THE WORLD BOOK ENCYCLOPEDIA,

c. 1955

CHAPTER SEVENTEEN

Ginny

1925–1928

Teddy got bigger and his scrawny legs filled out but he was slow about doin things other babies do. Rose and Edith had both sat up at seven months but Teddy hardly lifted a fist to his face, rarely cried. When he was hungry he'd open his mouth to make a sound but then seem to forget what he was doin. Henry went about his work like nothin had changed. He finally admitted the boy was slow, but said he'd catch up. Edith was leery of touchin the baby and Rose thought he was beautiful.

Durin the coldest of the winter months I would sit up in the dark with that child and feel his warm breath on my neck, his soft limbs curlin over my breasts and I'd feel a peace I'd never known. I'd felt so much anger at Henry before, but somehow that child could mold my hatred into something as pliable and mushy as his own body. I wanted to hate Henry but he'd given me my children and allowed me to keep the farm, so I couldn't. But I resented him.

He took to drinkin more and stayed out all night. When I was workin in the chicken coop I could sense Henry watchin me from the loft, too ashamed to show his drunken face to me. After I was strong and the baby was sleepin through the night, I still wouldn't let Henry back in our bedroom. I told Edith to move her sister's things into her own room and give Henry Rose's room at the end of the hall. Henry didn't say a word. He knew he'd gone too far by leavin me alone to birth that child. We spoke and shared our meals together but Henry had ripped a scar down the middle of us that was worse than any birthin could do.

When Teddy was eleven months old I got a smile out of him by clickin spoons together. I had him reachin for things too, like his bright colored rattle that Duffy had made and sent over. The first time I realized that he recognized me, when there was just a spark of somethin in his eyes that knew it was me who held him, then I knew he'd do all right. He might not've been like most children but I could see I'd be able to teach him things, and get a smile as a reward.

I didn't let the baby, or the girls, keep me from workin around the farm though, and there was a lot to do. Henry was sulkin and drinkin so it was up to me to figure out the best way to get things done. One afternoon I bundled up the kids and we walked into town. I had Edith stay with Rose and Teddy on the steps of Gossler's store while I ran down the street to Duffy's daddy's house. I knew Duffy lived out on Stanley's Point with his wife but he was usually tinkerin on engines in his daddy's dooryard or in the shed where he'd set up a repair shop. I hadn't seen Duff much since Teddy was born so I walked toward the shed a little slower than I wanted to. When I saw him he just looked up quick from an engine and looked right back at it.

"Can't say hi to an old friend?" I asked.

"Hi, Ginny. How's that baby?"

"He's doin all right." I stood close to him waitin for him to say somethin but he just kept on workin with his wrench.

"You mad 'bout somethin?" I asked.

"No," he said as he wiped his hands on his coveralls.

"Then what is it? Why are you so quiet?"

"I'm quiet when I'm thinkin. I been thinkin too much." Then he looked right at me. He'd never looked so serious before. I smiled and my face felt hot. Then he reached out his hand, held my chin, and kissed me.

"Why'd you do that?" was all I could think of to say.

"No one like you deserves a man like Henry. Don't he see who you are?"

"He's too drunk these days to see anything."

Then Duffy picked up his wrench and hurled it to the back of the shed. It clattered into tin pails and tools.

"If I hadn't o' found your girl that night, you'd be dead now. I can't forget it."

I felt I was standin behind that thick plank of wood I'd put up between us over the years, that wooden door that kept everyone out, but his green eyes dug right into it. Peeled away at the grain and the knotholes. I had the funniest thought when I saw his face just then. I thought about my daddy's loomin, ugly face comin through my bedroom door in the dark, and I wanted to run, run right into Duffy's big arms.

But I didn't, somethin of that wooden door held up to those eyes.

"Why'd you go and marry him? I just could never figure," he said softly and turned away from me.

"Duffy, I don't want to get into this," I walked up behind him and put my hand on his shoulder. "I came to ask for your help."

He didn't say nothin for a long time. I could hear Rose's loud voice from down the road singin some song. I'd told Edith to keep Rose at the store but Rose liked to be with me and not with her sister.

"What help do you need from me?" Duffy asked.

"I need you to get things goin for me at the farm. I can't pay a lot but you know what it takes. I can't watch these kids all day and do everything around there."

"I ain't workin for Henry," he said. "I'm tired of farmin. No rewards."

Now I knew that wasn't true. He loved the farm as much as I did.

"Now Duff . . ." I started to say somethin and he wrapped his arms around me. He kissed me again and then I kissed him back. I don't know how long the kids had been standin in the open doorway before I seen Edith's mean eyes starin at me. I pulled away from Duffy real quick and straightened out my coat. He put his head back under the hood of the automobile he'd been workin on. I went quick to the kids and fussed with Teddy's blankets in the buggy. Edith turned on her heel and took off up the hill.

"Ginny, I'll be to the farm on Monday, if you think Henry will want me around," Duffy said.

"He won't argue with me. He knows he can't win. He's not so drunk that he can't see he's ruinin the farm."

"Better go catch up with that girl," he said.

I turned the buggy around and with Rose at my heels made my way home.

"I hope Daddy won't let Duffy work here. I hate him," Edith said to me the next day as she was peelin some turnip at the kitchen table. I went right over to her and slapped her fresh mouth. She wouldn't cry though, no matter how much she was hit. Her face was red and she held her hand over the cheek I'd struck. Her eyes watered up some, but she wouldn't let em flow. She'd scream plenty and run to her daddy if she was real mad. I didn't want her doin that but I just couldn't let her say nothin mean about someone as good as Duffy. I knew there was a burnin hatred in her after seein Duffy kiss me, and as far as I knew, she hadn't said nothin to her daddy about it. I'd told Henry that I'd talked to Duff about workin for us and he didn't argue. He just stumbled off toward the Sorensen's place with a bottle of whisky.

"How can you say that about Duffy?" I yelled at Edith's homely little face. "You hardly know him. He worked here for years. He saved your life. He's gonna help us." I shook her but she wouldn't speak. I walked back to the counter where I was grindin some pork.

"Sometimes, Edith Gilley, you amaze me," I said.

"I saw him kissing you," she said softly.

"Well . . ." I wasn't sure what to say. I'd hoped she hadn't really understood the kiss.

"I did, right there in his shed," she kept peelin them turnip like we was talkin about her schoolwork.

"He was kissin me good-bye. He's like a brother to me. We grew up together. You don't know nothin 'bout what you saw," I said, but my hands were shakin. I was afraid if Henry knew, if he understood what was between Duffy and me, he'd take off and there was no way to keep the farm goin without his wallet.

"It didn't look like you were brother and sister," she said. She turned her little evil eyes on me like headlights. I had to admire her courage. Only seven and she knew when things were stacked up in her favor. I figured the best way to battle this situation was to keep actin like it was nothin.

"So, did you tell Daddy?" I asked, almost losin a finger in the grinder.

"No."

"Well, it's just one of those things. You'll understand when you're grown."

"I don't plan to tell Daddy."

"Well, that's a good girl. It really wasn't nothin," I said. I wondered now how much she knew about the birds and the bees.

"I don't want to peel these goddamned turnips," she said and threw down the parin knife. She stood up from her chair and glared at me. She waited for me to say somethin but I couldn't. She never used swear words before, and I knew it wasn't the last time she would to me.

She walked out of the room and outside. I heard the front door slam as she left. I wasn't sure what she was up to but I guessed she wouldn't say nothin to Henry. She liked havin this little secret over me.

Edith could be a sour taste, a bitter fruit, but Rose was a sweet, red apple. Rose was all giggles and forever good-natured. I could do things with her I'd never done with Edith. Rose would sit still on the sofa with me and I could read one book to her after another. Her eyes as big and round as pancakes. She had them kind of yellow curls all over her head like Henry. She was my little angel. She and my boy Teddy.

In the summer Rose and me would trudge up to the barrens and pick pails of berries and come back to the house and whip up some damned good pies. That little thing would stay right by my side if I let her. She'd roll the dough, sort the berries, and pinch the edges of the crust. Clever and sweet. But my attention to her didn't go unnoticed, Edith would stalk from room to room, starin at me, scowlin. I enjoyed bein with Rose, but I was careful not to go overboard. Edith might get me sprung in her trap at any moment if I wasn't careful.

"You never let me make pies with you," Edith said one day. Rose, Teddy, and their daddy'd gone to get some grain in Milbridge and Edith and me was alone. "All I do is watch that baby. I want to learn to cook, too."

"Didn't know you'd want to. You never much like to work in the house," I said and it was true. Edith was always with her daddy ridin alongside him on the tractor or helpin him in the dairy.

Edith put down the book she was readin and said she wanted me to teach her to cook. I thought I better cooperate with her. So, from that day on, I taught her how to make everythin. Just a child when she baked her first pie and it was better than mine. We never had the fun times Rose and I did, but we learned to work together. I showed her how to churn the butter, make jellies, can vegetables, and make good spicy sausage. She was fierce to learn all my chores and I had no choice but to show her and keep myself away from Duffy. Edith was always waitin around some corner to see the light in my eyes if I spotted Duffy in the yard. She had one goal in mind and that was to make her daddy proud of her and if she'd had her way, I'd have been pushed right out. I'd seen her get rid of people she didn't like.

We had an old woman work for us one year. Edith must've been nine or ten. The woman worked with the cows, doin the milkin and cleanin the stalls. She was a drifter from up north lookin for odd jobs when she wandered onto the farm. She was an old squaw who'd lost all her family somehow and had traveled down this way. There were a lot of Injuns comin around in the summers to pick blueberries. Her name was somethin funny like Dipsy or Delsey, I can't quite remember. One day she come into the house wearin a long face. She said some of the cows had dried up and some were producin sour milk. Now, I never heard of such a thing but she swore to it. First thing I thought was she'd done some Injun mumbo-jumbo and cursed our cows cause she wanted more pay or somethin.

"That's crazy talk, cows don't produce sour milk," I insisted.

"I'm all done here," she said.

"Why, what's goin on?"

"They've been cursed," she said.

"What are you talkin about?" I threw down the dishtowel and put my hands on my hips.

"The little birdlike one. Her eyes carry the power." That old woman stood there lookin at me with a stone face and expected me to believe in some magic.

"What? What do you mean?" Now I was convinced the old bat was drunk.

"You let that child around them cows and you won't have no milk," she said.

At this point, Edith came into the kitchen with her squizzled-up face just lookin for a fight.

The old woman pointed to her. "She has the evil eye."

Edith crossed her eyes and stuck her tongue out at the squaw and jiggled her fingers at her, like she was puttin a hex on her. The Injun's eyes got big and then she turned and practically run from my kitchen. She never did come back to work for us.

"What did you do to that poor woman?" I asked Edith.

"Oh, she's crazy. She's thinks I can curse her so I let her think it."

Things went on like that, me feelin at times like I was a prisoner and she was the warden. Duffy worked outside my cell and all that was between us was our thoughts and the mud of the dooryard.

Henry was proud of Edith and managed to cut back on his drinkin, spent his time dotin on her, but I didn't mind.

I tried to be good, but Duffy made it hard. His kind of look just got to me. A little rough around the edges, but strong and handsome. Henry was a good-lookin man, too, but his face was more gentle lookin, not so square or as rugged as Duff's. Henry liked Duff, too. Duff could tell a joke like nobody and seemed to find the worst things in life funny. Henry bein such a serious-type man, he didn't see things the same way as Duff, but he sure liked to laugh with him. So the time passed, my edgy nerves rubbed raw by Edith, but I was good. Just knowin Duffy was around seemed to be enough.

About two years after Duff had come to work for us, Edith

come home from school to find Duffy and me sittin at the table havin coffee. It was nothin but two friends talkin but she didn't see it that way. She threw a bunch of her schoolbooks on the floor and took off upstairs. I didn't know til the next mornin that she'd gone into my bureau drawers and shredded all my panties. And there wasn't nothin I could do about it, least nothin that might spurn her to tell Henry.

I decided I had to fight her somehow. She'd planted rows of eggplant and garlic, two things we never planted around here, nothin fancy like that. Henry thought she had good ideas and let her experiment with things. She had her daddy wrapped around her little finger. He gave her all kinds of space to grow things. After the war there was plenty of land to work with. Those eggplants were comin up beautiful and the garlic was in luck, too, cause we were havin a fairly dry summer, not a lot of rain that would rot the bulbs. Edith was preenin around about her work and I just got plain sick of it.

I couldn't go out to my chickens or the herb patch without her suspicious eyes followin me. I couldn't stand it. Duff and I had been good, no foolin around, and he was tryin to be a good husband to Coris, and a decent daddy to his boys. I didn't have no hard feelins about it neither. But that didn't stop Edith from watchin.

One day she went into town with her daddy and wouldn't be home til dark. I waited til the farmhands went home for the day and then went right out to the woodshed. I took two cans of gasoline up to Edith's gardens and sprinkled just enough over every one of them plants to kill em. Luck was with me, it rained like a son-of-a-gun the next three days so when Edith got outside and saw her gardens, she couldn't smell the gas. She screeched like a two-year-old for hours.

She might've thought the rains had drown her things, or she might've suspected me. I was never sure. But soon after that episode, I went out to collect the eggs and found that both the coops had eggs smashed all over the walls and floors. I had to guess she knew what I'd done, but she couldn't prove it. She got me back without tellin Henry, and I started to think she never would. She liked havin a hold over me. So from then on, our battles were fought like that, without sayin a thing to one another. I couldn't tell Henry about the rotten things she'd do and she didn't tell on me.

Edith was eleven when I went and slipped up. Duffy and me had passed each other everyday for two years now, without sayin much more than hello, but it was when I found a letter that Henry had written to his mother that I broke, and Duff was there to pick up the pieces.

The letter was hidden in Henry's coat pocket. I saw the corner of it there as I was about to go up the front stairs, and before I thought, I'd grabbed it. It was addressed to his mother. I figured he wrote to her from time to time but I couldn't imagine what he'd say to her. I thought he'd probably painted a pretty picture of our life but it wasn't that at all. The envelope wasn't sealed so I pulled the letter out and started to read.

> *Dearest Mother,*
>
> *As I've stated before the medical bills for Regina's condition continue to pile up. The doctors assure us that she's getting better but her medicines and the doctor's visits are very costly. If I had more time to devote to the farm and less to her needs as well as the babies, I'm sure I'd have no trouble covering the bills. If you can find it in your heart to loan me another 500.00 I promise I will pay it back along with the rest when times get easier for us . . .*

I had to stop readin. I couldn't believe he'd asked his mother for money along with lyin to her. His drinkin made more sense to me now. He felt like a failure to everyone, especially to the one who he wanted to impress the most, his beloved mother. I could only guess how much of these loans he'd turned right down his throat. He must've gone through Hell by crawlin to that cold woman, and was still goin through it.

I couldn't help but think how much easier things would be for him if I loved him.

"What's wrong with you?"

I jumped and crumpled the letter in my hand. I turned to see Duffy standin behind me behind the screen door.

"Oh, Duff . . . ," was all I could say. He opened the door and came in.

"Bad news?"

"Yeah." I moved down the front hallway toward the kitchen. I needed to sit down. I leaned on the table and sat. "Duffy, some days it ain't worth gittin outta bed."

"What is it?"

"Where's Henry?" I asked.

"Back pasture with Royce. I just wanted to git some water."

"I've done an awful thing by marryin him."

"And me by marryin Coris, I guess," he said as he sat down in the chair next to me.

"He's a broken man. I don't know how to fix him."

"We just keep goin, Ginny. I shouldn't be workin here at all."

"No, Duff, don't say that. I don't know what I'd do if I was alone." It was then I made a big mistake. I reached over to Duffy's hand and held it. The touch of him just made my insides burst and I started cryin. He pulled my head to his chest and kept smoothin his hand over my head. I was lookin at the floor through my tears but could plainly see the two feet step up to Duff and me. I lifted my head quick and come face to face with Edith.

Duffy and me both stood up. Edith didn't run like she had that time in the shed. She stood her ground, flarin her nostrils and squintin her little eyes.

"Don't start with me, missy," I said to her, trying to bully her away but she wasn't easily bullied.

"Daddy won't like this," she said with the same chill of frost her grandmother spoke with.

"You hold on. You don't know what goes on between me and your daddy. You just keep that trap shut. You don't understand things grown-ups do," I snapped at her, but she turned her back to me and started walkin out of the kitchen. I grabbed her by the shoulder and pulled her around to me too quick and she slammed her head against the door jamb. She crumpled to the floor like a lifeless wooden doll.

Duffy stepped over to her and lifted her head off the floor. Her eyes were closed but fluttered open. She looked stunned but it didn't take her no time to spit out her venom.

"Take your hands off me," she said to Duff. He propped her up before lettin go.

"You all right?" I asked, touching the welt on her head.

"Get away from me," she screeched at me. Again her voice reminded me of Henry's mother so I figured she must be Henry's girl. Or was she so damned angry all the time because somewhere inside her she felt she was Duffy's? I knew that was a crazy thought but who knows how deep the roots go, how many messages are passed through the blood of a parent to a child? If she was Duffy's then why did I find it so hard to love her?

"I'm takin you upstair to lay down," I said as I helped her up. "You can be as mad at me as you want but you're gonna lay down." Duffy went out the back door and I helped Edith up to her bed.

The rest of that afternoon I moved Rose's things back down the hall and put Henry's things back in my room. I promised Edith that her daddy and me was happy and would always be together. I don't know how much of it she really believed, or how much she just hoped for.

The drones have no stings and cannot fight back.
—from THE WORLD BOOK ENCYCLOPEDIA,
c. 1955

CHAPTER EIGHTEEN

Duffy

1925–29

The nights been the worse for me and Coris. I can't seem to sleep and she don't know why it is I don't slide in bed next to her and love her like I should. After our boys was borned, and her days was filled with them, I hoped she was too busy to notice I wasn't around. I think back on the talk I had with her daddy, years ago; he said I'd break her heart and I guess that's what I'm doin. She don't understand why I stay away. She don't know what eats at my mind.

I used Papa's old stable and set up an engine repair shop. I keep busy with it and make some money but I know Coris wants better things for us, more money.

Some nights I can forget Ginny and I can see Coris for the good woman she is. Then I don't want to stay away from her. I love her enough to keep the questions out of her face.

But somethin will happen and I'll be thinkin of Ginny again.

Like that cold November night when I was workin out in that

cold shed I heard a kid out back, cryin and rattlin around through the dump heap, her face was all tears.

You lost? I asked the girl.

She kept cryin and I took her into Papa's warm kitchen. Papa give her some warm coffee but she spit it out. Her eyes come around from cryin to bein mad. I see Ginny's scrappy look in the kid's eyes.

My mama needs help, the girl said.

Ginny? I asked her.

Yeah, I got lost on the road when it got so dark.

I'll give you a lift home. What's wrong at home? Why you out in the dark? I asked.

Mama's having her baby. Daddy's not home. Then she started up cryin again. I took her hand in mine and we went out to the truck. I had some trouble gettin the engine goin but soon we was on our way out toward Ginny's and I was feelin scared. Scared just to see Ginny face to face and not knowin what I might find out there.

Of all the kids to get lost and of all the places she could've ended up, why Ginny's girl in my dooryard?

She wasn't a handsome child. Reminded me a little of my ma. She had them same sharp features, same narrow eyes and olive-colored skin.

How long you been gone, you think? I asked her as we drove by Gossler's store. I don't know, she said and looked out the icy window.

Your ma in bad shape?

She's real sick. She doesn't think that baby wants to come out. We drove along real quiet the rest of the way while my insides were dancin around just thinkin about bein with Ginny again. I'd tried to forget her, done everythin to stay away from her, done everythin but spend more time with my own wife and love her like she needed.

Ginny fell into me like a ragdoll, pain lay a cold shadow over her pretty face. I got her to bed and did what I could do but it took too long, the baby was tangled in there and I thought it was dead for sure, but it wouldn't've been one of Ginny's kids if it didn't fight. Somethin more than that boy was born that night and Ginny and I seen it loomin larger than any child. It was knowin how we both really felt, and knowin how we'd hurt our own folk by thinkin it wasn't there. I kissed her just as though it had been our baby layin tween us. And that's what we both wanted.

Harder than the birth was havin to face Henry. He come home drunk and foolish, laughin about havin a boy and not seein how that child lay there, limp and red and wet like a smashed eye that don't see no more. I wanted to kill Henry. I thought I could do it, and feel nothin bad for doin it. I hung around the house for awhile til I knew Ginny was all right but then I had to leave fore I took a shotgun to Henry or throttled him with my own hands.

When I got home Coris was up with our youngest. He was colicky. She ran to me as I come through the door thinkin somethin terrible had happened. I patted her arm and told her about the lost girl and the baby bein born. Then I went to lay down on the cot in the parlor. I fell into a black sleep of guilt, as though I'd been unfaithful.

Next mornin I whittled out some wooden rings and knobs and fashioned a rattle for Ginny's baby. I sent it over to her house by way of Abel Gossler's wife, Maddie. I couldn't go back there.

I kept busy with engines. I learned my oldest boy, Austin, to ride his bicycle and took to singin to Matthew while I jiggled him on my knee. I did what I could bear, keepin any old shadows from comin tween me and Coris.

But I thought too much about Henry Gilley, drinkin himself away and lettin Ginny go to waste. The next year Ginny come to my shop and asked me to come to work for her, save what Henry was ruinin. I hadn't for a minute forgot how the two of us had messed up our own lives. I kissed her then and there and then I threw my wrench across the shed. That was me, all horny and mad. Her kids see me kiss her and I felt for a minute like I was standin on a wire about to lose my balance and fall. I shouldn't've done it,

I shouldn't't've gone back to work for her but I couldn't say no to them eyes.

I ain't as stupid as some. I sure got my shortcomins but I ain't all stupid. There's different kinds of stupid. There's those like us don't know books and then there's them who do and still are as thick as timber. Henry Gilley is like that. Knows all there's to know about readin and writin and figurin but his head must've been made from metal sure as a milkin pail is.

I come to work with my dinner bucket and thermos, Henry says what you got there? I come through his woods with an ax over my shoulder and he say where you been. Now if that ain't thick headed I don't know what is.

But Henry's a good man inside, when the liquor ain't got him all riled up. I don't know what drives him to drink so. Maybe he knows Ginny don't love him. Maybe, now, his excuse is that baby boy. It ain't right and I think it would eat me up a little inside too, to have a child that's gonna be no more than a face to feed, and clean up after.

Henry says, he'll be all right one day. Teddy'll grow out of this. But I don't say nothin, I don't believe the boy will catch up with other kids. Henry wants me to go with him to Milbridge to get a small load of firewood. I think, ain't this man some stupid, he'd got acres of wood to cut himself, but I go and do what I'm told.

I know a woman in Milbridge, got an idiot boy, a full-grown boy, so I think the best medicine for Henry would be to see this boy. We load our wood into the truck and I say let's stop over to Nellie's Lunchroom for somethin to eat.

Okay, he says.

We talk on the way bout woodin. I tell him he ought to harvest some of his own, stead of buyin someone elses. He says, he might next year. I think maybe he don't have the money to buy the equipment he'd need to make any money at the woodin, or maybe he can't pay no more wages to git the wood cut. I look him over all the time, wonderin how he keeps Ginny happy. It just don't seem to me he could keep his mind on lovin long enough for a woman to 'preciate it.

We go into Nellie's and order. I git the special, hot roast beef with gravy, and Henry gits a soup. I don't see the boy workin today and I start to wonder if I done the right thing by bringin Henry here. We're just bout finished up eatin when I see the boy come through the door. He walks right past us and I wave him down.

Eddie, I call. He looks at me with bulgy eyes and his mouth hung open. I don't think he recognizes me.

Hey, he says, more through his nose than his mouth. His head's bigger than it should be, he's droolin and movin the top half of him back and forth slowly like a pendulum. His eyes is as blank as snow.

Eddie, git to work, don't bother those men, Nellie hollers from behind the counter.

It's all right Nellie, I was just sayin hello to the boy.

Hello, Eddie says. He smiles like he just seen his best friend and puts out his hand for me to shake. I shake it and he gits laughin, then he turns to Henry and puts out his hand. Henry's face is hard and cold. His eyes look at me like he wishes I was dead. He ain't smilin. He shakes Eddie's hand, though, and we git up to pay our tab.

I'll git this one, I say to Henry.

He walks out the door to the truck.

I don't appreciate that, he says to me as I git in the truck.

What? I ask, tryin to act like I don't know what he means.

I understand what that was all about. Did Regina put you up to it? he asks.

Huh? Ginny? Hell, no. I just wanted something to eat, for Christ's sake.

We start headin along Route One and then he stops at Sutter's Tavern. I'm in need of a little drink, he says and smiles at me like he's forgotten all about Eddie. You can wait in the truck or come in and join me, he says. But I ain't in any hurry to go back to work.

I follow him inside and we start puttin em down. I know how upset Ginny'll be if he comes home drunk but I'm hopin to git him to talk. After four or five, his eyes git all red-rimmed and he starts talkin bout Ginny.

She never understands how it is to run a business, he says. I guess he keeps enough liquor in him so his talk don't even slur none.

Ginny? I ask, surprised. I always thought she was the one that kept em goin.

She's always at me about spending money. She just doesn't understand, he says.

She makes some money with the bees and eggs don't she? I ask, but then I remember I better not fight Ginny's fight with him. Best just to listen.

How do you keep Coris in line? he asks.

In line?

She knows her place doesn't she? A woman's place is to support her husband, help him, encourage him.

Well, I trust Coris to do what she thinks is right. Don't think I'd want her to keep her mouth shut bout somethin she thought was wrong.

What do you mean? he asks. I know I can't say too much but Ginny has told me how she tries to be quiet while Henry wastes money on new machinery or new roofs when they ain't really needed. I know how she struggles to plant ideas in Henry's head, ideas that might bring in some cash, not dole it out.

I just mean Coris knows her own mind, and it don't bother me none, I say. I go to the bar to get another drink. I sit back down and his eyes is closed, thinkin bout somethin.

Someday, I'll have the money I need to get that farm running properly, he says.

How's money gonna help? You ain't gonna get rich in farmin, not around here.

Oh, sure you can. If we had enough produce, enough beef,

lamb, milk, eggs, why we could sell all over the state, even out of state, he says with a flash in his eyes. I told you there was different kinds of stupid in the world and I've bout had enough of this kind.

I think we better git goin home, I say.

Regina thinks small. Can't make any real money thinking like that, he says.

So you gonna pay twenty, maybe fifty men's salaries, and have that food and milk and everything shipped all over the place? How much that gonna set you back? I ask.

Details, that's all. Can all be worked out, Henry says as he stands up, wobblin on his feet, knockin the chair over.

I take him by the arm and help him to the truck. I put him in on the passenger side and drive back to the farm while he snores and snorts in his seat.

I drive up the lane to the farm and see Ginny outside hangin out her wash. I pull the truck up next to the milkin barn and git out. Henry keeps on snoozin. I walk around the back of the house and watch Ginny struggle with a sheet that keeps fetchin up in the wind. I love her. I knew that before, but now I know it even more. She has shiny, long, dark hair and a body that's honed tight with hard work and a fierce temper. I love every bit of her. What foolish things she's done just to keep that farm, I think, when here I am, one man who understands that dark, boilin well of feelins that stews inside her. I don't knows I could've done much to help, I wasn't much for ideas, but I could've been right with her on what-ever she thought up to put food on the table. If only she'd seen that.

I walk back around the house and go find some work to do in the fields.

I've worked side by side with Henry now for over three years. I don't know's I can take much more. Winters ain't been hard. I usually git laid off for most of the season. Funny durin the winters

I don't have no trouble makin love with Coris. It's the rest of the year when Ginny lays in the bed between us, smilin like a child, like when we first loved.

Today is Austin's birthday. I can't believe how fast the time goes by. Seems like he was just a baby, now he's in second grade. It's the time movin so fast that gets me itchy. Workin these last years with Henry, watchin Ginny raise them three kids, seein how hard she works with Teddy. He's four years old and the doctors told Ginny he wouldn't live that long. But she won't never give up on makin somethin outa that kid.

Coris brings the cake she made for Austin into the parlor. It's pretty as can be. She has a way with makin things homey and pretty. We all sing and have some cake. Coris keeps takin hold of my hand at the table and pattin it. She's happy with these boys and with me. I been faithful but fought that dog everyday as I hear Henry sayin somethin stupid, somethin that makes me want to walk into Ginny's kitchen and pick her up, take her away.

I don't go to work today. I just don't want to.

It's afternoon and the boys have gone with Coris's ma and daddy to Milbridge to git ice cream. They give Austin a brand-new bicycle for his birthday. They're always givin the kids things I can't give em. Roland always watches my face when they hand over the presents.

Coris comes up behind me in my chair where I'm readin a beekeepin book I bought. She puts her hands on my neck and then down inside my shirt. It may have been my face that I see in the mirror across the room that makes me stop from turnin to her. My face looks older, I even see a few gray hairs around my temples. I'm not old but I'm gettin old. I'll only get older, alongside this woman. Never have what I want.

What is it, she says. She's used to me gettin randy quicker than her.

Nothin, I say. I stand up and hold her. We kiss some and then go upstair. There's never been a time in my life when I couldn't make a woman happy, but Coris keeps lookin at me, seein somethin in my face that I try to hide. I don't know if it's bein scared of gettin old or that I can only see Coris as a woman with dark hair, a woman whose thoughts are as slippery as black oil, her hands as someone else's.

We lay in bed, nothin happenin. No fire growin tween my legs. I sweat and get up from bed, out of breath, ashamed at myself for disappointin Coris. She dresses quietly and moves by me like I ain't there. There just ain't nothin I can say. She feels that somethin tween us just as though Ginny was standin right here.

I throw some more of my clothes in a sack. I'll take em to Papa's house. I can't stay here much. Can't keep hidin my eyes.

And tomorrow I'll go to work.

After the swarming season is over, or should the honey season prove unfavorable and the crop short, the drones are mercilessly destroyed. . . .

—*from* FIRST LESSONS IN BEEKEEPING
by C. P. Dadant, c. 1957

CHAPTER NINETEEN

Henry

1929

A man who believes he has it all, then one morning wakes to realize he has nothing, is a man who sees little reason in living. Henry woke to this realization after seeing a particular look in his wife's eyes when he moved toward her in bed one night; he realized this when his crops failed; when he wrote the first letter to Mother asking for money; when Mother turned her back on him.

Whisky was easy to come by in Washington County and Henry found some comfort in that. There were men who made it in galvanized barrels and copper tubing. It was gut-rot but like mother's milk after the first two or three sips. It cost money but soothed a thousand gnawing pains in one's head.

He would look at Regina silently, wondering why he'd married her. She moved through the days, busy, efficient, with extreme purpose. She didn't seem to notice him watching her, or she just didn't care, her work was too important. But why had he married her? She was pretty enough, smart, but not sophisticated. She lived here, on the edge of the earth, insulated from the real world. Was it because of Mother he'd plunged into this marriage? Was it as simple as proving to his mother and his father that he'd made the right decision to study agriculture? Had his reckless rebellion imprisoned him here, so far from the world he'd known? Trapped him in a crooked house with threadbare things, with dried-up cows, skinny pigs, empty, unplowed fields? A farmer! My good God what a fool!

Regina would go to her bees like some sort of charmer, she'd send them secret messages, collect the honey, move from one hive to another loving the bees more than her own husband. Then on to the chickens to collect pale brown, perfect oval eggs. She'd dimple a perfect pie crust, she'd wipe the tears from the children's eyes and change their direction, she could even fold a cloth napkin with such grace and speed that you were never sure if you'd just witnessed a magic act.

Her perfection was eating a hole in Henry and so he had to fill the hole with something. Whisky.

Oh, and how like Mother, Regina was. Not on the surface, no, not with her unsophisticated ways, her crude talk, but yes, like Mother in her ways of organizing, her capable and infuriating manner. Was that it? Was she like Mother so much that Henry had married her to be close to Mother? It couldn't be. But here she was, wiping his sweaty drunken face, cleaning his soiled bed, mending his clothes, feeding him, like a mother would her own child.

What the reasons were for his frustrations, his loneliness, he tried to forget. It all came down to one thing: He was stuck and in order to make it bearable he needed to drink. Things would improve.

His children would grow and they would be a comfort to him, but in the meantime, he drank.

Regina had moved him out of their bedroom, then she'd moved him back. Yet it was never the same. He felt unwanted there on top of her soft skin, she didn't look at him, she looked past him to someone else, or something else.

Henry had seen this sort of marriage before, where the two pass one another in hallways, in the yard, move above about like souls in purgatory. He'd seen this in his parents' marriage. It was nothing he'd wanted for himself. How had he fooled himself into thinking that a simple, country girl would look up to him, be devoted, and unquestioning? How had he thought he could make something of that dilapidated farm, those lazy farmhands, a backwards community?

Money ran short, the place couldn't pay for itself. The only consistent source of their income was from the honey that Regina sold and her damned pies and cakes. So, he wrote to Mother asking for money. His face was red with humiliation as he penned his first letter, asking to borrow against his inheritance. Mother made him beg. She ignored the first letter and then sent only half of what he'd asked for, after he pleaded for it, in his second letter. And now he was on this fifth. He realized that in order to get what he needed, he'd ask for twice as much and then receive a crisp money order in the amount he truly wanted. He believed each time that it would be the last time. But Regina had hidden their account booklets, their checkbook.

"You ain't drinkin' away every cent I make for us," she'd said with her nostrils flared, her tiny black eyes sparking. When his whisky was low, he wanted to slap her face, wanted to see her in pain, the same kind of pain he felt when he knew there was only one more drink left in the bottle.

And though Regina had never confronted him, he realized she had found his letter to Mother asking for a loan. Bitch. That was the same day that she took him back to her bed. He couldn't understand her. He would write another letter. He'd gone through his own money and Mother was the only answer. He made love to Regina to pacify her, to keep her at a comfortable distance. It was then he decided to do his drinking secretly. Let her think he had stopped.

In the spring of 1929 he received a telegram from his mother's lawyer stating that Mother was ill. She was bedridden and not long for this earth. He wept. He drank. He packed his things and told his wife that he had to go to be with Mother if this was indeed the end.

On the train home he wondered if he was strong enough to stay away from Josiahville forever. Could he abandon Edith? Rose? He had a dream on the train that Regina's arms were long and dark and hairy. She had several arms. She was holding the girls in her arms and Teddy. She was pushing Henry away from them with yet another long arm.

Through hot, windless days Henry sat by Mother's bedside and read to her from Trollope, James, and Eliot. He was never sure if she heard him reading those endless sentences or if his presence was enough. He deeply regretted the years he'd left her alone. How could he have abandoned her? Yet, as she moaned on, as he wiped her fevered brow, he thought about the advantages her money would present to him. He could send a large sum of money to Regina and the children, enough to support them for years, and he could travel as he'd always wanted. He could fade away and never again be Henry Gilley, unless he chose to be.

But could he do it? Could he abandon the children? Then guilt washed over him like the blood from the slaughtered animals he'd butchered. He gripped Mother's hand and prayed for another day, one more day of her life, one more day away from home.

Father had kept the liquor closet well stocked, and though he had been dead for over eight years, the closet still held the nearly full or unopened bottles of vodka, gin, rum, whisky. Armed with licorice candies, he stole sips of each bottle, then popped the candy into his mouth before reading to Mother.

Doctors came and went, shaking their heads. Henry was nearly through reading *Middlemarch* when Mother breathed her last. He looked at the clock, at the calender. When was it that he left his family? Had it really been six months? He pulled the bedcovers over her white face, her white hair. He didn't want to see her again. He went to the liquor closet and opened a bottle of whisky. He drank from the bottle, remembering how once he'd helped his mother in the kitchen. He remembered a time he'd walked into her room when he was a boy and saw her naked breasts. The thought now made him retch. He phoned the doctor and waited in the parlor as Mother was taken, cold and stiff, from the house.

Dear Regina, he wrote, Mother is gone. I will settle her affairs and be home by Christmas. Tell the children, Daddy will be bringing presents for them.

This was the beginning of October.

He thought again, something he hadn't thought for years, I have it all now. I can make a success of myself.

He worked with the lawyers, sorting through stocks, through a meager savings account, one Mother must have drained in order to loan her son money. He'd cash in the bonds, the stocks, he'd sell the house.

But too soon the shadows fell over him again. The world was overextended, the Crash took him by surprise. Men in the cities were throwing themselves out of windows. A blackness had encased the world. Henry had nothing but pieces of paper worth nothing.

When Christmas came and went, the world was struggling to get up out of the pile of debt. Henry sold the contents of the house for pennies, his mother's jewelry, his father's collection of guns. As the doors were sealed on the shoe factory, Henry stumbled, drunk and desperate along the streets of Concord and imagined the house, empty and useless, slowly falling into ruin, as he walked and walked toward nothing, out into a frightening world with nothing but pocket change and a fear of facing Regina. A fear that kept him traveling far from Josiahville.

PART FOUR

The Honeyflow

The nearly universal love of honey is what motivates all the study, experimentation, manipulation . . . honey tastes delicious to us. So we want it. It's as simple as that.
—from THE WORLD OF BEES
by Murray Hoyt, c. 1965

She eludes us on every side; she repudiates most of our rules and breaks our standards to pieces. On our right she sinks far beneath the level of our thoughts, on our left she towers mountain-high above them.

—*from* THE LIFE OF THE BEE
by Maurice Maeterlinck, c. 1901

CHAPTER TWENTY

Ginny

1929–1932

I knew somethin had to be done. I had children to feed, and just as important, I had my animals to feed. I didn't have no time to cry or whisper my wishes into a liquor bottle. If the newspapers were right, the world was spinnin itself toward some horrible endin, but I was gonna go with my head up. I was gonna go fightin.

Henry left us with no more than three hundred dollars in the bank. I got letters from him from time to time but I kept expectin them to stop. I thought it might be easy for him to forget us, go on with his old life in Concord, pretend he didn't have no family here. He was gone for over two months when the idea come to me. I knew if I thought hard enough, I'd figure out a way for us to get by.

I got Edith to sit with Rose and Teddy and I went off through the woods, through my property toward the old stable that sat beside the road, right on Route One. That building had been used as a stable for town folks and people passin through, over the years, but with the automobiles fast taking over the roads, it had been abandoned. My daddy had bought it over twenty years ago, along with thirty acres of land that adjoined ours. I'd never given the old building any thought before.

As I trudged through the woods, I could see Gunnar's place, his red tiled roof peekin above the birch and spruce trees. I thought I should be more neighborly with the Sorensens, especially with Noelle, but something about the way Gunnar always looked at me kept me away. He'd never gotten over how I'd thrown him aside for Duffy when we was kids. He was a funny devil, mostly friendly to me, and gave the impression of a lazy man, but I knew he lined his pockets with the rewards of his little still that he kept in the woodshed. I thought then, if I need some cash for my plans, maybe Gunnar would fork over a dollar or two.

I reached the stable. It was a big building. Had a hay loft in the top. A lot of sturdy thick beams and room enough for a barn dance. Some of the windows had been smashed out, and the doors were gone, but I could see the possibilities, I'd have the trees cleared in the front so that passing cars could see the big sign I'd put up. I'd get a couple of wood stoves, a gas range, a griddle, new windows, linoleum floorin, some tables, and a counter. I'd paint the outside a yellow gold. I'd have the front windows fitted with new panes of glass. I'd eventually have a road cleared from the house right down to the back of it.

I knew I had too many ideas and too little cash, but somehow I seemed to get the things I really wanted. And I wanted this.

I walked down Route One toward Gossler's. From there I could see Duffy across the road workin on a car, his head under the hood. I had a hard time keepin him busy at the farm, and if there was an engine that needed work, he'd jump up and start workin like a dog. I guess he didn't see it as work.

"Hey, thought I sent you out to the back pasture to find

Bessie," I said real loud, loud enough to make him jump.

"Oh? Hi." He rubbed the sore spot on his head where he struck the hood. His face got red. "I couldn't find her. I come out on the road, and well, I was sick of bein out in the woods . . ." he stammered. I scowled at him long enough to keep that red blush on his face, then I smiled.

"I need you to come look at somethin with me."

"Can't wait til I git this goin'?" he asked.

"Whose payroll are you on anyway?"

He put down his tools and stepped out of his coveralls. We went back across the road, walked a quarter of a mile til we come to the old stable.

"Is this buildin sound?" I asked.

"Well," he walked in through the doorway and then come to stand outside, lookin at the roof. "She ain't saggin. I guess it's still in good shape. What are you plannin to do with it?"

"I've just got some ideas runnin around in my head. Think you could round up a couple of men to fix it up?"

"Depends on what you're payin them."

"The goin rate," I said, not sure yet how I'd get the money I needed.

"It's gonna need new windows, doors, a floor. Probably some of the beams will need shorin up. I won't know what the sills are like til I take off the shingles."

"Round up some men and get to work on it."

"Have you talked to Henry bout this?" he asked.

"No, and why should I? He don't seem to be too worried bout me and the kids. I'm doin this on my own. So any idea what it'll take to make the place weather-tight and sound?" I asked.

"You're gonna need three or four hundred, I'd guess, what with shingles, windows, floors . . ."

"Well thanks, Duff. See what you can do 'bout findin some help." I walked back through the woods along the property line. If Duffy thought three hundred would do for the buildin then I knew I'd need another two or three hundred for stoves, counters, grills, tables, and supplies.

I thought I might live to regret it, but I went toward Gunnar's house.

On the ridge above his place I looked down at the roof, heard pots and pans rattlin in the kitchen. I didn't want to talk to Noelle so I sat down on a stump and waited til I see Gunnar's truck drive into the dooryard. I stood up and went closer, waved my hands. He looked up in surprise but came toward me. We went out behind the barn.

"What are you doin out here?" he asked. He'd been a good-lookin boy, but already, only into his twenties, he looked worn, his teeth were grayin, his blond hair was streaked with some gray, and he had lines around his eyes. He lived hard and drank hard, but seemed to be able to handle it better than Henry.

"I need some help," I said and looked down at my shoes as I scuffed around some gravel.

"What? Henry on a bender?"

"No, nothin like that."

"He ain't been by for my homebrew in awhile, he stop drinkin?"

"No. I doubt it. He's in New Hampshire. His ma's sick." Since Henry had written sayin that Mrs. Gilley probably wouldn't last long, I'd thought about what money he might get his hands on, but with all the troubles in the world I was afraid there wouldn't be none at all. If there was, I didn't want to ask Henry for a thing toward my plans. I'd sooner ask Gunnar.

"I came to see if I could get a loan from you. I know there ain't no point goin to banks now."

"No, I don't suppose the banks will recover from this mess. They're callin it a depression. Glad I never banked nothin," he said as he lit his pipe. He was startin to feel comfortable with me now, knowin I needed something from him. Mostly all he got from me was a wave or a nod. He'd made it clear back in school what he wanted from me and though we'd hidden behind woodpiles and bushes, I'd never given him all of what he wanted.

"So, you have cash layin around that I could borrow? We can make the whole thing proper, interest and all. I'll be able to pay you back."

"How much?" he asked.

"I need about six-hundred."

"Jesus Christ, Ginny, what are you gonna do with all that?"

"I have somethin in mind. You got it?"

"Christ no, I could come up with three maybe, but . . ."

"Then can I count on you for that?"

"Mighty fierce to get it ain't ya?" he laughed.

"Yes." He put his hand on my shoulder and lightly touched me.

"Well, Ginny I'll see what I can do. For you I'd saddle the moon, but I might have a better chance of doin that than gettin six hundred dollars."

"The three will do. You want me to have someone draw up some papers? I'll make good on this loan."

"Ginny, I don't know's I can get that much money together. Maybe in another year or two things will be different . . ."

"Well, sorry I bothered you," I said softly, tryin not to show how mad I was.

"Now, hold on," he said and took hold of both my shoulders. He looked into my eyes with that same devilish look he'd had as a boy. "Ginny, we go back a long way. I'd like to be able to help you."

"Well, if you can't, you can't."

"I'll see what I can do," he said, and sat down on an over-turned washtub. I folded my arms waitin for him to say somethin, but he smoked and looked off like he was tryin to come up with some way to help.

"How would you pay me back?" he asked. I wanted to kick him. He wouldn't've been askin me that if he didn't have the money.

"I better get goin," I said.

"Don't rush off." He stood up and held me by my wrist. I hated what was goin on in my head but I couldn't stop it. I knew what he wanted. He wanted to work out an arrangement between us. He had the money but he wasn't partin with it easy. I'd have to come up with more than interest on the loan, if I was to get anything. I pulled my wrist away from him. He just smiled. Then silence hung over us like a water bag about to burst. There were things he wanted to say. I just stared at him, I didn't smile, I didn't make it easy for him to speak. I didn't want him to embarrass himself.

"I'll be seein' you Gunnar," I said as I started to walk toward the woods. As kids I could play him like a fiddle. Just one pull from me of the bow across his strings and he'd bust. But it seemed the bow was changin hands.

"Wish I could come by to visit sometime, Ginny. Especially if Henry ain't home," he said and I had to turn around. I opened my mouth about ready to tell him off, expectin to see that shit-eatin grin, but all I saw was a sad man. There were streaks of meanness in him, but right then he was lookin lonely, lookin like the boy he once was when I told him I was seein Duffy.

I didn't say nothin. I walked through the woods and headed home.

"Where you been?" Duffy asked me when he see me comin through the woods and down through the pasture.

"Why, you been lookin for me?"

"Yeah. After I come back a telegram come for you." He held it out to me. It was from Henry. His mother had died. He said he'd be bringing home Christmas presents for the kids. It was October and the last thing I wanted to think about was the cold months ahead. I didn't want to think about him either. I tossed the telegram down on the ground and walked ahead to the house.

"Ginny, you all right?" Duff asked. He put his arm around me. I jerked away quick.

"Don't do that. Remember Edith could be anywhere watchin us," I snapped. He looked like I'd slapped him.

"She's with the kids out by the apple trees," he said.

I didn't listen. I walked up on the porch, leavin Duff outside, and went upstairs to my room. I sat down on the bed and thought it all out. If Henry come home with some money, then I could ask for some to set up my business. But he wouldn't agree with me. He'd sink every cent into some new machine, a new truck, more cows. If he didn't come home, and I'd learned by now not to trust his words, I had no way to get the money. Earlier that day I'd been so sure of myself when I showed Duffy the old stable, but now I felt like a pitcher of water and I'd been tipped over, everything was runnin out. I laid down and closed my eyes.

Later on as I went about gettin supper, I read through my recipe books, made a dozen lists of things I'd need to buy for the business. I kept on plannin, couldn't stop.

Edith, like always, helped with the supper. She was quite a cook by now and I appreciated the help. She moved from counter to cupboard without talkin. Held everythin inside her. Her daddy's leavin had hurt her right through, but she wouldn't say nothin bout it. Rose, pretty and quick, would dance around the kitchen, fill the milk pitcher, feed Teddy some raw carrots that he liked so, and she'd chat on and on about what she'd played that day, or how much she liked her teacher, couldn't wait to get to school on Monday. If she felt her daddy's disappearance she pretended not to. Edith was a dark night compared to Little Miss Sunshine.

I looked at my girls durin the meal, both of them hidin their hurt in different ways. I just wasn't the kind of mother that could give them the sort of things they needed. I knew that, I was too much like my own mother, and I remember how I waited for my ma to reach across the table to take my hand, or scoop me up in her arms when I'd scraped a knee, but those things didn't happen much.

Rose seemed to glow in her own lantern light, but Edith was starvin. Henry had given her some of the things she needed to loosen up her pinched face, but I just didn't know how. The kinds of things I could give them was a warm house, food on the table, clean dresses. And I wouldn't be able to give them those things without money. The word "depression" bout summed up the times. I thought, well, we might not starve, I could grow enough for us, I could get enough wood cut to keep the place warm, but what else could I give?

"Edith, you done a good job on this hake and pork scraps," I said as I swallowed a bite. She looked at me but didn't say nothin.

"I like yours better," Rose said. She and Edith always fought, but Edith ignored her sister that time.

"I think Edith's might be better than mine," I said. I scooped up some of the fish that Teddy had let fall from his fork. I straightened the towel I kept around his neck when he ate. "You done enough work for today Edith, I'll do up the dishes."

Edith just looked at me and then slapped Teddy's hand as he reached out for some pickles. Then she served him some.

"Don't hit him," Rose said.

"He's got to learn," I said and then I got a scowl from Rose.

After supper I read a story to Teddy and put him in his crib. He still tried to get out of it but even at four he couldn't quite figure it out. Then I went and sat in the parlor with the girls and did some sewin, and kept thinkin how much I wanted to throttle Henry. Edith read until bed and Rose cut out paper doll clothes she'd drawn on old newspapers.

That night, after the kids was all asleep, I went out on the porch and listened to the fadin sounds of fall. The air felt chilly. There'd be snow fore I knew it. I decided to have some of the wood lots cleared and sell off what I could of the harvest. It wouldn't help with my business plans but it'd keep things goin on the farm for awhile.

Before I went indoors I heard someone walkin up the lane to the house. For a minute I panicked thinkin it was Henry.

"Duffy, that you?" I called out.

"Yup,"

"What are you doin back out here tonight?" He came up on the porch and held the door for me. We went into the house.

"I was worried bout you. You were all excited bout fixin up that buildin this mornin, and then you come home lookin like the world ended. What happened?"

"I just got carried away. I don't have the money to fix that place up," I said as I sank down in a chair in the parlor. Duffy sat in front of me on his knees. The only light come in through the windows from the moon. Duffy looked helpless.

"Never known you to give up. What's your plans?" he asked.

I put my fingers in Duffy's hair and kept strokin his head. I saw all our lost chances there in the air between us.

"I guess sometimes I have to realize I can't have everythin. I was hopin to open a lunchroom. A place to sell my baked goods, my honey and jams. Right there on the main road I could get the summer people and anyone else to stop in for a muffin or a donut, cup of coffee, a lunch. I think I could make some money, but I need money to get it goin." Duffy reached up and took hold of the long strands of my hair, twirled them in his hands.

"When's Henry comin home?" he whispered.

"I don't know as he is. Think this place and me was too much."

"Ginny . . ." Duffy said as he put his head in my lap. "He ain't no good for you. Why'd you do it?"

I didn't answer him. I knew what he was askin, why'd I married Henry. The whole mess of my marriage, the burden of the farm, my wasted love for Duffy, all fell down on me. I felt like I was gonna cry, and it made me mad. As I stroked Duffy's head, feelin like the only thing I'd ever held onto in my life was that man's sweet head, I got madder. How'd it all happen? How'd I been foolish enough to think Henry could give me anythin? If I was ever to have Duffy or the things I wanted I had to fight harder than I ever had. I had choices to make that might hurt people, choices I wished I didn't have to make, but there they were.

"Duffy, I should get some sleep," I said softly.

"Ginny, let's go somewhere, just for tonight," he said, lookin up at me with those big eyes. I almost choked on my shame for what I was plannin, but it had to be done. Duffy was married and my husband might come home, and we were too far away from bein those lovesick kids we'd been.

I stood up, gently pushin Duffy off me. "Duffy, you got a wife that's wonderin where you are. I need some sleep." I turned and walked into the hall before he had a chance to get to his feet.

"Night, Ginny," he said as I started up the stairs. I didn't look back to see his face.

When I went to bed that night I almost let myself cry but fell asleep fore the tears come.

It was a few days before I could bring myself to do what I'd planned that night that Duffy toyed with my hair. I started avoidin him. I couldn't let him see anythin in my face. Maybe one day, if things went my way, Duffy could lay his head in my lap again, and maybe I'd be able to touch him without feeling like a wrung-out dishrag, or an empty water pitcher.

I sent the girls off to school and got Maddie Gossler to watch Teddy for a few hours. I looked over the stable again and then trudged back through the woods to the rise that overlooked that red tiled roof. Gunnar had never come by my place to talk about the loan again. He'd made it clear what he wanted in return for the money. I knew just what I would become by workin out this arrangement with Gunnar and I wasn't proud of it, but there were worse things in the world. When I thought about it, I'd done the same thing for Henry. I'd married him cause I thought he'd be able to provide for me. All the names for a woman like that rushed through my head, but I turned the course of that stream to head another way. I just didn't have the time to listen to the current.

I stayed out behind Gunnar's barn and waited just like I had a week earlier, til I saw him. I waved and he strutted over to me like Cock Robin. The deal was done with just a look of his glassy eyes. I let him know what time the kids went to bed. Told him I'd be workin in the milkin barn that night. On my way home, knowin what that night would be like for me, I had to keep pinchin myself, hard on my arms and legs to remember what it was like to still be livin.

A few weeks passed while I added and re-added my accounts. I sold a fair amount of wood to a man in Cherryfield and I had the three hundred I'd need to get started. I still had to have money to keep the farm goin, pay the salaries, buy feed for the horses and cows. But I had the extra cash for my little lunchroom. I kept busy with figurin, plannin, and swallowed hard every time I was interrupted by Gunnar's knock on the back door.

November come with a light snow and low temperatures. Every mornin I bundled the girls up good and sent them off to school. Teddy played on the kitchen floor with blocks and wooden spoons while I baked and jarred jellies. I sketched out plans for the lunchroom. I knew, no matter what the times were, people would pay for good food. While I worked I was always lookin over my shoulder, afraid Henry would be there. But time went on and he didn't come home. Christmas passed by and still he didn't show, and neither did the presents he promised the kids. I'd never told them about what he said, so they weren't expectin nothin.

The winter was a white blizzard outside, and inside my head the storms were just as fierce. Duffy and his crew worked on the old stable when they could, but mostly they couldn't. I'd told Duffy not to come by the farm for work, just wanted him to oversee the buildin. I told him that I was doin fine at home. I'd hired Walter back to help out and I didn't want Duffy to see the boot tracks in the snow that led from my back door down the road.

By the time spring rolled around Duffy had a lot of the work done in the stable. New windows, new doors, floors, and plastered ceilins. He'd gotten together two good men from Milbridge who'd work cheap and he made sure they done a decent job. I'd started jarring more honey than in the past. Had some fancy labels made sayin GILLEY'S GOLDEN HONEY on it. I made a honey spread and some jams and got hold of a food distributor from Bangor. I started selling my products in dribs and drabs. Made just enough money to buy more jars, labels, and hire a woman from the village to help with the bottlin. I wasn't gonna be rich but along with my baked goods that I sold at Gossler's, I was able to eat and keep up with some of the repairs around the place and save a little.

The work on the stable was a little less than what Duffy had thought, so with another hundred from Gunnar I started orderin my equipment. I can't say I still wasn't afraid that Henry would come up the lane, but the unopened door never filled up with him. Eventually I stopped lookin.

Within the next year and a half, I had thirty hives all together, in groups of four or five, situated between the storage barn and a windbreak of spruce trees. A few queens would die over the winter and some of the colonies would die out from the cold, or a few years they was victim to diseases, or bee mites, or mice would get in the hives and destroy everythin. But mostly I was lucky. I'd order new queens, comin in the mail in little crates, wrapped in mesh. I'd set them in the center of the queenless colonies, and in no time they'd mate. New cells, new eggs, wax, honey. The healthy colonies would split up and half of them would swarm, followin a new queen outside. It was just as though they'd discussed who would go and who would stay. The ones that left the old hives would take over the empty ones that Duffy built for me.

I never suffered much loss with them. Early spring the whitening at the top of the combs, in the brood chambers, would start up. But I seemed to know when the time was right without even lookin at the top of the combs, as though the bees had told me. But still I checked anyway, never trustin if I was gettin the right signals from them. Then I'd add the supers for the surplus honey.

Henry had been gone now for almost two years. Two productive years for me. I'd jarred up so many bottles of honey that I had to put up shelves in the dining room and make a stockroom. We'd never used it anyway. I was havin no trouble keepin my lunchroom, the Queen Bee, full of people. Anyone travelin downeast would stop in for hot soup or baked beans, or one of my cinnamon rolls. I was generous in my portions and people appreciated it. Frank Backman, my distributor, was gettin more and more orders for honey. There was talk at the time that honey was good for keepin fit. People used it in their tea and over biscuits. Frank kept tellin me to raise my prices but I didn't. I knew everyone was havin hard times and I didn't want to make my honey somethin they couldn't afford.

I kept three girls workin at the restaurant, part time. I had two girls at home bakin and cannin and I kept Duffy, Royce, and Walter busy on the farm. We didn't have the cows no more but I still had a lot of land planted, vegetables for the business and for us at home, and though the bees got what they needed from the evergreens, the clover fields, and wildflowers, I had a fair amount of flower gardens planted just for them. Sometimes I felt just like a queen bee with all my workers scurryin around me to help. There was a few goods years that I thought of as my "honeyflow years," my best.

Some nights, after I come home from work with sore feet and an achin back, I'd go out to the hives and sit in the grass, listen to the hummin. I felt they needed to know what was goin on with the business. It kept them happy and busy to know it was all workin. I'd whisper to them, tell my ideas, my hopes. I didn't have no one else to tell.

It is well for the beekeeper to become acquainted with
the principal honey plants of the region in which he lives
and to increase the honey flora in all practical ways.
—from FIRST LESSONS IN BEEKEEPING
by C. P. Dadant, c. 1957

CHAPTER TWENTY-ONE

Caleb

1956
It's nearly morning and I have not left her bedside. She has whispered her secrets, her confessions, into her pillow, not to my face. She tells me of her few happy times. I remember too that there were years when the honey flowed from hive to house, to Ma to Duffy, and to me, though I seem to be remembering only those years that were dry and sad, and filled with my mother's anger or grief. But there were, like in all households, some good times.

Edith moved away before I was born, or before I was old enough to remember her, but for her few visits. Rose left soon after Edith. It was Teddy and me for a handful of perfect years. Now as I sit in this dark cavity of time, waiting for answers, hearing whispers and footsteps of ghosts, watching the sunlight slowly rise above the tree line, daring me to move into the new day, I can remember the sweet times.

I was five. Lois, the woman who looked out for Teddy and me while Ma worked at the lunchroom, was busy bottling honey, and Teddy got it into his head that he wanted ice cream.

"Come," he said to me. He started to walk toward the trail that led to the back of the Queen Bee. I knew we weren't supposed to leave the yard, but it was hot and I wanted a scoop of chocolate ice cream too. I kept looking over my shoulder for Lois as we headed into the woods. Along the trail, Teddy would crouch down and start laughing. He knew what we were doing was wrong and he was thrilled with the danger.

When we reached the restaurant we opened the back door slowly and peered inside. Maude, one of my mother's employees, was washing dishes in the big metal sink.

"What are you boys doin' here?" she asked.

Teddy laughed, hugged Maude, and we went through the back room to the dining room. Ma was chopping vegetables and turned to us with wide eyes.

"Where's Lois?" she asked, dropping the knife and putting her hands on her hips.

"She home," Teddy said. He was older and a lot taller than me. My big brother. But Ma looked at me. Even at the age of five, she expected more of me.

"Caleb, you know better," she said. Teddy grabbed her around the waist and hugged her, grinning.

"I want choclit," he said, pointing at the freezer.

"You bad boys," Ma said, but she held onto Teddy and kissed the top of his head. He was overweight and nearly knocked her over as he swayed, repeating over and over "choclit, choclit." She smiled at me and told Teddy to sit down on one of the stools. "Caleb, get some bowls."

I took two from behind the counter and handed them to her.

"Don't you want some?" she asked.

"Yes," I said.

"Then you better get another. I'm havin' some, too."

I did as she asked. We sat together at the counter and ate big bowls of ice cream. Ma between my brother and me. She'd shake her head as if she couldn't believe that we'd escaped Lois, but she was happy we'd stopped by. She let Maude wait on the few customers that were there.

When we were done she held my shoulders and looked at me with a serious face. "Now, I'm leavin' it up to you to watch out for him," she said. "You're a big boy. You make sure he don't go nowhere but right home."

"I will." I felt important and loved. "Can we come down here again? Another day, I mean?"

"Well," she started, then straightened up, squinted her eyes at me. "You mean just the two of you?"

I nodded.

"If you think you're clever enough to slip by Lois again, then I guess you deserve to."

She lightly slapped our rear ends and sent us off through the woods. I'd never felt better about myself.

Then it became a game. Every few days during the hot months, I'd make sure Lois was busy, or tell her we were playing in my fort in the apple orchard, and we'd sneak off. I think Ma was impressed with my deviousness, and she trusted me.

Duffy was living with us by then and he was part of the game too. He'd keep Lois busy while we scurried down the path. Maybe Lois knew, eventually, but I couldn't believe my good luck at the time. She never caught us.

And there were times when the four of us, Ma, Duffy, Teddy, and I would just spend quiet afternoons or evenings on the front porch. Ma would work with Teddy on his lessons and Duffy and I would sketch airplanes together, play cards, glue tiny red ant carcasses, or butterfly wings, into my scrapbook, or he'd whittle a sword out of a strip of pine for me to play with.

There were good times that didn't change until I was seven. That was the year World War II broke out and the economy started to decline. Men went away, and so too did many of the women, to work in factories and help out any way they could for the war effort. Ma's business quickly dwindled. No one was spending money to eat out. She still had a few regular customers who would gather to gossip and nurse cups of coffee, but everyone was afraid of what would happen to the country, so very little was spent on her pies and stews. They were not only afraid of what would happen to the economy, but to the government, and to their families as well. I felt the gloom even as a little boy.

The Depression hadn't affected the state of peoples' minds in Washington County as much as the war did. Everyone here was poor, a lack of money was something they coped with by growing more crops or salting more fish. No one worried about the money for schooling. No one had college degrees, so their children and grandchildren didn't need them either, certainly not to be farmers and fishermen. But with the war, workers were needed in cities, in the factories. Newspapers and radios brought us more news of the world, news that we hadn't paid much attention to before. Soldiers were offered money to go to college after they served. Washington County picked up its sleepy head and looked beyond the swamps, the shorelines, the tree line, and was interested in what it saw. Families moved on, and for a stretch of years, houses sat empty, some of them, eventually, fell in upon themselves. Cellar holes, not front porches or backyards, became children's playgrounds. At the end of our lane there once stood a small white house where a German family lived, and with the war they disappeared. Teddy and I often played in the house, creeping through the broken windows. When the place started to fall apart it was burned down. Trees now spring thirty feet high from its scar.

Ma probably would have survived the death of her lunchroom, or brought it back to life after the war, if it hadn't been for Teddy's death. If I'd never tempted him with the bees.

At six, Ma started keeping me with her when she opened the hives to scrape the honeycomb off the frames. I wore long sleeves, string around my ankles to keep my pant legs tight, and I wore a veil. Ma never wore one but she didn't want me to be scared, so in the beginning I dressed for work with her. It wasn't long before

I went into the beeyard with a bare head too. She told me her father had taught her at a young age to tend to the bees and though I doubted she'd relinquish her power, I was anxious to learn. We would work together, me taking the honeycomb back and forth to the house while she opened another hive. We would even laugh together over something trivial. If I dropped comb on the grass and broke it up, she didn't respond the way she would today.

She was so young then, so much more than what she has become. Though Duffy only lived with us, and wasn't married to Ma, I felt we all completed each other. I couldn't have had those thoughts at age six, but now looking back I realize why I've been hurting for so long. If I'd always lived in gloom and anger I wouldn't know there was anything different, but I had understood love. And like those abandoned houses, I was suddenly deserted after losing Teddy and then my mother's love. Over time the frame of who I was has collapsed, and green trees have not yet sprouted up from this foundation.

With the bees I was anxious to show someone all I'd been taught by Ma. I never should have brought Teddy near them. But how was I to know? He had pills that he took for beestings, so I saw no danger.

And after he died I felt Ma's grief and my guilt. When I became aware of the anger in her I thought it was justified. Wasn't it all my fault? Wouldn't I feel the same way?

His death ruined us. A disease had entered the hive and what was left was dust, and paper-fine wings that crumpled when touched. We three lived in a doomed silence. She would reach out to Duffy at times, but I was useless. If she reached out to me during those first few years after Teddy died, then I didn't see it, or wouldn't allow myself to see it for the size of my guilt. And so I forgot. For awhile. I forgot what I had felt for Teddy, or Ma or Duffy, and though I didn't realize it then, I became someone new. No longer open and friendly, I was silently angry and creating a world inside my head. Each new insect I collected was a new member of the tiny family I belonged to. Each butterfly, another mother;

every dragonfly, a new father; the others, brothers and sisters. Taped or pinned in their places, precious, moving only in my mind.

Grief, or what my mother thought was a proper period of mourning, eventually passed, at least on the surface. She went about her business. Worked a bit at the restaurant, until she closed it, and continued on with the bees, selling her honey wholesale. When she looked at me I saw no softness in her face and I was never asked to help harvest the honey crop again.

She erased most of Teddy's existence from the house like one might take a soiled tablecloth from a table, careful not to spill the crumbs, gathering up all four corners neatly and discarding it. But in doing so, she exposed the badly marred surface of an ancient wooden table, where the wood is so dark and hard and pitted that you can't ever eat at it again, because the memory of the bright flowers and colors of the cloth have ruined you for anything less.

The sun is rising. The day we bury the dead. I stand from the chair to stretch. I know there is more to learn from my mother, but if the sun intrudes I'm afraid she will not speak.

In a few hours it will be over. Duffy will be gone from us. I think of leaving Ma's room but instead I face my chair away from her and sit back down. She can only tell the truth if she is not seen. The shades are still drawn. I know that our darkness forms a contract between us. I wait for her to begin her story again.

PART FIVE

Enemies of the Hive

Honey attracts many would-be thieves. Mice stuff them-
selves with honey and beeswax and even eat the bees.
Bears are also age-old enemies. . . . They like nothing bet-
ter than honey.

Certain moths, ants and lice prey upon honeybees . . .
reptiles . . . toads, and so do certain birds.
           —*from* THE WORLD BOOK ENCYCLOPEDIA,
                                          c. 1955

*The fur coat of one of these huge honey-lovers is heavy
enough, and the hide under it is thick enough, to frus-
trate the would-be defender. Mostly she can't get close
enough to the bear's hide to ram her stinger home.*
                    —*from* THE WORLD OF BEES
                       by Murray Hoyt, c. 1965

CHAPTER TWENTY-TWO

Ginny

1932

Gunnar was makin my life uncomfortable. I hadn't been able to
pay him all that I owed. I expected by the next year I would, but
til then he kept comin by whenever he wanted. I still kept Duff at
a distance from me, acted as though I had no feelins for him. I
thought it was best. And Gunnar, he was the rotten apple in the
barrel. Other than him, my barrel was pretty full of good, sweet
apples.

One hot June night I stood out by the hives, listenin. The
swamp was throwin out croaks and whistles and the bees was settlin
in from a hard day of work, singin soft like a smooth engine. I'd
hoped Gunnar wouldn't be comin by, til I looked ahead of me in
the dark, and see a black bear comin toward the bees, lumbering
along on all fours like a calf. I caught my breath and stepped back.

I thought, this is it, there go all my bees. Then I did wish Gunnar was around.

I stepped backwards, slow, didn't want to wrestle no bear. He didn't pay no attention to me. He moved in on the hives, had only one thing on his mind. Honey. I slipped around the corner of the barn and run just as fast as I could to the house. I hadn't handled a gun in years and wasn't too sure I could do it. But I grabbed one of Daddy's shotguns, the one he'd shown me how to use as a kid. Duffy used it quite a bit to kill off the coyotes and foxes that tried to rob us. I fumbled with it, got it released, and checked to see if it had any shells. It did. I thanked Duffy for that. I scrambled outside and around the barn. That goddamed bear had tipped up two of the hives already. I lifted the rifle, cocked it and let it go. I wanted to kill the damn thing, but I hadn't even taken the time to aim right. The shot rang out and the bear dropped the lid of a hive. He moaned and for a second I wondered if he might come after me. But I think he could tell I was mad. He took off up through the pasture.

That night I dragged some blankets from the house and slept outdoor with the gun in my arms, mad at all the useless men in my life who'd left me somehow.

I think it was then that I decided I had to find some way to git out of my arrangement with Gunnar.

He was some company for me, though. On the nights he'd come by, I'd hear the chickens squabble or his feet crunchin over the gravel in the yard. I always felt like his gettin nearer the house was like one of them slow, quiet calms before a good clap of thunder. His silences and somber moods reminded me of Daddy. But a good swallow of whisky could smear clouds over in my mind. He'd come in, whisperin through the kitchen door. I'd let him know if the kids was asleep or not. How he got away from his own wife so often, I don't know. If Noelle was the kind of woman my mother'd been, then she enjoyed her hours away from him like a fox savors a stolen hen.

The night after I'd driven that bear away, I kept walkin out to the hives to make sure he hadn't come back, but on one of my trips out there, I saw Gunnar's dark figure movin slow toward me, with the moon behind him. I'd suffered men before and told myself I could again, til I didn't have to no more. Sometimes he'd just come to chat and that's when I appreciated the company.

"Evenin Gunnar," I said, meetin him by the toolshed.

"Ginny," he nodded at me and we walked up to the porch. I listened to the screen door to make sure there were no more sounds from upstair.

"Didn't see you at the diner this mornin," I said as I sat down in my rocker. Usually, Gunnar and Duffy, along with a lot of local men, would come to my place in the mornins for muffins or donuts with coffee.

"Been to Ellsworth. Noelle's doctor."

"She over her sickness?"

"They say she won't never be over it," he was lookin down at the floor, leanin against the railin. She'd never been so sick that she wasn't busy with the wash and cleanin, but she'd always been pale-skinned, and caught colds from every draft in the air.

"Oh? Anythin I can do?"

"No."

Then he sat down in the other rocker. He was often quiet if he wasn't all fierce to start pawin at me. But that night it was more than bein quiet. He looked torn up. Even at times when I found myself enjoyin lyin next to him, I didn't for a minute think there was anythin as messed up as love between us. He loved his wife. When it first dawned on me that he loved her, I remember wonderin why he was always so antsy to be with me. But over the course of time, I'd learned another thing about him, he was stubborn and bitter, and wanted to be able to lay his finger on something, anything, anyone, and know it was his. He'd have stolen his own mother's teeth if he thought he could get away with it.

Duff had won me from Gunnar when we was kids, and now I'd been taken back, like a lost marble in the schoolyard. He believed that he'd picked me up from the dust and he kept me tight in his pocket.

"She still takin her medicines?" I asked.

"Yup, but she's awful weak at times. Doc says she's got a weak heart. And she don't eat right."

I rested my hand on his knee. He took it as a sign that I wanted more. He stood up and we went out to the milkin barn. It was never like the lovin had been with Duffy, or even with my Henry. Those men had a better idea what it was that a woman wanted. Gunnar wanted only one thing and usually it was over in a few quick seconds. Or it seemed like that to me. I had a way of keepin my mind on other things, like how I'd make shepherd's pie for the next day's special, or how I could make a quilt out of the girls' worn dresses. It was just passin time for me.

On school days the girls would dress quick and eat whatever I put down in front of them. Teddy wouldn't eat nothin unless I made him. He didn't seem to remember what hunger was from one day to the next. He'd moan about bellyaches, usin the few words he knew. Pointin to his stomach he might say somethin that sounded like "truck" or "book." I usually had a fight on my hands, all the while tryin to get out the door so's I could get to work.

Edith might fuss about her clothes, or cause some little argument with her sister, but when it was clear to us that Henry wasn't comin back, her edges seemed to curl up like burnin paper. I knew that one day there might be hot embers sparkin at the edges, but so far, she'd blackened and silenced herself. She spent too many hours readin in her room, doin her chores without complaints.

"Edith, come by the lunchroom after school, will you?" I asked.

"Why?" she looked up from her bowl of oatmeal. Not scowlin. Nothin.

"I got an idea. You come by and I'll leave with you. I need some things over at Gossler's."

"Can I come?" Rose asked smiling.

"Honey, you come back here and help Lois with Teddy." Lois had some cannin to do, and the laundry; she could always use the extra help watchin over Teddy.

"I always have to do that," Rose sulked.

"I'll bring you a surprise."

The girls left for school without me gettin an answer from Edith, but I knew she'd do what I asked. I sat down with Teddy on the floor and played a game of knockin over blocks and each time he stacked them up, I'd get him to take a mouthful of oatmeal before he got to knock over our wooden tower. In the fall he'd be seven, but still my baby. When I'd sit with him on the floor and the house was empty, I didn't care if I'd get the lunchroom opened on time or not. Those watery blue eyes of Teddy's and his crooked teeth had a hold on me that made what I'd done with Gunnar all worth it. With the girls, I'd lose my patience when they wouldn't do what I'd told them, expectin more from them, but with my boy I didn't expect nothin, but that nothin grew around me into a fancy coat that I wore. On the lapels I pinned every smile, every new word, every hug that was never asked for.

After Lois got to the house, I went down the path that I'd cleared myself, to the lunchroom. Some days I had Maude MacClellan open the place and git the fires goin, heat up the grill. She was a good worker and I never had to find somethin for her to do. When I walked in the door, she'd already fried the donuts and was at work scramblin eggs for some woodcutters that were rentin rooms in the village.

One thing I didn't like to see each mornin was the lonely face of Duffy. He'd come there to eat and to try to get me to chat. He'd asked me a few times over the last year if I was all right, if I needed anythin, and I would smile and say I had it all. He'd given up askin, but his eyes still questioned me.

"How's Coris?" I asked him as I took my apron off the hook by the counter and tied it around me. I didn't look at him. I knew he couldn't really see the thoughts and secrets in my head but I was always afraid my eyes might show him the trail that led there. One night, not long after I'd started up the work on the lunchroom, Duffy had come by to get some tools he'd left at the house, and just missed seein Gunnar comin through the woods by only a few minutes. I don't suppose I should've worried so much that Duffy might find out, after all he had a wife and I had good reasons for what I was doin, but all the same, I did worry.

"Coris is fine," he said. He sipped his coffee and I went about fillin salt shakers.

"There's some lettuce ready to be picked and I need some carrots. If there's any onions left down cellar, I need them too." I told Duffy. "And I'd guess you could get a hell of a lot of green beans for me too."

"Royce is gonna pick them this mornin."

"See if you can think up a way to put a fence around the hives, somethin that will keep out a bear."

He nodded and got up off the stool. As he went out the door my decision to find a way out of my arrangement seemed to harden. Duffy wasn't but ten yards from me, but more like a hundred miles.

I got to work on a beef stew and then spent the rest of the mornin and into the afternoon packin up an order to send to Bangor. I went over my books tryin to figure out a way to pay Gunnar back what I owed him. I was still short a hundred dollars and a good idea.

When Edith come by, I closed the place up and we walked over to Gossler's. She didn't say much, just that she'd won a spellin bee. At the store I took her over to the table where Abel cut fabric. He had some new wallpaper books that I started thumbing through.

"Look at this one," I pointed to a pattern that was all flowers, blue and yellow, with green leaves.

Edith nodded and adjusted her spectacles that she'd had to get last winter when her teacher told me that she thought Edith was havin a hard time seein the blackboard.

"Well, do you like it?"

"It's pretty," she said and took the book from me. She started flippin the pages and come to one that was copper pots, spoons and forks, and plants in baskets. "This would be nice in the kitchen," she said.

"The kitchen? I was lookin for somethin for your room." Her bedroom hadn't been papered since my mother did it over thirty years ago. It was all water-stained and peelin. I never knew how to make Edith happy and I'd thought the paper would do it. I was tryin hard to save what money I could, all the while the salaries and the business drained most of it, but the wallpaper wasn't more than a couple of dollars. I needed those rolls of paper to unroll a bridge to my daughter, though flimsy it might be.

"Oh."

"Wouldn't that flowered one look nice on your walls? I could make you some new curtains."

"I guess. I like the kitchen one."

"I just had Walter repaint the kitchen. This would be somethin special for you."

She looked at me, pursed her lips, and waited for me to speak.

"What is it?" I asked.

"How come? Why not get something for Rose's room? She likes flowers."

I wanted to slap her. No matter what I did, it wasn't enough. Rose got happiness out of all kinds of things, but I couldn't figure out Edith.

"You're fifteen years old, almost a grown woman. Don't you want to git rid of that paper with the ballerinas?"

"Sure, the blue and yellow. I like it." She set the book down and started lookin through the dress patterns. I didn't want to fight with her. I was hopin to make her smile, but there was no point in tryin. I went over to the counter and showed the wallpaper to Abel, put down a deposit, and he promised to order it.

On the walk home I thought of different things I might say to get Edith to talk to me, but kept quiet. She hated me and I guess I was never gonna win her over. She thought everythin to do with her daddy leavin was my fault, and a good part of it was. But I still held it up that if Henry was any kind of a man, he'd have had the strength to stay, to fight, to make his plans work out with the farm. Or maybe I said that to myself to keep me company durin the quiet nights I lay alone in bed, with the smell of Gunnar's hands still on me.

It was movin toward another fall. Edith had fought a smile the day I finished paperin her room. I pretended not to see it. The room was some pretty though. I made some new curtains with blue gingham and took the old braided rug from my daddy's office, a room we never used, cleaned and repaired it and put it on Edith's bedroom floor.

During the rest of the summer Edith kept to herself, never did the things other kids did, like swimmin, or playin Mother May I, runnin to the store for an ice cream. Rose had some friends to play with, but Edith wandered the woods with a book or stayed in her room. Some days she watched out for Teddy, but I wondered if she paid enough attention to him, she was in her own dream world and it scared me.

I'd had a busy summer at work. By the end of August, after nearly two years of owin him, I had enough money to pay Gunnar back. I held the money in an envelope, put in the back of a drawer, waitin for when I could tell him that the time had come for our sneakin around to be over. I knew he'd give me a fight, or try somethin mean just to get back at me. I wanted to do it carefully, but I didn't know how. Didn't know what I'd say to him without causin a big fuss. I thought I'd just have to wait and see when the waters were calm, or icy enough for me to walk over.

When comparing the head of the drone with those of the queen and the worker one readily notices the compound eyes, those crescent-shaped projections on each side of the head. The facets composing those eyes number some twenty-five thousand in the head of the drone, so that they can see in all directions.

—*from* FIRST LESSONS IN BEEKEEPING
by C. P. Dadant, c. 1957

CHAPTER TWENTY-THREE

Duffy

1932–33

Coris takes the boys to church every Sunday but I don't go. I don't stay out at the house on Stanley's Point too often, though there is seasons when I have to, or feel close enough to Coris to want to. Or guilty enough to try and be close. I watch them dress in their best. Kiss Coris good-bye, and they take off in the old vehicle I put together with my own two hands. It runs smooth for bein pieced together.

I'd had hopes when Henry left that Ginny and me would pair up again. But it was plain stupid to think that. If we had, what would I do bout Coris and my boys? I couldn't just forget I was married to a good woman like Coris. She didn't deserve that. I should've gone to church with my family, to keep my thoughts clean.

When I was a boy my ma would make me go to church with her, wanted me to listen for the voice of the lord, but all I heard was kids' feet scuffin on the floors, hittin the back of pews, and the drone of old Pastor Green. Now I think I should've listened harder.

I go down to the shore. I hear waves, see sunshine, watch the terns struttin on the rocks and through pockets of sand and seaweed. Is that the voice I should be listenin to?

Turned my back on the lord as a boy. Didn't see his good works in my worn-out Ma with red, calloused hands, or in my drunk papa. Didn't hear nothin of God in a shack of a house, with a torn, tar-papered roof flappin in the wind like it might come right off. Didn't feel him under layers of quilts to fight off those twenty-below nights when we all see our breath standin in the air like another brother or sister, another mouth to feed.

I found some sort o' religion in my love for Ginny, but that never give me sleep at night. It just ain't easy to forgit. And yet Ginny gives me awful good reasons to. On a day like today, when I ain't got nothin I want to do, I let her seep into my head and I git mad. I read them few books I could find on beekeepin and then I tossed them in the woodstove. Weren't no point in keepin them, or holdin on to what I'd learned. Ginny never heard me when I talked bees or farmin. Just like she didn't hear the farmhands and the girls at the diner.

So I sit on the shore, look back at the house, think of my boys, think of Coris's gentle little heart, and know now this must be God givin me his sounds and touches. I been sittin out here every Sunday for the past year, waitin, watchin, hopin. It was the way Matthew held onto my pliers this mornin, wantin to stay to home and work on his bike. That's what wakes me to the voice of God.

I go back up to the house and look through my drawers for my pants that ain't so ripped-up, my clean shirt, the tie I wore to my weddin. I shave and slick back my hair with water. Get lookin real nice and walk to town. On the road I see one of the Hollis boys from Milbridge, comin my way. Put out my thumb. He gives me a ride to the church.

I stand outside the doors, listen to the voices singin pretty. I don't know how to go in. I go around to the side of the church and just listen. Voices of God, up through the throats o' them people. The pastor talks and I hear some words but ain't quite sure what they mean. Holy spirit. Damnation. Saved. I sit huddled in an alder patch and wait.

When I see people comin out I go over to where Coris has left the vehicle. I git in and wait. Coris and the boys come out. They talk to the preacher and then come over to where I'm slumped down in the seat.

What're you doing here, she asks.

Thought I might git some religion, I say. She reaches her hand across the miles I put between us and touches my face. The boys say they want to go fishin.

We go home and change up. Coris says she's comin too. She usually spends Sundays visitin folks or makin a big dinner. Today, she says, is different and she goes about packin a big lunch in a clothes basket. We drive out to Smith Pond.

I go to work like every Monday mornin. Stop first at the Queen Bee and git my coffee and somethin to eat. Ginny tells me what she needs from the garden. Tells me to work on the fence I been puttin up around the hives. I ain't nothin but a farmhand, a handyman. No man at all.

I do my chores up quick and it's half-past noon when I go out through the woods to hide out. If no one sees me they think I'm workin somewhere. I have a smoke and wander up to the huntin camp where Ginny's old man used to go for weeks at a time. He'd come home with deer and rabbit and sometimes even a moose. I hated trudgin through the woods with wagons or sleds to haul them damn carcasses back to the house. From up here I can see a bit of ocean way off to the east, and then I see the church steeple from Steuben.

I lay down in the cabin on a cot and sleep out the day.

Sunday I git all dressed up again and drive Coris and the boys to church in Milbridge.

You comin in? Coris asks me. I shake my head and have a smoke in the truck. Listen to the singin. I know inside them doors is a feelin I missed out on. I keep my feelin close to me like a flask that I sip from only once in awhile. I ain't sure I want to share it around.

Coris says the boys are goin with the other kids on a church picnic. She says why don't we go home. I was thinkin a cuddle would just hit the spot, so we drive home laughin and run to our room like school kids. I let down her pretty yellow hair and smell her good smell. She says she likes my face when it's clean shaved. We git under the sheets and move together.

The next Sunday I will go in the doors of the church.

Some nights I can't sleep. 'Specially since Papa's been gettin worse. He ain't drunk liquor in a few years cause his doctor told him it was ruinin his insides. But Pa's gotten worse just the same. He won't come and live with me and Coris, still lives in the old house that ain't fit for no one. I make sure he gits his food and Ginny gives him things from the lunchroom. I lay awake in bed wonderin what mornin it will be that I go down there and find him dead.

I get out of bed and slip on my overalls. Coris sleeps on while I dress. I leave the house. Kitchen clock says it's a little after three. I don't want to wake no one with startin up the engine so I walk to town. I like a good quiet walk. The moon lights the road even though it's just a thin slice in the sky.

I get to thinkin bout the church and bout Coris. Wonder if my wantin to go is just some old guilt pushin me that way. Sometimes I feel like I ain't really who I am. I was always me with Ginny, but Ginny hasn't looked in my face for so long now, I'm wonderin if I'm real. When she gives her orders is she seein anyone standin there? Or has ol Duff just gone up in smoke?

I can't never think of Ginny without thinkin how we rolled together as kids, touched parts of each other that no man or woman ever touches. But it made me close to her, close to somethin more stronger than any church, any God or Devil could claim for themselves. I head off the road, into a nice spot under age-old spruce trees. Sit on the floor of soft needles, lean into the tree trunk. I try to feel it again, that way we had.

It's been at least an hour and I'm comin toward town. I look around my pa's place. Don't want to wake him. I walk the old lane out to the farm and watch as the moon slips behind the hills, beyond the back of the house, and I see the first splotches of light refectin off the upstair windows.

I hear the back door shut quietlike, but I hear it. I see movin around on the side of the house. I think it might be the bear at first. I take a few steps. I don't hear nothin else.

But then I see somethin, someone movin, walkin along the barn, heading toward the wood's road. I know who it is. Now I know how things stand.

I never cried in my life. Well, maybe as a child, but not once I was old enough to know how silly it is for a man to cry. But there is somethin wet on my face, and it is hard to see the lane back to town through blurry eyes.

I go to Papa's and he's still in bed. Says he don't feel like gettin up today. I make him some tea and some toast. I go out to the shed, open the big doors, and start up workin on Abel Gossler's truck that's been givin him some trouble. Lose my thoughts in the wires and gaskets and belts.

The sun gits high and leans in the windows of the shed. Out of the corner of my eye I see a shadow comin closer toward me, spreadin across the dirt floor like a stain. I don't want to talk to her. Don't never want to see her again.

Why ain't you at work? You didn't come by for breakfast. Walter and Royce are wonderin where you are, she says. I keep my head under the hood.

Well, Papa ain't too good. I'm stayin close by, I say.

You comin to work tomorrow? she asks.

I don't think so. You got enough help.

You quittin? she asks and I pull lose a burnt fan belt. I guess I am, I say, and I watch her shadow movin away.

At church I listen to what the preacher says bout judgement. We don't got the right to judge, he says. We're just people. Not Gods. We shall not judge our neighbors, somethin like that. I take Coris's hand and feel she ain't never been this happy. All it took was for me to come through them doors. I feel the river of sweat runnin down my back. I watch my boys scuff their feet against the back of the pews. I forgit to listen and sit there quiet, peaceful but judgin everythin I know.

Winter comes, colder than the last. I stoke the stoves in the house and drive to Papa's. His windows is thick of ice and I don't see no smoke comin from his chimney. In the kitchen I hear nothin. Quiet as the frozen cup of coffee on the kitchen table. A spoon froze in it like a fallen limb in a bucket of ice. My breath clouds out in front of me as I walk to his bedroom. He went to bed without rememberin the stove. He's as frozen as the coffee. A sheet of gray ice from his last breaths is coverin the quilts under his chin.

I go and start up the woodstove. Git a good fire goin. I heat up some water and make coffee. Once the place is warm I take off my coat and gloves. Sit down to the table and have my coffee. Think bout my boys. What'd they do if I was frozen in my bed?

I sit there til nearly noontime. Go through his papers, look for any signs of who I was. Any old pictures. Letters. There's only pictures of me with my brothers and sisters. Most of them died fore I knew them. I got a brother in Holden and a sister in New Brunswick. An old aunt in Mariaville. If they was to put together all their money there wouldn't be enough to send any of them home for a service. I find a picture of Ma and Papa. An old tintype. Probably their weddin day. I slip it inside my shirt pocket and walk over to Gossler's to phone some people.

I sit with Papa til the people from the funeral home come to git him.

It's the middle of February and I haven't got much repair work to do. I wander from Stanley's Point into town a few times a day. I go across the road, past Gossler's and just fore I walk around the corner to Ginny's lunchroom, I stop and backtrack.

She sent me a nice card when Papa died but we didn't have no service. Coris asked her mama for some money to bury my Ma and Papa and a pretty granite stone. I felt proud to have it there. We both prayed over the graves, but I know my prayin is not so good as hers. I don't know how to ask for things. Don't understand prayin for ones already in the ground.

I keep waitin for God to whisper somethin to me, teach me

how. Show me how to keep prayers and sin and Ginny from gettin all twisted up in my head. Seems like it all comes down to good and evil. If evil is what I feel for Ginny then how do I know that good is what I feel for Coris. Coris is good, but my achin for other things can't be evil.

But evil is what Ginny is doin with the Devil. She been bargainin with the Devil most of her life, I think. I walk into the woods where I can see the luchroom through the trees. I lean on my knees in the cold and pray for Ginny's soul.

Coris is havin her hard times like I had. Her daddy is sick and her mama wants her to come to Bangor to help nurse him. Coris doesn't want to go and leave me alone. She thinks I been too quiet since Papa died, but I say I always been quiet. She thinks it over. Tells me she'd have to take the boys out of school if they was to go with her. I don't think schoolin is more important than seein her daddy. She says she won't stay long, but as much as I try to make things work right with her, I look forward to bein alone for awhile.

Alone ain't that good. I miss the talk, the warm bed. I stoke my stoves. Keep the wood split. I work a little on engines but it's too cold, even with the stove goin in the shed. Nighttime I go over to Sutter's Tavern and drink a few. Find I can't sleep. Find myself fightin with God. Every day been the same.

Morning time I wander into town to bullshit with Abel. We talk bout the trouble the world's in. Everyone's talkin gloomy now, people in other places is goin hungry, everyone's poor. Here, I don't see's it's any different than it's ever been. We all live off the land and always have. That's just the way it's always been. Not enough money around here for anyone to miss.

You all done workin with Ginny? Abel asks. He's weighin nails
and puttin them in a paper sack.

I'm done, I say.

Not enough work out there? he asks.

Nope, I say.

She's doin good business over at the restaurant ain't she?

I guess.

You two have a fallin out? he asks.

Just don't want to work for a woman no more.

Too much like bein a husband, ain't it? Abel laughs.

Somethin like that.

When's Coris comin back?

Not sure. Depends on her daddy.

You must miss her.

I miss her.

I walk back home, wishin I had a dog for company.

There's a bangin noise starts up in the night. I wake, git out of
bed, and head into the kitchen. A rappin against the house. The
moon's full and I see out in the dooryard. The lights brighter'n I
ever remember bein at night. The trees and my truck is almost
glowin like hot coal. I grab my coat and head out the door. I hear
voices comin through the trees, like a whole group of people is
whisperin and comin toward the house. I see shadows movin. I
think maybe they's comin for me. Hello, I holler but no one answers. The light is almost like daylight now, all yellow and wavy
like a hot August day on the tar.

I go over to my truck. It's still glowin and I touch it. Hot as
Hell. The moon's comin down, closer to me. A big white snowball.
The voices sing to me. A song I never heard. I call out again, think
I've lost my mind livin here alone for the last few weeks. I think I
hear my Papa callin my name but it's way off and cracklin like the
radio.

Papa, I say, but there ain't no answer. Now the light's so bright I can't see the movin shadows in the trees no more. I go back in the house. Close the curtains but the house is all lit up from the glare outside. I think I'm dead if I'm not crazy. I keep hearin old voices. Voices of Ginny's daddy, my daddy, my ma, my dead baby brothers and sisters. I grab an ax and think of goin out there to fight them off. I pray.

The light gits softer and I open the door. The moon looks right now. The truck ain't glowin. I walk around the dooryard, tryin to make some sense of what I see. Down the road I see someone comin through the dark. It's a woman. Wearin a long dress, a big cape. I only see her shadow, not her face.

I ain't goin with you, I say. Holdin the ax handle tight. But she keeps comin. I can tell the way she walks. Familiar but I ain't quite sure. Looks like Ginny's ma. I go back inside, shakin like a fool dog in the thunderstorm. I huddle up to the stove, close my eyes, crouch down. I wait for a knock on the door. I wait for a long time. When I dare to open my eyes again, I see it's still night. It's quiet. I git up and look out the door.

Nothing.

I go back to my bed still holdin the ax.

The mornin light brings with it a foolish feelin in me. I ain't no coward but I ain't never been that scared. I go outside and look for footprints, for scraps of cloth that might've tore off on branches. I check the engine in the truck. Cold as a witch's tit. I wonder if I'm sick in the head. When I was a boy Old Man MacClellan had somethin they called a disease, a sickness in his mind. I think my only sickness is love for Ginny.

What brung the dead to my door? I wonder. Wasn't it enough that I can't keep Ginny out of my head?

Indoors I go bout gettin some coffee, then go back outside to work. I lift my ax and slam it down on the wood, sendin bark and splinters sprayin out around me in a circle. I try to sum up the years that I been waitin for Ginny. I say waitin, cause that's what it feels like. Even though I got my own wife, I still wait for one word, or one look from Ginny to know the time ain't been wasted. I think it's been forever. Been bout fifteen years since she married Henry, maybe that ain't so long to some, but still it seems like forever to me.

I chop the wood, throw it into a pile, and later I'll stack it. Stack it up neat and high. Every chunk of it like a day gone by.

You think everyone gotta read the Bible to be good? I ask the preacher after church. We're sittin in the front pew. The church is empty.

I can't read so good, don't understand it, I say.

No, don't try to read it if it's difficult. But understand what it says.

How can I understand it if I can't read it?

Understand the meaning behind it. The message.

Message?

Listen, you'll hear it.

I think of tellin bout what I see outside in the night. But he'd say I was dreamin. Tell me I need to be with more people.

I'll try to listen, I say.

I know some of what he's talkin bout. Like understandin an engine but not readin the manual, or understandin a cow but not readin books bout cows.

Intuition, he says.

You hear voices from the Lord?

I hear it in here, he thumps his chest.

Then I don't need to go to church to hear God, I say.

He smiles. The church is the common thought, the common voice that we're all listening for. I hear it when we're all together, or when I'm praying. Don't you hear it when you pray?

David C. Fickett

I hear it when I don't.

Are you talking about the Devil? His voice can be louder.

I think on this. I never liked Ginny's ma that much, but she weren't no Devil. Neither was my pa or those dead babies.

Duff, are you talking about the Devil?

No.

We all feel we've heard or seen things. We often convince ourselves that we're following God's direction, but misinterpreting circumstances. The Devil does the same thing. He tries to trick us, the preacher says.

God. The Devil. What's all this mean? I wonder to myself. First I go to church and then I think I see dead people. My mind's achin with the preacher's talk. Achin with my own thoughts. Achin.

Thank you. I say and stand up to go.

I hope I answered your questions, he says.

Yup, I say, but I don't feel no better.

If people's supposed to follow God's path, but they ain't real sure it's the right one, then how do you ever know? Seems to me all the preacher's talk just left it open to explain things any way he needs. If I feel that Ginny's ma bein there is somehow mixed up with Ginny, then maybe I'm s'posed to go back out to that farm. But I'm married and if the preacher knew all bout Ginny and me, he'd tell me the Devil was talkin to me, tricked me. But he says you gotta hear it inside, understand it, these signs from God. I feel like I was told to do somethin. Somethin good. Ain't no way the Devil talked through Ginny's ma.

On my way back to home, I chuck my Bible into the gully longside the road. If I can read it, understand it, without openin the damned thing then what good is it?

When he (the beekeeper) thinks fit, he will peacefully violate the secret of the sacred chambers, and the elaborate, torturous policy of the palace.

—*from* THE LIFE OF THE BEE
by Maurice Maeterlinck, c. 1901

CHAPTER TWENTY-FOUR

Caleb

1956

I wake. I had fallen asleep in the chair in Ma's room. She is breathing softly. I don't remember when she stopped speaking, when I drifted off, but clearly Duffy was with us, here in this room adding his words to her story.

I dress and go downstairs. It is still early morning and the sky is clouded over. I go into the parlor.

I should close the lid. But I stare down at Duffy. It is impossible to be as still as he is. I can't believe that we will be burying him today. I should be able to close this lid but I can't. I know Ma can't either. It will be up to me. But I still have questions. Will I forget them if I can never see his face again? Why was it that of the people in my life, he seemed to love me more than they did? Or was it only that he understood my isolation and tried to reach me? I may never know, but I know I can't close him in there. Not yet.

I hear Ma getting up, walking overhead.

I go outside and walk the fence line along the back pasture. I have dreamed of leaving this place, of finding a place where I truly fit in, but will I ever be able to leave? I want to finish my education. I want to study insects. I want to live without sadness.

The dark morning is still, and frost has settled over the tall, dried grasses and branches of the trees. It smells like snow. As I near the Sorensen's property line I can see Olaf sitting on the stone wall through a stand of spruce trees. He's swinging his feet and smoking. I climb over the fence and approach him.

"Morning," I say.

"Hi." He smiles.

"You're out early," I say.

"Couldn't sleep."

"No, I couldn't either. What keeps you awake at night?"

"Just stuff." He looks down over the slope to his house. His shirt collar is open wide and I can see the dark flat mole on his neck. He drops his cigarette and steps on the butt with his boot, as he stands up.

"Don't rush off," I say.

"Nora will be lookin' for me. I have to help her with the wood, and the bed." He shakes his head and puts his hands in the pockets of his jeans.

"Nora? I thought she left."

"Came back. She always comes back. Scared of my dad, I guess."

I can't believe she'd go back to him. Did she think I was using her, like Gunnar, or other men she may have known? Or did she have no home to go to? I have to tell her that I will help her somehow. She needs to get away from all of the Sorensens.

"Olaf, I had a crazy thought," I begin, not quite believing that I've found the courage to tell him what I'm about to.

"Yeah, what?"

"You know how people talk?"

He nods.

"Do you think that old Gunnar and my ma had something going a long time ago?" My face is hot and I know I'm red.

"I've heard it said. Don't know as I believe it. Funny to think of old people doin' it."

"Yeah," I look down at the ground, swing my feet out from the stone wall.

"Why'd you ask?"

"I don't know. I guess with Duffy gone, well it's got me thinking about my dad. I never knew him."

"You think my dad could be yours?" Olaf squints his eyes and shakes his head. "You gotta be crazy. We ain't brothers. Shit." He pulls out another cigarette and lights it. He turns his head and rubs his eyes. "What got that into your head?" he asks. His voice shakes. He turns his back to me.

"I don't know what to believe. It seems funny to me that my dad would take off when my ma was going to have a baby. He never even came to see me. Never sent a letter. I think something bad must have happened to send him away like that. Anything is possible. There's enough secrets in my ma's head to sink a ship."

"Look, you ain't my Christless brother, all right?" he yells at me, turning so I can see his red face. He is furious and I can't imagine why. Would being my brother be that bad a thing?

"Hey, calm down. I've just been turning a lot of things over in my head. I thought I could talk to you about it."

"Well, I don't want to hear it," he yells again, his voice catching in his throat, his eyes wet with tears. He is beyond anger. This is grief.

"Hey, Olaf, what is it?"

He starts walking away from me, down the slope, walking fast, until he is running. The last time I saw him fall apart was the night he took me home with him when I was too drunk to drive. He cried that night and wouldn't let me out of his arms. He had always cared for me in a peculiar way, a way that made me think he was simply lonely and thought of me as his only friend. But it is not that. Partly, it is, I guess, but now I think it is more. The idea of being my brother must negate his secret love for me.

I walk back to the house unable to worry about Olaf as I have my own worries right now. Like Nora, Ma, Edith, the burial. I slip quietly in the back door, through the kitchen, and down the hallway to the parlor. I hear Ma and Edith talking softly. I peer through the crack in the doorway and see them, their backs to me. At first I think it is Ma who is sobbing, but it is not her. It's Edith. Her head is bowed and her shoulders shake. Ma is comforting her, patting her back with one hand and wiping the tears off my sister's face with her other. This sort of motherly love I've witnessed so infrequently that the shock of it nearly makes me call out, as thought I've witnessed a serious crime. But I keep quiet.

Mostly what I hear is only what I can imagine, or piece together from overheard conversations that have been whispered in this house long ago. Their words are soft, disjointed to me. As I listen I hear the unspoken beneath the timbre of their words.

A few birds, among which we shall name the kingbird,
eat bees. But their damages are so insignificant that they
are hardly worthy of mention.

—*from* FIRST LESSONS IN BEEKEEPING
by C. P. Dadant, c. 1957

CHAPTER TWENTY-FIVE

Edith

1933

At school Edith was a good student and Mrs. Ballard had told her
she'd make a fine teacher, but Edith wasn't sure she could tolerate
the noisy kids with their backtalk and lazy habits. She tried to
imagine a future for herself but conjured up only a blackness, covered in a fine dust. A blackboard with occasional words written
there, in bold pennmanship, words she couldn't erase. Words that
somehow told her all she was, all she could ever be. Daughter.
Sister. Or in the bleakest of winter's nights, she'd see Ugly. Useless.
Abandoned.

She was sixteen and had never been kissed. She wasn't sure
she wanted to be kissed, but she resented the other girls at school
who had been. When Mrs. Ballard had to leave the school to run
an errand, she'd leave Edith in charge and the oak desk under
Edith's palms felt warm and smooth. She felt in control, protected

by its wide surface and distance from the students. The feeling excited her. She didn't quite understand it. It frightened her too, maybe like a boy's kiss would make her feel.

The wooden pointer was something she knew could hurt the other girls if she were to strike them with it. And using the chalk could change the course of her classmates' day. She could write the names of the ones that misbehaved. The ones that called her "Miss Bird" and taunted her about her spectacles, or her pointed nose, or her gray dresses. Always she put Rose's name on the board for very little reason.

"But I didn't do anything!" Rose yelled out. It was a spring morning and Mrs. Ballard had gone to the Post Office and to see the mother of one of the students.

"You were whispering to Marie. I saw you," Edith said as she completed the s and the e of Rose's name.

"You always pick on me," Rose said and slumped back in her chair.

"Hey Bird, why don't you take some of us boys out to the woodshed. Show us who's boss," Sven Sorensen hollered. All the boys started to laugh.

Edith kept her face to the board. She knew she was blushing.

"Yeah, I need a good spankin'," Sven's bother, Erik said. More laughter.

"Open your arithmetic books," Edith sat down at the desk. "Mrs. Ballard wants the upper grades to work on page eighty-seven. Do the problems. I have to work with the lower grades," she said, not looking up. She turned to the children on the right half of the room and told them to start reciting their times tables. A tiny wet ball of paper hit her in the head. She stood up slowly and went to the board. Under Rose's name, she wrote Erik.

"That wasn't me!" he yelled.

"What wasn't you?" she asked.

"That spit ball. I didn't throw it."

"Then how do you know it was a spit ball?"

"Ah . . . cause I seen who throwed it."

"Threw it." She turned to face Erik. "Tell me who it was."

His face became red. He rolled his eyes but didn't say anyone else's name.

The small children were nearly through with their five's times table, when someone tossed a paper airplane. She could see in her peripheral view that it was Sven, but as she stood to write his name she thought better of it. She had an idea. The perspiration beaded up on her forehead. Her hands sweat as she wrote down another boy's name. Ralph.

"That wasn't me," Ralph protested.

"Then who was it?" she asked, knowing no one would dare tattle on Sven. He was the biggest boy in school, and the oldest. Ralph said nothing. If she kept Sven's name off the board then she'd have the chance to talk with him after school.

As the morning dragged on, Edith managed to get all of the older children's names on the board. All of Sven's friends. All of the girls who spit venom at her as she walked home from school. Mrs. Ballard would keep them all after school. She always believed Edith, no matter how much Rose or the other students would protest. As she'd hoped, Sven behaved the remainder of the day and Mrs. Ballard did not have to add his name to the list.

That afternoon as a handful of students were dismissed by the teacher, Edith hurried to get out the door behind Sven.

"Hey Bird, you know who throwed that plane at you, don't you?" Sven walked beside her. He was tall, and his legs and arms were powerfully built. Edith had thought about his arms ever since she first noticed that they were filling out, nearly three years ago. She'd watched him chopping wood through the schoolroom window. His shirt was off. At the time, she thought, how ugly the bulges were, covered in blond hair.

"Don't call me Bird," she said. She took off her spectacles and slipped them inside her pocket.

"I could call you a lot o' things," he said and walked a little faster, ahead of her. The younger children raced ahead and scattered in different directions.

"I could call you names too!" she shouted.

He stopped and turned to her. "Yeah, like what?"

"Like . . . like . . ."

"You don't even know no bad words." He waited for her to catch up. He was laughing.

"I just won't say them," Edith smiled, hoping her smile was pretty.

He took a cigarette from his jacket pocket and lit it. "You won't say them cause you're too goody-goody."

"I am not." She thought she might cry but closed her eyes tight and held the tears in. She had practice at doing that. She thought crying was foolish and a waste of time. Rose would cry at anything.

She knew boys like Sven were impressed easily. She reached out for his cigarette and took hold of it. He watched her, wide-eyed, as she took a drag. She'd never smoked before but she was careful not to inhale too much. She didn't want to start coughing and gagging in front of him.

She blew the smoke out and handed it back to him. "You don't know anything about me, Sven."

She walked past him but he followed.

"What else don't I know?" he asked, handing the cigarette back to her. She smoked again, inhaling more of it, liking it.

"You just think I'm a bookworm, but I've got a boyfriend. Over in Milbridge. He takes me to the picture shows. Mama doesn't even know." Edith invented a boy that resembled her father. Blond wavy hair, tall and thin, with a new car and a job. This boy was a man. He was out of school. He worked somewhere, where? At the telephone office. He was a supervisor.

"You don't have a boyfriend," Sven laughed.

"I do. I'm more grown-up than you think."

They'd reached the four corners. The Queen Bee was across the road and further on was Gossler's store. Edith hadn't wanted to go by her mother's restaurant yet. Not yet.

"I don't believe you," Sven crushed out his cigarette under his boot and crossed his arms over his chest. "You never been to the pictures either."

"You're just a boy. You have no idea."

"Yeah, well then let's you an me go the pictures sometime," he challenged her. She was excited and terrified at the same time.

"You don't have a car," Edith said as she walked ahead of him.

"Well, I can git my daddy's truck."

"A truck?"

"Yeah, what's wrong with that?"

Edith was facing the diner now. She hated the idea of seeing her mother, but she wished she could go inside to hide from Sven. She didn't know what to say to him. She hesitated, wondering what it would be like to kiss him. Now that she'd made up the boyfriend, he might think she'd go all the way. Was that what boys wanted, even though she'd been called names by everyone, even though she knew she wasn't pretty, would he still take her on a date if he thought . . .

"Well, I have a b . . . boyfriend," she stammered. "I couldn't go out with you."

"To Hell with you, then." Sven turned and headed in another direction. Edith fumbled to find her glasses and put them on. Her heart was racing. She felt relieved yet anxious. Had she ruined her chances? Would she have enough courage to try again? Her mother was looking out the window. Edith ignored her, looked down at the ground and walked home, not wanting Mama to see her eyes.

As she went through the front door, she passed Teddy, gently pushing him aside, not wanting his grubby hands on her. She ignored Lois who was folding laundry on the kitchen table. She headed upstairs and went into the bathroom. Daddy had turned one of the small bedrooms into a bathroom before Teddy was born. Edith felt as though they were rich to have plumbing upstairs. She turned on the tap and splashed cold water on her face. Then scrubbed away the awful taste of tobacco from her mouth.

She took her books and went to her room. The walls were papered with blue and yellow flowers, green vines, and white ribbons. She loved the paper. Mama had let her pick it out at Gossler's from a book filled with beautiful colors, flowers, trellises, fields of horses, farmhouses, and even patterns of palm trees, bamboo, and pine boughs. One pattern was of pots and pans and plants. Edith had asked to buy that for the kitchen but Mama had said no, she liked the kitchen painted green. Even though the pattern Edith had chosen for the bedroom was her favorite, she sulked about the kitchen paper, and pretended as if she didn't care about her room.

She'd rearranged the room so that her bed was near the window that looked down the lane toward town. She lay on her bed watching the road. She wondered if she'd ever leave this place. She dreamed of having her own home, a place like the farm, but with better things, more animals. Maybe she'd marry someone like the man she'd dreamed up to make Sven jealous. Someone like Daddy.

If only Daddy would come home, she thought. It was Mama's fault that he'd disappeared. Mama could be so mean. But why wouldn't he come back to get his daughter? They used to work together in the gardens, in the milking barn. He used to bring her penny candy when he went in town. Now she resented candy, anything sweet.

Daddy's going had something to do with that idiot man, Duffy, Edith was sure of it. Edith had caught Mama kissing him once. Daddy must have found out, maybe he caught them himself. Poor Daddy, she thought, to be driven away by Mama and a common farmhand.

It was easy to hate Mama. Easy. When Edith remembered that brittle, cold night that Teddy had been born, when she'd been pushed by her mother into that November darkness, she'd cradle her hatred gently, warming it with her hands, protecting it from harm, as though it was kept within a fragile eggshell. She'd keep it with her in her room, in her bed, take it with her to school.

That cold night, her mother's labor pains filtered through the dim light of the parlor until they reached Edith. Edith could feel them. Mama looked afraid. The baby wouldn't come. Edith was sent to find help, and for a few minutes, she felt like a heroine. But the cold air and an uncomfortable blackness in the sky lowered itself like a dark dome over the girl. She walked ahead, thinking she was still on the road, until her foot struck a stump or a rock and she fell into icy puddles and wet grasses. She jumped up, looked around, hoping to see a light to follow, but there was none. She couldn't see her way and then the hate for Mama pecked away inside.

Edith wondered if her mother had planned it. Had she wanted her daughter, her ugly daughter to get lost? freeze to death? starve to death? She kept walking until she found help. Duffy. She brought him to Mama, and then she foolishly fell into Mama, crying as that stupid man took Mama's pain away.

Teddy, her idiot brother. That was the result of that heroic night. Another reason to hate Mama. But that night, and so many afterwards caused the hatred to grow. When Edith realized that Mama loved Duffy, she used it against her, blackmailed her, but now with Daddy gone, she had no control over Mama. So she'd stopped fighting so much. She'd retreated into a cold silence.

She turned over on her bed and stared at the ceiling. She thought about Daddy too. It wasn't easy to hate Daddy. Even when another year passed and he hadn't returned, she wanted to hate him, but she couldn't. Daddy loved her even if Mama didn't. But he'd been gone so long now it was getting harder for her to believe in him.

The anger, the hatred was cracking the delicate casing that housed it. By warming it, nourishing it with her self-pity, she was allowing it to grow into something she could touch.

"You didn't stop by the lunchroom today," Mama said to Edith as she filled her plate with creamed potatoes.

"I had homework." Edith pushed the potatoes around with her fork.

"I made gingersnaps. Thought you'd like them."

"Mama, Edith put my name on the board at school. I didn't do nothin'," Rose said.

"Mrs. Ballard wouldn't have Edith in charge if she didn't think your sister knew what she was doin'."

"But I didn't do nothin'. She's just mean when she's teacher," Rose took another roll from the basket.

"You like teachin'?" Mama asked.

"It's all right," Edith said.

"I talked to Mrs. Ballard. She thinks you should go to Castine Normal School, get your degree. You want that?" Mama asked.

"I don't know."

"What do you want to do? Stay on this farm? You wouldn't be happy."

"Edith ain't never happy. Old sourpuss," Rose said with a mouthful of food.

"Shut up," Edith said.

"Are ya? Happy, I mean?" Mama asked.

"Talk about something else," Edith said. She pushed her plate forward.

"Don't like the supper?" Mama asked.

"I can't eat. I'm going to bed." Edith stood up and walked toward the hall.

"Hold on Missy. What's the trouble?"

"Nothing. I don't feel well."

"You don't look sick. You got dishes to do. Did you make up Teddy's bed?"

"I'm not your hired help," Edith turned back to her mother.

"Are you tryin' to git a fight goin'?"

"No."

"I don't know what to do with you." Mama got up from her chair and came toward Edith. She hated to have her mother touch her and she knew what was next. Mama would grab her arm and hold on while she yelled. Edith stepped away from her.

"I don't want anyone to do anything with me. I want to go upstairs."

"You ain't goin' nowhere til you tell me why you're so god-damned mad all the time. I try to give you kids a good home and . . ."

"Shut up!" Edith screeched out. She was surprised at how loud her voice was.

Mama grabbed her arm, pulled her closer. Edith could see pieces of potato in the corners of Mama's mouth.

"Don't you never yell at me like that. I'll boot your ass out of this house so fast you won't know what hit ya." Mama's eyes were fierce. Edith could feel the heat of her hatred.

"You won't have to kick me out, I'll go on my own. Anytime you ask." Edith pulled her arm free. "And don't touch me either."

"You git up those stairs and make up your brother's bed and then I want you to git goin' on these supper dishes. You ain't livin here for free."

"What about her, what does she do?" Edith pointed to her sister.

"She does plenty, and without any backtalk. You got no reason to sass me. You been doin' it all your life."

"I've got good reason," Edith said. Her mother stood closer to her, her hand raised in the air.

"What reason? What in Hell did I ever do to you?" Edith thought she saw her mother's eyes moistening. It wasn't possible that she would cry, though.

"You boss us around. You make me take care of that fool . . . and . . ." Before Edith could finish her sentence, her mother's hand landed on her face with such strength that Edith fell back against a chair and tumbled over the back of it. Her glasses spun into the middle of the kitchen floor. She threw her hair out of her face and looked up at her mother.

"Don't you call your brother a fool," Mama was bending down, glaring at Edith.

"Don't you ever hit me again," Edith said slowly, feeling that fragile shell cracking open, peeling away from the bloated monster that had grown there. She felt a sharp pain in her head. She tried to hold her skull together, it seemed it might burst. "You fucking whore!" Edith screamed out. She stood up quicker than she thought possible, so fast that she was on her mother before the woman realized it. She pulled her mother's hair, she raked her face with her fingernails, she hit and hit until her mother cowered, helpless under the fury of this wonderful demon that Edith let rise out of her. "I hate you, hate you, hate you," Edith kept yelling. Edith saw Rose coming at her. The child was crying and swinging her fists. Edith grabbed hold of Rose's shirt and threw her back on the floor. Teddy had wandered downstairs and stood watching, unthinking.

"You and your sneaking around . . . It's your fault that Daddy left us, your fault," Edith ranted. She stopped only when she realized that her mother was not fighting back, just holding her arms up to protect herself. She stood back, her heart racing. She couldn't remember ever feeling so alive.

Mama looked up. She wasn't crying, hardly looked upset, but then, that woman was made of stone. Rose ran to Mama and cried.

Edith went to her room, locked the door and lay awake all night.

In the morning, before anyone was awake, Edith went downstairs and took some food from the pantry. She grabbed her schoolbooks and walked into the woods to wait for the sunrise.

She sat on a log and ate an apple. It was still dark and the sounds of the early morning excited her. She felt odd, as though her encounter with Sven and then the fight with Mama, the day before, had freed her of her fear. From where she sat she could see the top of the barn and the toolshed. She had an inspiration. She got up and ran quickly back into the yard, wrapping her sweater around her head, leaving enough of an opening to see where she was going. When she reached the beehives, she opened the gate of the fence and quickly kicked over two hives, then ran with her head protected, back up the hill, into the woods. A few bees followed, but she ran fast. She swung her sweater free and swatted the damn things. She crushed one under her foot.

She'd thought of running away. But where would she go? What if Daddy came home and she was gone, she'd have no way to know that he'd come back. No, she knew she had to stay. She had to go to school, had to face her mother at some point, but so what? What could that woman do to her to punish her? Nothing. She could try, but Edith knew she wouldn't take it. She was as strong as Mama.

She knew too, that she'd see how far she could go with Sven. It was obvious to her that he was curious about this other Edith that he'd never noticed before. She could be whatever he needed her to be. It was fun seeing how much she could manipulate these people, Sven, Rose, the students, Mama.

She picked up her schoolbooks and her paper bag of food and started walking along the wood's road. A dim morning light was seeping through the trees. She would wait on the Sorensen's dirt road for Sven. She looked back toward her house, took her hair out of its tight ponytail, and shook it free. She started to take off her glasses but noticed someone walking away from the house. A man. He was coming up the wood's road. She moved quietly, revolted at her mother's indiscretion. It had to be Duffy. How she hated him, hated them both. She hid beneath large branches of a pine tree that hung out in the trail. She waited, wondering if she should say something to him, threaten to tell his wife about what went on.

As he came closer, she thought she might be sick, but closed her eyes to control the retching, forcing the queasiness down deeper into her. She opened her eyes as he walked past. He looked taller, his shoulders broader. It wasn't Duffy at all.

It was Sven's father.

He passed, went down the slope toward the Sorensen farm, then she let the sickness overtake her. Silently she retched and retched, but the only thing that came was anger.

*Of all the diseases of bees the most dreaded is foulbrood.
Foulbrood attacks the larvae, which die in the cells. It is
infectious and must be treated with promptness and care.*
—*from* FIRST LESSONS IN BEEKEEPING
by C. P. Dadant, c. 1957

CHAPTER TWENTY-SIX

Ginny

1933–1957

I was happy with the way things was goin with my business, happy
not to have Henry around, too. But I couldn't say I was happy
about my oldest girl. Sometimes I'd look at her, her eyes always
lookin at the floor, her hair messy, her clothes with no color, and
I'd see myself as that same lonely girl I'd been sittin across from
Mama at the kitchen table. Or maybe she was more like my sister,
Dora. She had been plain and taken for granted. Both of us was
always waitin for Mama to reach across the table and take our hand.
I'd sat too long on my side, waitin.

Of course, Edith and I weren't alike in most ways though, just
that we were orphans. I couldn't reach her and her father had left
her. Both of us deserted her but in different ways. I felt some
disaster headin her way. I remembered what Dora had been driven
to do with that shovel. I didn't see signs of that kind of hidden
anger in Edith, but I wasn't lookin close enough.

There was a spring mornin when I went to wake up my girls to get ready for school, and found that Edith had gone. She and I'd had a terrible fight the night before. I had two fingernail scratches across my cheeks. When I'd seen how wrought up she was at me, I just let her hit and scratch away. It was somethin she needed to get out. I guess I thought I deserved some of her wrath. I wondered if she'd run away.

I looked through her drawers to see if she'd packed anything, but all I found missin was her schoolbooks. I wondered what time she'd left, and why? Was she doin a special project at school, or had she gone off early cause she was fillin in for Mrs. Ballard? Had she left so early that she'd seen Gunnar leavin the house?

I'd taken too many risks with Gunnar. I had to end it. After I got Rose's and Teddy's breakfast and Lois had shown up, I went to the lunchroom, hopin Gunnar would come by as he usually did. I got the stoves goin, chopped some onion for a chowder, washed down the counters, and waited. I wished Duffy would come by, but he'd taken to avoidin me. I wasn't sure why, just figurin he was makin things work with Coris. I prayed to God he'd never learned about Gunnar and me, but the thought crossed my mind more than once.

I'd told Rose to come to the lunchroom if Edith wasn't in school and by eight o'clock she didn't show up, so I knew Edith was there. I fed a few of the regular men their breakfast and kept lookin at the door, hopin I'd see Gunnar. It was half-past nine before he walked in.

"You're late," I said and put a hot cup of coffee on the counter.

"Been workin on my boat," he said. Most men around had a boat or two to go lobsterin, or fresh-water fishin. Gunnar dabbled in farmin, fishin, loggin, and carpentry. He liked makin money and would do it any way he could.

"Need to talk to you," I said quietly, waitin for an older couple to finish up their eggs and pay. When they'd left I refilled Gunnar's cup and folded my hands on my apron pocket, feelin the lump of cash I'd slipped in.

"What's with you today?" he asked. He bucked up his chin and narrowed his eyes. He knew somethin was goin on in my head.

"I've got your money."

"My money?" he asked, but he knew what I was talkin about.

"Yeah, the loan. Remember?" I felt hot. I was gonna play this out with a level head, I hoped, but still he made me nervous.

"All of it," I said. "Plus, I give you some interest."

"I don't want your money, Ginny." He swallowed down some coffee and turned on the stool, facin the door.

"It ain't mine. It's yours." I took the money out of my pocket and placed it on the counter. "Take it."

He turned back. His black eyes looked darker than usual. I'd never seen a shade of black that deep. He lit up a cigarette and blew out the smoke, tryin to gain some time to think.

"What happens if I take it?" he asked.

"I've paid you back. I appreciate the loan. Couldn't've done this without you."

"Ginny, I don't want the money," he said softly.

"Gunnar, it's yours. I've paid in full." I met his eyes, spoke in a low voice, he knew I meant more than what I said.

"Just like that?" he asked.

"Just like that."

"You bitch. Can't tell me our little setup hasn't worked for you?" His face was gettin red now. He stood up, a tall man and built strong. If he wanted me bad enough he could take me. I wasn't the one in the driver's seat. I'd merely gone along for the ride, always waitin for a chance to flip the door handle and jump. I'm sure he realized that in the beginnin, but he must've hoped I'd come to like him, maybe love him. But I think love to him meant ownership, like his boats or trucks. I wasn't no Ford or Chevrolet.

"Gunnar, keep your hat on. No reason to get mad. You didn't think it was gonna go on forever did you?" I slapped down my dishrag on the counter. He stepped back away, scratched his head.

He couldn't think of nothin to say. "Now, you go on home to your wife," I said.

"Goddamn. I don't believe you. Little slut like you tellin me . . ."

"Hold on, don't need to get nasty. I thanked you for the money. You got more than what you deserve."

"You liked every minute of it, rollin 'round on that barn floor just like a cat in heat. You'll want it again 'fore long." He laughed, threw down some change for his coffee and took up the stack of bills. "Well, it's over when I say so."

"No, it's over. I'm tellin you. You should be thinkin about your wife. I got kids. We've risked this too long. Now face it, it's gotta stop." My voice rose up in a shriek. I was gonna lose control if I didn't cool down. But I'd waited so long to tell him. The excitement had built up in me like steam in a kettle. I wanted to scald him with my anger but I knew I had no chance of convincin him unless I stayed calm.

"If I come in here for a hot meal, you're gonna make it for me, and if I stop by your place, you're gonna serve up the goods just the same. Once a whore, always a whore. You hear me?"

"I hear what you're sayin, but don't try it out. You show up at my door and all you'll get is a shotgun 'tween the eyes. Now, I've had enough. You listen to reason. Don't want Noelle to find out about it do you?" I knew I couldn't tell Noelle nothin, but I thought it might shut him up for a minute. It wasn't much of a threat though. He probably didn't care what Noelle knew about it. She wasn't gonna be able to keep him away, if it was what he wanted.

"Better keep a close eye on things 'round here, Ginny. You might come to work one day and find just a pile of burnin rubble," he said as he turned and went out the door, slammin it behind him. I waited til I heard his truck spin up gravel in the driveway and then I sat down at one of the tables. I waited til my hands stopped shakin before I started cookin up the chowder for my lunch crowd.

When school let out I saw Edith walk by the restaurant goin home. She never said a thing about leavin so early that day and I knew better than to ask.

When I got home that afternoon, Royce told me that two of the hives had been knocked over and the bees were goin crazy. Duffy had built a big fence around the hives, so I didn't see how a bear could've gotten in, and when I looked I could see that the honey hadn't been touched. I spent a few hours settin things right and coaxin the bees back in. I figured Edith was behind the mess, but I never said a word. I wished then that Henry was home. He might be able to help her.

No one ever asked me about why he'd left. In the beginnin, they asked when he might be home, but I dodged the questions best I could. I guessed that most people around thought I'd driven him away. Probably thought I'd driven him to drink, too. I'd never cared that I wasn't well liked. I'd never had many close friends, never any girlfriends, and I knew I put people off with my quick answers and the frown I'd inherited from both Mama and Daddy. Folks must've thought Henry'd had enough of me, and that didn't bother me. What bothered me was wonderin if they'd known about Duffy. I didn't like to think his name had been dragged through the mud.

But the people I'd hired thought differently about me. They knew I was fair with them. Walter and Royce had watched me grow up, so they knew I wasn't all bad. Walter, Royce, and a few others were the only peoples' opinions I really cared about.

That was til I had girls that were nearly grown. I didn't like to think about Edith and Rose gettin wind of stories about their mother. Rose had come home one day, not long after Edith and I'd had our fight, sayin that Abel Gossler's girl, Irene, had had a fight with Edith. There was no fist fightin, just words strung together like barbed wire that stuck in my girl's skin. Irene had told Edith that she was plain rotten, and no better than her whore of a mother. I knew too well that Edith had a bad disposition but she was such a wallflower, I couldn't imagine why Irene had called her that name.

"Rose, people say awful mean things when they're mad. What did Edith do to make Irene so mad?"

"Irene said Sven was *her* boyfriend and Edith laughed at her, said he didn't like Irene anymore."

"Ain't Sven and Irene goin together?" I was sittin in my daddy's old office. I hadn't used it much since he died, just a place for me to store cannin jars and file my old receipts, but lately I'd cleaned it up, dusted off his framed butterfly collection, and was usin the desk to do my figurin.

"I guess, but Irene said something I couldn't hear. The girls were making fun of Sven too. I don't know what's going on." Rose stood beside my chair, leanin over the desk. She put her arm around my shoulder and looked down to see what work I was doin. She never had trouble reachin out for me. I never found it easy to reach out for the girls, but Rose didn't seem to notice. Edith and I had walls thick as brick between us.

"Well, I'll talk to Edith, not that it will do me any good."

That night I went up to Edith's room and I asked her about the argument with Irene. There was no point in me askin about the overturned beehives. I figured she'd done it. Up to her old tricks.

"Rose has to run and tell you everything," Edith said.

"She was worried. Irene said some awful things. Why'd she call me that name, any idea?" I had a pile of folded laundry that I started to put away in her drawers.

"Why do you think?" Edith said, lookin at her textbook.

"I don't know. I don't know what people say about me. I don't care much, but I worry about you girls hearin it."

"Don't."

"Are you sweet on Sven Sorensen? Is that why Irene was mad?"

I'd never imagined Edith likin any of the local boys, especially

Sven. He was a rough boy, a boy headin down the wrong road. I thought of Edith as likin a boy like Henry.

"I don't ask you about who you like, do I?" She slapped the book cover down and sat up on her bed.

"What kind of question is that?" Then I realized what she meant. She'd never forgive me about Duffy. She probably thought we were still sneakin around behind everyone's backs.

"If anyone thinks you're a whore it's your own doing," she said, glarin at me.

"You watch that mouth. Don't you call me that ever again. What's got into you?"

"I don't want to talk about this," she said.

"I do." I sat down on the bed beside her and picked up her book. I thumbed through the pages not seein the words. She waited for me to say somethin. "You worried about me? Me and Duffy?"

"I don't give you much thought."

"I think you do. You're old enough for me to tell you about Duffy, and I think you ought to hear it."

She sighed and looked away from me.

"Duffy and me was once in love. It was a long time ago. Before your daddy. We was kids. He wanted me to marry him, but I didn't think I should. I was tryin to keep this place together. My mama was sick, my daddy gettin sick too. Sick in the head. I didn't have things as easy as you do. When I met your daddy I thought things would change for me. We had big hopes for this farm."

"I know what I saw . . ." she mumbled, still not lookin at me.

"You mean that time with Duffy? It wasn't what you think. He still had strong feelins for me. It was just a kiss. We stayed good friends. I never hurt your daddy. He never knew about it."

"Well, he left . . . for some reason."

"Henry had his own troubles. Just remember who left and who stayed behind to pick up the pieces. Remember who made them dresses you wear, and who makes the money to buy you your hairbrushes, your shoes, everything else we got around here."

"I want to go away to school," Edith said. I stood up. She didn't want to talk about me or her daddy.

"School costs money too. I don't think you want to go to learn nothin, you just want to be away from me." I started to walk toward the door.

"I'll make my own money."

"And how do you plan to do that?" I turned around to her.

"I don't know, same as you I guess."

"Cookin? Waitin tables? You don't want that. I know you can do more."

"I'll borrow it."

"No one's lendin money these days. I want you to get a teachin degree like you want, but we'll work somethin out."

"I can get it from Mr. Sorensen. Isn't he like a bank?" Edith looked at me, darin me to say somethin. I had no idea she knew where I got the money to start the business. She'd either gone through my desk or had heard something in town. It would be like Gunnar to brag to one of his buddies when he was drinkin. I watched her, waitin, but she clammed up. Pursed her lips up and adjusted her glasses. I couldn't hold my tongue for long.

"What are you talkin about? Tell me."

"Nothing." She got red in the face and started fiddlin with a tuft of thread on her bedspread.

"Tell me what you're talkin about."

"Irene said that Mr. Sorensen gave you money to start the Queen Bee, that's all." She looked close to tears. I went back to the bed and sat down. I lifted my hand to put it on hers but thought again and set it on the bed.

"Did she? Where'd she hear that?"

"Said her daddy told her mother once and she heard it." She looked up from the bedspread and directly into my eyes. There was a scared little girl there, but a spark of me too. Edith wanted answers and she decided to challenge me on it.

"So what if I got loans from people? I've paid him back."

"You have?" She took a deep breath and looked down. She

opened her mouth to speak but didn't. She looked up, then down again. I knew she knew the truth. How many times had I told myself that the kids couldn't've seen Gunnar comin or goin from the barn at night?

"I've done things I thought were the best way to keep a roof over our heads. Don't you worry yourself about me."

"I won't."

"Keep in mind all I've said. There are some things in this world you might never understand. And keep away from them Sorensens. Set your hat a bit higher." I got up and looked down at her.

"When I leave here, I'm never coming back," she said. I could see the tears fillin her eyes. I walked out of the room before we said things we could never take back.

One afternoon a week I'd put Teddy in the truck and we'd take a drive. I left Maude in charge at work. I'd fill up a sack of gumdrops at Gossler's and Teddy would chew on them til his jaws hung slack from the work. We'd go over to Point Francis if the weather was good, or sometimes into Ellsworth to look in the stores. With Teddy I could forget most of my troubles. He seemed to be the one person in this world that I could take love from without nothin bein expected in return. He loved me like nothing else, enjoyed touchin my face, combin my hair, feedin me gumdrops. I let a little bit of that kid out of me that must have been hidin under my stubbornness. I couldn't remember playin simple games when I was a kid. It was work all day, or fightin, or hidin. But I could chase Teddy on the grass, try to teach him to jump rope, and even play marbles with him. He shook away the old grump's clothin I wore, and opened my face up with smiles that I'd been ashamed to show before. It was cause of him that I felt so bad about Edith. I wanted her to know this sort of thing before she was boxed into hard work with a drunk husband, and a pile of bad choices lookin her in the face.

David C. Fickett

It was early fall when we stopped by Newberry's for ice cream sundaes. Teddy dribbled gobs of hot fudge down his shirtfront and jabbered to me about the cherry, but I couldn't understand much of what he said. I read the newspaper, Roosevelt promised to help all the farmers in the country and to see us out of this depression, but the words made no sense to me. I couldn't see how he'd ever help those who were really sufferin. I wondered how Henry's family had made out after the crash. Was he out there in the world spendin his daddy's money or was he stone broke like most who had kept their money in the bank? Henry wasn't a bad man, so I couldn't believe he'd got a dime out of his mother. If he'd had any money he'd've come back to the farm. I could only guess that he'd felt like a failure and was too ashamed to face his kids.

Teddy and I finished up our sundaes. I scowled at the waitress, who was eyein me and my boy. She must've thought I was foolish to bring my retarded son out in public. Most folks thought people like Teddy should be in a state home, learnin nothin but the routine of three meals a day and how to tie his shoes and brush his teeth. I knew he'd get a lot more from me than he'd get in any old hospital. I took his hand and left, not leavin the waitress a tip.

As we went out the doors of Newberry's I saw Edith and Sven across the street, gettin out of his truck. They didn't see me. I hauled Teddy back inside and watched from the window. Edith's hair was hanging down long. She usually kept it tight in a bun or pulled back with hairpins. She wasn't wearin her spectacles. She was smilin. I'd rarely seen that. She looked like a young girl, a happy girl, not my Edith. I watched till they disappeared down the street, then Teddy and me went home.

. . . the bacteria are transmitted easily from one colony to another through the honey . . . or through careless handling by the beekeeper. . . . Foulbrood seems to be transmitted otherwise, possibly through the queen.

—*from* FIRST LESSONS IN BEEKEEPING
by C. P. Dadant, c. 1957

CHAPTER TWENTY-SEVEN

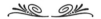

Caleb

1956

My mother has always had a deeply rooted hatred toward the Sorensens. I've never completely understood it. If Gunnar took advantage of her, if that's how she saw it, then I can understand somewhat, but the hatred seems to run much deeper. And, as I suspected, her affair with him may have resulted in creating me. Does she hate him for that? Does she see him in me?

Every year in August the county has a Blueberry Festival, a fair where we sell our honey. This past year I saw the anger between the Sorensens and Ma, after we'd set up our booth and they happened by. My mother had spent days bottling honey and wrapping breads and pies she'd made. Duffy and I loaded everything into the truck. He was already showing signs of illness but he wouldn't give in to it. This event was one of the few things that brought Ma,

David C. Fickett

Duffy, and me together. Ma always loved cotton candy and the crowds, Duffy and I loved the Ferris wheel rides, but this past year he showed no interest.

When we got to the fairgrounds we were told where our booth was and we set up. My mother moved her pies to the front of the table and shelved the honey on the wall behind. Her quick movements and narrowed eyes told me how important it was for her. Next to our booth was an Indian woman who was selling braided yarn dolls, dressed like Indians. She also had beaded bracelets and moccasins, rabbits' feet attached to key chains, and tommyhawks made with carved wood and brightly colored feathers.

"Hi, we're the Gilleys. I'm Caleb." I put out my hand to the Indian woman and she smiled at me. She had only a few teeth in her mouth. Her face was large, round as a pie and dimpled like the crust. Her black-and-gray streaked hair spilled down over her broad, plump shoulders.

"I'm Twilight," she said and giggled. When she smiled her eyes became tiny slits within her flesh. I liked her immediately.

"This is my ma, Ginny, and this is Duff," I said and they smiled at her.

As we waited for the crowds to start filling the fairgrounds Ma chatted with Twilight, as she moved things around on the table. I could see the Sorensen boys coming toward us. Erik is tall and heavy and Sven is thinner. Both of them are intimidating with their brash talk and broad shoulders. Olaf was not there. I walked over to another booth and when I looked back at ours I saw Ma talking with them. I walked back to her.

"No, I ain't givin' you boys none of my pie for nothin'. You pay just like everyone else," my mother was saying to them.

"Hi," I said as I went behind the booth with Ma. They nodded and kept teasing my mother for some free pie.

"After all the free whisky we usta give your ol' Henry, I'd think you'd let us have some o'your good blueberry pie, Ginny," Erik said with a big grin.

"A dollar a pie," Duff chimed in, coming from around the back of the booth.

"Well shit, then I don't want none," Sven said and started handling Twilight's dolls, throwing them around and rifling through the basket of bracelets.

"Don't manhandle all my things," Twilight said as she struggled to stand up.

"Now you porked-up little Injun, do you know who you're talkin' to?" Erik said as he tipped the basket over onto the ground. Duff walked up to Erik and grabbed his wrist.

"Git outa here if you're just up to no good," Duff said, and Erik threw Duff's hand off him. My mother headed around the back of the booth and I heard her open up the truck door.

"Old man, don't never touch me or you'll find your sorry face down in that mud," Erik said.

"You ain't got a reason to harass this woman or Ginny neither. Now go find your fun elsewhere," Duff said.

"Don't want no pie from a whore, anyway," Sven said and I reached out to grab him, but Ma took hold of my shirttail and I turned to her. She handed me Duffy's rifle that she'd got from the truck. Before I could lift it Sven grabbed hold of Ma and pulled her to him. I lifted the gun and shot it off. Erik and Sven both jumped at the sound, and stared at me with wide eyes.

"Let go of her," I said.

"Well, now here comes her shining knight," Erik laughed.

Sven still held onto Ma's arm, though she was struggling to pull free. "I said let go of her or I'll blow your goddamned arm off."

Sven let go and walked toward me. "Now ain't this just a priceless moment," he said with a grin. "Thinks he can take me on. Put the gun down and fight like a man, shithead," he said. My throat went dry and my legs were shaking but I didn't put the gun down.

"What in God's name are you defendin' her for? Or don't you know about her screwin' around with my old man?" Erik says as he leans on Twilight's table. Sven stood still waiting to see if I would fire a shot at him. People started to mill around us now and I could hear kids crying.

I saw their father coming toward us.

"Let them alone," he said quietly, staring at me, looking ashamed.

"Wait Dad, let me see if this shithead can shoot at a target as big as my brother here," Erik said. He turned to the crowd and smiled, showing his yellow stained teeth. Sven walked closer to me but I couldn't seem to pull the trigger.

Ma saw Gunnar and me looking at each other. She looked scared, and then she looked angry. She walked between Sven and me, and said something to Gunnar, but I couldn't hear it.

"Come on, Sven. Let's git outa here," Gunnar said.

"Caleb, put the gun away and calm down," Duff said from behind me.

I lowered the gun and Sven lunged for it. We wrestled for it, but I couldn't keep a good grip on it. He stood with it, pointing it at me. Erik started laughing, went over and clapped his brother on the back. Gunnar walked up to Sven and slowly eased the gun away from him, but I believe, looking at Sven's eyes, he would have pulled the trigger. Then Sven turned and laughed with Erik and some of the people in the crowd. Next to me, Twilight lifted a big chunk of wood and handed it to me. I didn't think what I was doing as I slammed it over Sven's back. His eyes bugged out and he went down on his knees. I think I saw pride in Gunnar's eyes. In my mother's I saw pain. Then the sheriff hollered to us as he approached. Sven stood back up, pulling Twilight's table over, spilling all her wares.

"Come on, let's break it up," the sheriff said as he took hold of Sven's arm. "You two get the Hell out of here and don't let me see you back on the fairgrounds again." He said nothing to me. He knew that normally I wasn't a troublemaker. But they were.

Erik and Sven scowled at us as they walked toward the front gates. Gunnar handed me the rifle and before I could think of anything to say, he was nearly out of sight, walking in another direction.

"They're crazy," I said to Ma. She had tears in her eyes, looked away from me, and started to help Twilight collect her things. Duff picked up her tabletop and put it back on the saw horses.

"Thanks for the club," I said to Twilight and we started to laugh. But Ma didn't laugh. The rest of the day she sat silent in a chair behind the counter, while Duffy and I sold her honey and pies. She wouldn't ever talk about the incident.

Now I wonder if both she and Gunnar had seen the anger in my eyes, and both understood the strength of the Sorensen blood in my veins. Or was my mother upset because I hadn't pulled the trigger when I should have? Or was she afraid that in time that scene would come to solidify my suspicions about who my father is?

Would I see myself in him?

. . . then there are bears; I hope you are not so unfortu-
nate as to be afflicted by bears.
—from BEEKEEPING: THE GENTLE CRAFT
by John F. Adams, c. 1972

CHAPTER TWENTY-EIGHT

Gunnar Sorensen

1933

He lies on the bed, smelling of hay, manure, oil. He sees the cracks in the ceiling, the brown spots, hears his wife coughing in the kitchen. He hasn't told her what Doc Proudy said to him this morning. How can he? She is bound to break into pieces. He lights a Lucky Strike. He thinks about Ginny.

"You lay dere all day?" Noelle asks with her Swedish sing-songy accent. Her big eyes. Her white, white skin.

"I need a little rest," he says. He runs his hand over his bare chest and belly, thinking how Ginny's hand would run along the trail of dark hair. She knew how to please him. Why has she shut the door on him? Sometimes he wished that Noelle would get worse. He has thought about her funeral. He's imagined Ginny there at the graveside, brushing her hand over his, telling him that, now, they can be together. He thinks about their union and how owning all of her land, along with his many acres, would make him feel.

Without Ginny, though, he wants nothing to happen to Noelle. He doesn't want to live in this house without a woman. He enjoys the soft sounds, the soft skin, he likes big meals.

Putting out his cigarette, he gets up. He stretches. He watches out the window as his son gets out of the truck and opens the passenger door for Ginny's daughter. The girl is not pretty. Not like Ginny. The girl is a bad reproduction of Ginny, a faded copy of her mother. But if she is like Ginny, then he understands his son's infatuation. He smirks, thinks of the warm place between Ginny's thighs.

"I'll be home in awhile," he says to his wife. Noelle smiles, her eyes look old to him today. He kisses her. He already sees her as a ghostly image, transparent, and through her, the muted tones of the wallpaper, the kitchen table, the stove. He goes outside.

"Who's this?" he asks his son who is sitting with the girl on the porch swing. He knows who she is, but she looks different. He has seen her at Gossler's, a stiff, thin girl, bound in dull clothing, hair of no particular color, a face pinched like an old woman. But now, she is smiling, her hair is moving in the wind, long and teasing, like her mother's hair, but without the secret brilliance of Ginny's.

"Dad, this is Edith Gilley, you know who she is," Sven says, his face red, heated.

"Well, I didn't know she was so pretty," Gunnar laughs, takes a cigarette from the pack his son is holding. He laughs loud, lets his large belly jiggle. Watches the girl to see if she is looking at his bare chest. She is squinting, but looking at his son.

"What're you with Ginny's girl for? You don't want this child's mother out here after you. Ginny ain't one to tangle with." Gunnar lights his cigarette.

"I ain't scared of her," Sven says. His face is getting redder. Edith takes hold of Sven's arm and smiles. Not a pretty smile. Gunnar doesn't understand his son's choice. Irene is a pretty girl with a figure, why would he push her aside for Edith? Then he thinks on it. Sven must be getting more from this one than the other. Irene is a good girl. Edith must take after her mother.

"I'd be careful, you two," Gunnar says. He walks across the yard to his truck. He feels the need to be with Ginny like hunger. He can't understand her new rules. The bitch.

He sits in the truck, watches his son and Ginny's girl, the girl's hair, her tiny waist, looks for something of her mother in her.

Ginny's girl.

Mice may enter the hive in winter when the bees are sleepy and slow.

—*from* THE WORLD BOOK ENCYCLOPEDIA,

c. 1955

CHAPTER TWENTY-NINE

Ginny

1934

Edith had been spendin a lot of time over at the Sorensen's. It didn't set well with me. I was still waitin for Gunnar to get back at me for cuttin him out of my life. I didn't want Edith in the middle of no crossfire. But it seemed havin a boyfriend changed her. She smiled more, and though we hardly spoke, she was kinder to her sister and brother. I'd hoped the girl had sense enough not to marry Sven, or worse, get in the family way. I was hopin come fall, she'd go to school. I was able to start puttin some money aside for her education.

I found out soon enough, after Gunnar and me, that I didn't like bein alone so much. I missed Duffy, and more than once, I closed up the restaurant and walked partway down the road to where his daddy had lived. Duffy ran his engine repair business there. But before I could turn the corner I lost my nerve. There wasn't no point in me tryin to be close with him no more. He must've worked things out with Coris and I had no right to mess things up for him. I just had to keep my mind in other places. I worked harder, jarred up a lot of honey, made pies, and spent my evenins readin the paper, or playin cards with Rose.

In the summers my business always took off. A lot of people would drive by on their way to Quoddy Head or go to the beaches for an outing. The rich folks, the ones that'd held onto some money durin the crash, would come up Route One and spend the months of July and August in their big cottages.

But by fall things had slowed down and I was usually working the place alone. One particular rainy day my spirits was down. I'd been spendin too much time alone, I guess. I felt a funny gnawin inside me. I don't know if I was lookin into my future, afraid of what I saw there, or just scared of waitin for Gunnar to get back at me, but that day brought two strange happenins that made my insides twist and wrestle.

First thing come in a big, shiny black car. I knew the president and his family had a place way down east in Campobello, but I never dreamed that I'd be lookin him in the face on that rainy, September mornin. There was no questionin that it was him. FDR come in the doors of my place being helped along with a couple of men. One of them set up his wheelchair and they eased him into it. They settled around a table as though they was anyone. I walked over to them and smiled.

He was a handsome man, all tidy and in a suit and tie. His hair was grayin, but his long thin nose and full jaw and laughin eyes made me feel like he was just one of the regulars.

"Do you have pies?" he asked.

He wasn't more than ten or twelve years older than me, but he had that strong, sure-of-himself look, like every girl wishes their daddy had. I felt like sittin down with him and tellin him my troubles, leanin on him like I would've liked to lean on my own father.

"Yes sir," I heard myself say. The words were caught up in my throat. I just couldn't believe who was sittin at one of my tables with half-filled salt and pepper shakers and a dirty ashtray. I scooped up the ashtray and wiped down the table real quick.

"I love a good pie," he said and winked at me. Here was the man who claimed he had all the answers to save the world. I hoped someone from town would stop in to be a witness.

"I got blueberry, apple, chocolate cream, and cherry. But the cherries are canned, I better tell you that up front." I put the ashtray on the counter and took out my pad of paper.

"Blueberry. You boys want something?" he asked the men that sat like stone soldiers.

I took their orders, went back in the kitchen and wiped my forehead, splashed some water on my face, and hustled to cut the pie. Two blueberry and a cherry, three cups of coffee. I still remember how my hand shook while I poured out the coffee.

"Nice place you've got here," the president said to me.

"Thank you. Hard work, maybe not as hard as yours," I said and smiled. His smile lasted the whole time he sat there eatin. It calmed me down.

"We'll see an end to the hard times, Miss . . . ?"

"Ginny. Ginny Gilley."

"Gilley? You aren't the Gilleys that sell the honey are you?"

"That's me." I pointed to the shelves full of my honey, jams, and honeycomb on the far wall.

"Well, I'm glad I came by. Mrs. Roosevelt and I love honey on our toast. Jim, grab me some jars of that." FDR pointed to the jars. "Better yet, I'll take a case of it, if you've got it."

I nodded and went out back, bringing a boxful with me. One of the men paid for everything and they headed toward the door. Mr. Roosevelt turned his chair back to me before leaving.

"Best pie I've ever had," he commented. "Your hard work pays off. You keep at it." He laughed and then went out. I watched as his big black car headed out of the drive and down the road. I stood dumbstruck til I heard my pot of potatoes boilin over on the stove.

I couldn't stand not tellin no one about the president of the United States sittin in my place eatin a pie I made myself. His visit got me all excited, forgettin those gloomy thoughts I'd had earlier. I latched the door and put up a note sayin I'd be right back. I walked toward Gossler's, hopin to go in and tell Maddie, but Gunnar's truck was parked outside so I headed further on. I could hear the sound of metal bangin on metal and the smell of gas in the air. When I went up to the door, Duffy just looked up at me like I was nobody.

"How ya doin, Duff?" I asked.

"All right. You, Ginny?" He was sittin in an old wooden chair at a table, in the shed. Looked like he'd been doin some figurin. There was a small pile of dog-eared papers under his hand.

"I'm all right, too. I guess." I wanted to blurt out all about FDR, but the sight of seein Duffy after so long took over me. I took off my rain hat and shook it out. I walked closer to Duff, hopin he might say somethin. He looked at his papers. Didn't write anything, just looked.

"Just thought I'd stop by," I said.

"Yeah?"

"Heard you been goin to church," I said. Maddie Gossler had told me that Duffy and his wife had been seen together at services. I had a hard time believin it but I didn't know what it took to keep a marriage together. It was none of my business, but I blurted out the words before I thought twice.

"I was goin for awhile," he said.

"No more?"

"I found religion bout as reliable as friendship," he said, and looked up at me.

"I don't know what I believe," I whispered.

"I know what I believe, but I don't need no book, or preacher tellin me how to worship."

"Duff, I came by to tell you somethin."

"What's that, Ginny?" He stood up and started fiddlin with some fan belts that were laid out on his workbench.

"You'll never guess who come by the lunchroom."

"Henry, I suppose." He turned to me and looked like an old

man for a second. I could see the battle scars of our love all over him.

"What?"

"Yeah, I heard he was around. Marvel Dinsmore said he found him drunk in his barn yesterday. I figured it was only a matter of time fore he showed up." Duffy took one of the fan belts and shoved his head under the hood of the truck that was in the shed.

"Duffy . . . No. I . . ." I didn't know what to say. No wonder I was feelin down in the dumps that mornin; it was like I already knew what was ahead for me. FDR or no, there was no reason for celebration.

"You talked to him? What's he got to say for himself?"

"Duffy, no, really?" I pulled my flannel shirt closer to me. "You sure about Henry?"

"You ain't seen him?"

Duffy stood up and looked at me. He looked angry. I'd given him every reason to hate me.

"Guess you better lock the gate to your back pasture," Duffy said as he lit a cigarette.

"What?"

"Henry home, you won't want any late-night visitors. Someone'll git their head blowed off."

I turned and walked out into the pouring rain. It felt good comin down hard on me. I was walkin past Gossler's again before I really heard what Duffy had said about lockin the gate. How many other people knew about Gunnar and me? And why did Duffy have to hear about it, of all people?

I stopped in at the store and asked Abel if I could use the phone. Gunnar's truck was gone, thankfully. I got the switchboard and asked Alice to connect me to the Dinsmores. Not many of us had phones then, but the Dinsmores lived way outside of town and Marvel's parents were always on the brink of death, so they'd had one installed.

"Yes?" Marvel answered.

"This is Ginny Gilley. I heard Henry was out there last night. Is it true?"

"Yes, scared me to death when I come upon him in the barn. When he wakes up I'm bringin' him over there. I don't need no drunk to take care of."

I thanked Marvel and hung up. I walked back to the lunchroom in a daze. What was I goin to do with Henry back in my life? I just couldn't see the two of us makin a go of it, now. Not after he left us for so long. How would Edith feel? Would she tell him about Gunnar? I guess it didn't make no difference now if she did tell him. He had no claim on me no more.

I put up the closed sign and walked home. The rain was comin down to beat the band, but I didn't care. I walked through mud pockets and puddles along the trail I'd cut to the house. I sent Lois home for the day and made Teddy some peanut butter cookies. He was munchin away on them when I realized I hadn't even changed out of my wet clothes. I went upstair and threw on an old skirt and a blouse. I combed out my long wet hair til I couldn't stand the comb gettin caught in the tangles no more. I pulled out Mama's old sewin scissors from the dressin table drawer and started hackin away. When I was done I'd cut off nearly a foot of hair. It hung limp at my jaw line. I didn't care, it felt good to be free of it.

I waited around all day, jumpin up every time I heard a truck on the lane, but it was only Royce workin around the place. The girls come home from school, looked at my new haircut, and asked what had happened.

"Someone told me today that your daddy's back. I expect he'll be comin home," I said as I set aside some socks I'd been darnin.

"What? Really?" Edith looked like she'd just won a first prize.

"I don't want him back," Rose said.

"Shut up," Edith said as she threw down her books in a chair.

"I don't know's I want him back here, either." I stood up and put my arm around Rose. She wasn't gonna forgive Henry as quickly as Edith was.

"I want to see him," Edith said.

"Why? After he just went off and left us?" Rose turned to her sister.

"You don't know why he left," Edith said.

"And you do?"

"There's no point in fightin about it." I walked into the kitchen with the girls followin.

"Mama, what are you gonna do about it?" Rose asked me.

"I don't know. He can't come back here like it's his home."

"It is his. Where is he?" Edith stood in front of me with her eyes all afire. I had to remember to keep my temper.

"Rose, you wanna let me and Edith talk this over? Go check on Teddy for me, will ya?"

As soon as I was alone with Edith I sat down at the kitchen table. I waited for her to start, not knowin for sure what sort of attack she might come at me with.

"Well, doesn't this mess up your plans?" she said, still standin and lookin down at me.

"I don't have no plans."

"What about him?" she said real loud, pointin in the direction of the Sorensen's farm.

"There ain't no him. You got everything mixed up girlie. What do you think your daddy will say about you and Sven?"

Edith sat down, lookin like I'd knocked the wind out of her.

"Daddy won't have anything to say about me having a boy-friend," she said softly.

"He won't like who it is. And he'll think you're beddin that boy. Sven's just like his daddy. He wouldn't be hangin around you 'less he was gettin more than what he got from Irene Gossler."

"Well, I guess you'd know all about that."

"Your daddy was drinkin buddies with Gunnar, but he won't like the idea of his girl gettin pregnant with a Sorensen. They's just trash."

"And what in Hell are we?" she screamed out at me and then run from the kitchen all tears.

The evenin went by with hardly a word between any of us. We kept listenin at the door, holdin our breath. I let the girls stay up late but still no Henry, so they went to bed quietly. I sat in the dark, front parlor wonderin what tomorrow would bring.

It was nearly dawn when I heard the front door open. I'd fallen asleep but jumped up quick. I went into the hallway and watched as Marvel Dinsmore came through with an older, weathered version of my husband, slumped alongside him, leanin on Marvel's shoulder.

"Ginny, I'm sorry," Marvel whispered.

"Put him on the sofa." I moved ahead of them and cleared the sofa of books and newspapers. I turned on a lamp and Marvel dropped Henry down quietly. I walked Marvel to the door.

"He's awful sick. The booze I guess," Marvel said. "I wish you luck, Ginny." And then he was gone and I was left alone with the sounds of Henry's raspy breathin.

I went over to him. His face was lined and bloated and red. His nose was crooked now, like he'd had it broken at one time. His mouth was a deep line, down-turned and scabbed in places. His hair was almost all white. He was too young to be such an old man. What had prompted him to come back this way, I don't know, but here he was again and I was left to clean up his mess.

I went in the kitchen and ran some hot, soapy water into a basin. I washed his face and hands, opened his collar, took off his boots. He smelled of whisky, mud, and shit. By the looks of his clothes, his whiskers, and long shaggy hair, I'd guessed he'd been livin like a bum for the past few years. I covered him up with a blanket and sat back down in my chair.

After awhile I heard someone comin down the stairs. It was Edith. She came into the parlor and put her hand up to her mouth when she see him. She looked at me and then walked close to the sofa and knelt down.

"He looks awful," she said as the tears come down over her cheeks.

"He'll look better when he comes out of it and gets cleaned up."

She stared at her daddy for a long while. I didn't say nothin, just sat there watchin her heart break again. He wasn't the man she thought he was. I got up after awhile and handed her a handkerchief.

"Mama, what are you going to do with him?" she whispered.

"Get him sober to start with."

"You're going to let him stay?"

"Yeah, I'm gonna let him stay." Then I reached out to where she knelt. I laid my hand on her head and when she didn't flinch I stroked her hair.

*Were the drones almost blind, had they only the most ru-
dimentary sense of smell, they scarcely would suffer. . . .
Out of a thousand one only will have, for one instant, to
follow in space the female who desires not to escape.*

       —*from* THE LIFE OF THE BEE
       by Maurice Maeterlinck, c. 1901

CHAPTER THIRTY

Duffy

1934

Coris and me got along pretty good for our years together but we've
had our fair share of troubles. I look back on them early years of
ours and can plainly see why I chose to marry Coris, even though
I still loved Ginny. I'd say our first two or three years was good.
But I never shoulda taken on a job at Ginny's. It wasn't long after
workin at the farm when I think Coris knew what my feelin's for
Ginny was all about. Then we just grew apart. We still share a bed,
if I don't stay all night down at my shop. And if one of us tries to
love the other, moves their hand under the sheets, it never seems
to work out. I know she sees Ginny in my eyes. We stayed together
for our boys, Matthew and Austin.

  Some nights I go to my pa's house to sleep, some nights I come
out here to the house on the shore. Tonight she's been cookin a

beef stew and says it's on the stove if I want some, but she already ate. She reads in the living room and I go out onto our screen porch to watch the waves whip around in the wind. The boys are already in bed.

I think bout Ginny. When I told her that Henry was around I know it was like I'd stuck her with a sharp knife. But I shouldn't be worryin bout her.

I guess the reasons Coris and I stayed married all these years is first, she's too proud to divorce a man, and because she's come to be comfortable here. She's got a lot of good friends and she has her faith. I don't think she'd like to leave her church. And then the boys, though I don't know's I've been too good a daddy. But somewhere in our odd little setup there's two people who like one another, though I must have hurt her a hundred times over the years.

Coris says to me when I come back in the house, I was reading in the Farmer's Almanac how you should move your crops around to a different garden each year.

Yeah, I say, that's what we used to do out at Ginny's. Her daddy was a stickler bout that.

I always wanted a garden, she says as she sits down to the table.

Her hair is always just as neat as a pin. She keeps it twisted up in a knot of some sort and she wears the prettiest little earrings and bracelets and pins. Sometimes she looks like such a lady and then I look around at the faded wallpaper, the mismatched kitchen chairs, the torn upholstery on the sofa that she keeps coverin over with blankets she knits. She was meant for better things. I get a hurt spot in my chest wishin I could give her them things.

Didn't know you cared bout gardenin, I say.

A flower garden, she says, a rose garden, but I suppose here on the shore I'd have only trouble raising rosebushes.

The whole Christless shore's covered with them pink rosebushes, I say.

Cultivated ones, that's what I'm talking about, she says, and then she laughs at me and pats my hand. If we moved inland, maybe up to Bangor with Mama and Daddy, I could grow roses there, she says.

She opens up her magazine and starts in readin. I eat some of the stew she made, wash up for bed, and then stand there in front of her. I know it's time I should say somethin. She's too fine a woman to let her wait on me forever. Why she don't say nothin bout our marriage, I don't know. 'Cept she's too proud, maybe.

Coris, I say, this don't work, does it?

She looks at me, don't smile, don't frown, don't question what I mean.

It hasn't worked for quite awhile, she says. She straightens up her sweater, pushes a piece of hair behind her ears.

I know it. It ain't fair what I've given you. You here alone and me livin my own life.

I loved you, she says. And we have the boys.

I'm sorry I ain't a good husband. Most nights I don't come home no more. Ever since you went to help your ma with your daddy, it ain't been right tween us. Livin out here don't seem natural to me. I want to be in town.

And I guess I want to be where I can grow roses, she says.

I'm sorry. I didn't mean it to be like this. I tried.

I kneel down by her chair and hold her hand.

Is it still her? she asks.

I'd been expectin that question for a long time. I just stare down at the floor but she knows the answer. I look back at her, she just keeps that little half-smile smile on her lips.

I'm sorry, I say again.

I knew when I married you. I knew there was someone else and when I met her, I knew for sure. Thought I could change things, but I haven't. I'm worn out with it though. I knew I'd leave this place sometime, I was hoping it wouldn't be until the boys were older.

I nod, embarrassed for myself. I know if I had half a brain I woulda loved her more than Ginny.

David C. Fickett

Henry's back, I say. She's gonna need me.

I've needed you. Your sons have needed you. But no more, she says and stands up.

Coris, I can't make up no excuse bout my feelins. They's just what they is, and I been tryin to outsmart them for years. I see Ginny today, I know nothin's changed for me.

Coris walks around the kitchen, rubbin her hands together. I stand up and walk toward her, but I don't try to touch her, though I'm hurtin for her.

I've done without for years, she says. I've let my sons exist in this house, this dead house, all the while letting them believe we loved each other. It was for nothing, she says.

I'm sorry. How many times can I say that, I wonder.

What do you want? What should I tell the boys? she asks.

That I tried. But I'm just a man. A stupid man.

You know what I'll do, don't you? she asks.

I'd like to help if I could.

You can't. I won't stay here. I thought when we had this out that I'd want to throw something, hit you, anything but this civil little conversation. But now, well, after waiting for it for years I can't feel much. But I don't want to be made a fool of anymore. I'll go home to my mother and father. Do you want the boys with them?

No, but I know this ain't right for any of us. What about your church? Your friends? I ask.

Don't concern yourself with any of it.

I can see that there are tears in her eyes and I want to take her in my arms but it's too late for that. I tried to love you best I could.

She turns her back to me. I think about the insects that Ginny's daddy used to pin to fabric on boards and put up on the walls of his office. He knew just about everythin bout them bugs. I feel just like one of them, pinned, not able to move.

You might as well leave now, Duffy, go back to that hovel in town, she says as she looks back at me. I'll make plans for the boys

258

and myself, and I'll let you know what they are. But there can never be a divorce. I can't do that. I'd never be forgiven. That's all I ask. If you care at all for me you won't fight me on it. But go, you do what you need to.

I start to speak, but there ain't no point. I take my coat from the peg on the wall and leave for my pa's house.

Mice may invade the hives, especially in the fall, seeking a snug wintering place as much as the substance of the hive. Restricting the opening of the hive in the fall will prevent their invasion, although some beekeepers further make their hives proof against invasion by a series of little teeth between the bottom board and the front of the hive.

—*from* BEEKEEPING: THE GENTLE CRAFT
by John F. Adams, c. 1972

CHAPTER THIRTY-ONE

Ginny

1934

My Edith was some glad to have her daddy home, though I don't know why. When he woke from his drunk he just stared at us like we was strangers. Edith smiled and took hold of his hand but he just kept on starin. I knew he hadn't forgot who we was, or he never would've made his way back to Maine.

"Ain't you some sight," I said to him. "What do you want from us?"

"I . . . I . . ." he started and then cleared his throat. "I don't want anything." He smiled a little and held on tight to Edith's hand. He looked at her. "You've grown up," he said.

"Daddy, where have you been? Why?" Edith asked with teary eyes. I'd been standin over the two of them with my hands on my hips, but I wanted to hear some explanation so I plunked myself down in my chair and waited for him to open his mouth.

He just looked down at the floor and shook his head. He didn't have no reason for desertin us. He was just a coward.

"What happened to your mother?" I asked. I really wanted to know what he'd done with her money.

He looked up at me. His eyes, like a picture show, runnin the reels of his past five years over and over. I could see drunken nights, fights, him sleepin in any alley or barn he'd come upon.

"She died." The words hitched up in his throat. She was still the center of his world. "Lost everything in the Crash. I couldn't come home." He held his head like it hurt, scrunched up his eyes, his skin was all gray and weathered.

"You better take a hot bath and get to bed," I said and got up to leave. The sun was up and I had work to do. I went in the kitchen and tried to busy myself with breakfast, but heard them talkin so I went to the doorway to listen.

"I don't suppose your mama will forgive me for running off, but can you?" Henry asked Edith.

"Yes," she said too quickly. I wanted to slam somethin against the wall, run in there and scratch out his eyes, anythin to let him see my anger. I don't know why I was so mad. I didn't mind much that he left, just that he left us without much money, but I guess after seein how it'd got to Edith, it had built up in me like the way the pile grows under an outhouse. After a while you should move it, cover over the stink, and dig a new hole somewhere else. I wondered if I should forget the rottin inside me that Henry had caused, or dig a new hole, one that I could put him in and cover over.

"Where have you been, why didn't you write?" Edith asked, her voice shaky, uncomfortable. She'd been waitin for him all these years and here he was, a total stranger.

"I've just traveled around, found odd jobs. I was too ashamed to write. I haven't made much of myself."

"Daddy, don't say that," Edith whispered.

"I shouldn't stay now, don't really know why I'm here." I heard him stand up and pace around the parlor floor.

"You can get better. Start farming again," she said.

"I'm not a farmer. Your mother always knew that. I just wanted to see you girls, and then I should be on my way. Your mother won't want me around."

"Don't worry about her," Edith said. I noticed how Henry didn't mention Teddy's name.

"I need to make a little money, enough to get me back to Boston. I know someone there who'll hire me."

"Daddy, don't go. I want you to stay."

I'd heard enough. I walked to the stove wonderin who was the bigger fool, me, for lettin the man in the door, or Edith, for wantin him to stay. He wasn't home to see his own children, he was here for money. Money that he thought he deserved to have.

I heard him go up the stairs and Edith came into the kitchen.

"He's sick," she said.

"Looks like he is, but it's just the look of a drunk. Don't fret over it." I slammed down a skillet on the stove and then dropped the egg I'd been holdin. I swore as I bent down to clean up the mess. I was so mad, but wasn't quite sure what I was mad at, Henry comin home or Edith's excitement.

"What are you going to do?" Edith asked me.

"You asked me that earlier, I don't know."

"This is his home, isn't it?"

"This is my home, yours, Rose's, and Teddy's. I don't know who elses. All I know is what I've done to keep it goin while he was runnin around, like some kid, a brat, a spoiled brat. I can't get it outa my head."

I expected Edith to start defendin him but she didn't say much for awhile. I scrambled some eggs and heated up some biscuits. My mouth tasted like metal where I'd been gnawin at the inside of my cheeks.

"He isn't Daddy. He seems like someone else," Edith said in

a soft voice, lookin down at the table. She looked afraid. I went over to her and waited for her to look up at me, but she was frozen in her hurt. I put my hands on both sides of her cheeks and slowly moved her face toward me.

"Edith, don't let this eat at you." She gently pushed away my hands, stood up, and walked out of the kitchen.

When the girls had gone to school I went upstair and found some of Henry's old clothes. I set them outside the bathroom door and went back down to the kitchen. He looked a little better when he came down, all washed, dressed, and clean shaven.

"You need to have that hair cut," I said. "Sit down, it'll just take a minute."

He nodded and sat down. I put a dishtowel over his shoulders and got out some scissors. I started in cuttin his hair. He sat still like a guilty child, not sayin a thing. I moved his ears aside as I cut behind them, they were soft like kitten fur. I thought about cuttin one of them off, just to claim my piece of flesh.

"If you're thinkin things will go back to the way they was, you're wrong. I've lived alone too long. I run this place now."

He nodded. The things that had happened to him since he'd left had changed him, damaged him. I don't know as there was anythin left of him inside.

"What made you come back?" I asked.

"I . . . I don't really know," he said, and then started coughin. When he got his breath he spoke. "I guess I wanted to see the children."

"They don't need you." I rested for a minute, leanin my hand on his shoulder, layin the scissors over his collarbone, just under his throat. I thought about how he squandered away most of his money on foolish farm tools and plows we didn't need. I thought about how he'd secretly written letters to his mother askin for money and then spendin it on whisky. I wanted to cut his throat.

I could just tell the girls and anyone else who asked that he'd up and left again. I could hide him somewhere on my land, deep in the ground. It wouldn't take three springs before new trees would grow up and the roots would anchor him good down there.

But even as I let those thoughts race through my head, I knew I was as much to blame for the way things had turned out for us. If I'd loved him I mighta been more patient with his crazy ideas, he might never have turned to drink.

He gently shoved the scissors away and turned his head up to me. "I wouldn't blame the girls for not wanting me here. Maybe I should just go. I wanted to know how you were making out." I finished his hair and then shook the towel over the side of the back porch.

"How much do you need?" I asked.

"Need?"

"Money? How much?" I set the scissors down and walked over to the spice cupboard. I didn't know it then, but I made a big a mistake by showin him what I kept in the bakin soda tin. I reached in the cupboard and took it out. I lifted the lid and held the roll of bills in my hand. I thought he might take the money and leave for good. His eyes sparked up, but then he looked down, actin like he wasn't interested. Maybe he was too smart to ask for a handout now. He'd wait and take as much as he wanted, when I least expected it.

"Regina, I don't want your money," he said. I stared at him for awhile, tryin to look into him, but I couldn't. I put the money back in the cupboard. I should have counted it, or hid it somewhere else, but I wanted to catch him stealin, I wanted Edith to see what he'd become. Until she saw him for the coward and the drunk that he was she'd never try to understand me.

He stood up and looked out the windows.

"The farm looks good. How have you managed?"

"By sellin what I could. Doin whatever I had to. I got a little lunchroom now. It makes ends meet. That and sellin honey, wood, whatever." I was tempted to tell him about Gunnar, just to see his face when he realized what I'd been forced to do. But it really didn't matter.

"You plan on stayin around here?"

"I wouldn't expect you to want me here."

"I don't, but Edith might. You've got a lot to make up to her. I don't know as Rose gives a fig about you. Teddy won't even know who the Hell you are."

"How's he doing?"

"Just fine." I cleaned up the dishes and Henry went outside and wandered around. Keepin my hands busy in the sink somewhat settled my nerves.

Teddy came downstair still in his pajamas. I fed him and took him outside to find Henry. He was sittin on a bench by the hives.

Teddy put out his hand to shake, like I'd taught him, but Henry just smiled at the boy. I think he might've been afraid to touch his own son.

"I'll be goin to work as soon as Lois gets here. She watches out for Teddy." It wasn't quite time for Lois, but I wanted to see Henry's reaction to Teddy. He didn't show no interest, didn't care that I'd taken so much time to teach the boy how to behave proper. He'd never know the hours I'd spent showin the boy his letters and how to turn his hollow, rounded words into somethin you could understand. I sat down on an old crate and watched the bees with Henry. Teddy wandered over to pet the cow inside the fence. "I don't know what's keepin Lois, but I got to get to work," I said, lookin down toward the lane.

"You've got a lot more bees now. More than twice what you had."

"Best little workers I know." I felt good that he noticed. My creatures all buzzin and cluckin and snortin were more for me to be proud of than anythin.

"You can go on if you want," Henry said. "I'll be here with Teddy til the woman gets here."

"There ain't no liquor in the house if that's what you're plannin."

"I'll just stay out here with him. Don't worry that I'll drink."

"I'll worry all I want, til I understand why you're here. If you plan to drink while you're under my roof, then you might as well clear out of here before I get home. I don't need to try to piece together the girls after another one of your drunks. I want you to decide what you're goin to do, how long you're stayin. I don't much like you comin back here." I stood up to leave. He still had that same faraway look in his eyes that he'd had all mornin. I didn't like it. "If you get hungry, don't be botherin Lois, come to the diner. I'll fix you somethin."

"Thank you, Regina," he mumbled, lookin at the bees.

"Remember what I said." I left him there, knowin Lois was on her way. I met her partway down the lane and told her that Henry was at the house but that she was to stay til I got home. I didn't know if I could trust Henry to keep a close eye on Teddy.

I cut through the woods to the lunchroom listenin to the mournin doves cooin in the branches. I had to sit down on a stump and rest for a minute, afraid I might get to work in such a state I'd chop my own hand off, or snap at all my customers. I needed to pull my thoughts together.

The last thing I needed was another kid to take care of. I felt wore out with raisin my own. Didn't have it in me to watch out for Henry too. If he was goin to stay awhile, I figured he had to find another place to live. He could visit the kids when it suited him. The thought of havin him around for good seemed wrong. He didn't have no right to be under my roof anymore. I wouldn't see the kids hurt by him again. I wished, like I had so many times over the years, that it had been Duffy I'd married. But if I had, chances are I'd've lost the farm long ago. It had been Henry's money that had got it on its feet. Maybe I owed Henry a warm house, a bed, and some good food for awhile. At least for awhile.

After I got to work and busied myself with things I felt better. It wasn't like Henry was a bad man, just weak, a coward, a bullied boy who'd been tied to his mother's apron strings, didn't know how to unknot them. When we'd first been married, we'd been happy for a short while. We'd played cards and he'd read to me from his leather-bound collections of classic novels. He'd been company for me. Maybe we could work out somethin, learn to be friends. But there was no way I was going to sit idle, keepin my mouth shut like I once had. He was gonna learn that I made the rules. He wasn't my husband no more, not a father to my kids.

I had a surprise visit from Duffy that mornin. He'd steered clear of me for a long time, but since I'd visited him the day before, he must've felt different about me. He came in and ordered coffee. I had a few other tables filled with men, so I couldn't sit and talk with him. But he waited til the place cleared out.

"Glad to see you here," I said as I refilled his coffee cup.

"Nice to be here." He didn't smile. Hadn't since he walked in.

"You were right about Henry. He showed up this mornin."

"How is he?"

"A wreck. We ain't talked much. I'd guess he's been drunk since he left here. Looks like an old man."

"What does he want?"

"Nothin. I think he just ended up here. No place for him to go." I washed down the counter and tended the baked beans in the oven. I kept lookin at Duffy but he was either starin out the window or at the floor. "Can I get you anything else?" I asked.

"Nope. I oughta git to work." He took out his money and set it in on the counter. "Why'd you cut your hair?" he asked.

"Oh, I don't know." I waited for him to speak but he stood up to leave. "Duff, what'd you mean yesterday, bout me keepin the back gate locked up?" I had to ask.

"It ain't my business."

"Well, it's all over, you know. I guess you figured Gunnar give me the money to get this place goin. I had to do somethin. I didn't want to lose the house."

He looked me over. I noticed he had a few flecks of gray in his hair. We were all gettin older. I wanted to jump over the counter and ask him to love me again. He was still what kept me from losin my mind. No matter how far away from me I'd pushed him, he was still all I had. I felt somethin hot boilin up in me, wantin to spill over. If only he'd reached his hand to me I would've come apart.

"I don't know what you want me to say," he said.

"Nothin, I guess. I just wanted you to know. I think that farm has meant more to me than it ever should have. I've run right over everythin that I should've tried to hold on to." I smelled the eggs boilin dry on the stove but I didn't move. I could always boil more.

"Ginny," was all he said. He sat back down on the stool. He strummed his fingernails on the linoleum countertop. Went to light a cigarette but couldn't get the match lit. We both started to say somethin at the same time and then stopped.

"Things might be a lot different if we'd had that baby," I said.

"But you weren't even pregnant. Water under the bridge."

"And we was just kids, but sometimes I guess I think about it."

He lit his cigarette and went out. I had to throw out the pot that'd burnt on, scorched my hand on the handle.

When I got home that day the first thing I did was check the tin for my money. I wasn't sure, cause I hadn't counted it, but I thought I'd had another ten-dollar bill in it, and maybe another five. I put most of it in my pocket but left some there for bait. Twelve dollars and some change.

"You didn't come by to get a lunch," I said to Henry when I saw him comin up on the back porch with Edith.

"No, I got something here." He smiled and came into the kitchen. Edith seemed quiet, like she was disappointed. They'd been for a walk up along the woods road. He wasn't the daddy she'd invented in her head and I think it hurt her. She went up to her room and I started supper. Henry sat down in the rocker while I cooked like he'd always lived there.

"I don't suppose you'd sit somewhere else?" I asked.

"I'm sorry, I should be helping." He got up. I handed him a stack of dinner plates and he went about settin the table. I felt just like someone had come back from the grave and was at work in my kitchen. My arms broke out with goose bumps.

When Edith came down to supper she was smilin again. Durin the meal she startin reminiscin about when Henry had lived with us. Her eyes shined and I couldn't believe it was her talkin. I thought that must be the pretty girl that Sven knew, but I'd never seen before. I chewed my food and got some of it down. I'd planned all day to tell Henry that he had to leave, find a room in town or somethin, but I never said a thing.

He did up the dishes with Edith, and Rose even helped them without fightin her sister. That night I helped Edith move her things down to Rose's room and Henry slept in the room with the pretty wallpaper. I don't think I slept more than two hours all night. I kept waitin to hear Henry sneak out to buy whisky with my money, but if he did I never heard him.

He started to help a little around the house, but mostly he kept to himself. I let the days go by hopin he'd up and leave, checkin my money each day. Every once in awhile I'd notice a dollar or two gone. I warned him that he better not drink, better not come home drunk. If he did I never caught him.

I kept believin Edith needed him around but he slipped more and more into the shadows, didn't want much, expected nothin. It was clear to me, after a week or two, that Edith was thinkin hard about him. He started stayin out nights, rarely joined us for a meal. When he was around, I'd catch her lookin at me, and then lookin at him. I guessed she was comparin us.

One night after I'd cleaned up from supper, I asked Edith what she thought about him, wanted to know how she'd feel if I told him it was time to leave.

"You hate him, you always have," she said.

"I don't hate him, but I sure as Hell don't need another mouth to feed." I went to puttin away the dried dishes. Edith was still dryin the silverware. "I thought it was important to you that he stay, but you don't seem too interested in him anymore."

"It's not me. You've driven him away again."

"Me? Christ I've let the freeloader live here, I keep him fed, his laundry is all done for him. What have I done?"

"You could treat him like a husband," Edith said as she slapped down the last of the silver in the drawer.

I walked right over to her and took hold of her arm. "You listen here, he gave up any rights as my husband five years ago. Doesn't it even bother you that he's never even called Teddy his son?"

"He probably isn't sure who Teddy's father is," she said.

I raised my hand to slap her one, but it would do no good. She was mean right through to her bones. I caught my breath, closed my eyes. When I opened them, Edith was just glarin at me, smirkin. Somethin in her voice reminded me of how Duffy had warned me to keep my back gate locked, his mean way of lettin me know he knew all about Gunnar and me. It was then I was certain, no more denyin it. Edith was Duffy's child as sure I was my daddy's girl.

"If that's how you want to think, girlie, maybe you better look in the mirror and try to figure out who your daddy might be." I let go of her and walked away. I would have killed her if I'd stayed near her.

Time moved by slowly. Edith spent more time with Sven, goin over to his place to visit, but I didn't see any excitement in her eyes about the boy anymore. When she told Henry that she was Sven's girl I thought he might show some signs of life by tellin her that Sven wasn't good enough for her, but he smiled and patted her hand.

Then she stopped comin home after school, goin somewhere with Sven. She lost all interest in her daddy, started avoidin him, but he didn't seem to notice. His head was driftin somewhere out on a far shore. He wasn't really home at all. At night I could hear Edith cryin in her room, but I knew even if I opened the door there'd be a wall keepin me from comfortin her. I know I never should've said nothin to her about who she was. She'd probably never given it any thought. I wondered now, how often she looked at Rose and Teddy and saw Henry's eyes and hair, and long legs.

Duffy kept comin to the restaurant each mornin, but with the crowd of regulars there, we didn't get much chance to talk. He'd been out to the farm one day to see Henry. Lois had told me he was there but when I asked Duffy about it he just said he was curious to see Henry, and that they hadn't found much to talk about. Now that I'd admitted it to myself about Edith I couldn't help but look for her in Duffy's face. It was obvious, maybe others around had seen it. Maybe Henry had. But I'd avoided recognizing Edith's and Duff's similarities. Their chestnut-brown hair, hazel eyes, the strong nose that was handsome on Duffy and homely on Edith.

When Gunnar heard that Henry was home he started comin into the diner, smilin and eggin me on with vulgar words that he mumbled quietly so that only I'd hear them. He was still mad at me.

It wasn't long before Gunnar started showin up at the house in the evenins. He wouldn't come in but sit in his truck waitin for Henry. I thought, this might be Gunnar's revenge, gettin Henry on the bottle again, seein what kind of mess he could cause me through Henry.

"I told you if you start comin in here drunk, I'm throwin you out," I said to Henry. He gave me a look like an innocent child but I could smell the whisky on his clothes in the mornin. I started to hope he'd come in drunk so that Edith could see him, and so I could get rid of him, but he managed to control himself, and was up some mornins before me, sometimes collected the eggs, or milkin the cow. I couldn't catch him stealin from me. The little bit of money that disappeared I figured was his pay for doin odd jobs on the farm. Edith watched him comin and goin out of the corner of her eye. I knew I'd ruined whatever there was of a child in her.

"There ain't nothin to what I said to you. I was just mad," I said one afternoon when I'd stayed home from work. Edith was sittin in the parlor readin. She didn't look up at me.

"What's your daddy said to you about stayin around?" I asked.

"Nothing. He thinks I should go to school though." She kept her face buried in a book.

"Tell him to find a job so we can afford it. You'll have to pay room and board in Castine if you go there."

"I don't think I want to go to school." She looked at me over the tops of her spectacles. She was holdin somethin back from me but it would've been pointless for me to ask about it.

"I can't believe you want to stay here," I said. "What kind of work will you do?"

"Same as anyone, I guess."

"You're better than that. You're smart. Put your brain to use. You don't have any ideas about marryin, do you?" I asked.

"I . . . I don't know. I like to be with Sven."

"After you've lived with him for six months you'll regret it."

She kept readin and I finished knittin a sweater I'd been makin for Teddy. After she went to bed and the house was quiet I went outside. It was cold and would probably be a harsh winter comin. But I needed to walk. I thought of tryin to find Henry, see what he was up to, but I lost interest in him as I walked along the lane toward town. I'd made my mind up though, I had to ask him to leave. There was no place for him on the farm.

The street lamp in front of Gossler's had gone out and the clouds had hidden the stars. I walked in darkness to Duffy's shop.

I opened the heavy door and nearly ran into a car he'd parked inside. I felt my way around to his workbench and then found his chair. I sat down and wrapped myself up in one of his thick flannel shirts that he'd hung over the chair. It smelled of Duffy. Under the smells of oil and smoke, I could just pick up the scent of his skin, sweet and acidic, somethin like pine needles and cut timber.

I closed my eyes and breathed in all the odors of our days as kids: the hidin out under fir boughs with our clothes tossed around like they'd been wind-whipped from a clothesline; the whiff of bee balm from the gardens with honey on our hands; the musky scent of milk and cowhide in the dairy barn; the fresh smell of tilled soil and bundled hay.

When I opened my eyes I noticed a dim light reflected in a Nehi bottle that sat on the bench. I turned around and looked out the window at the old shack that had been Duffy's daddy's house. In the house, through a torn window shade a candle flame flickered. I stood up and went outside. I slogged through the muddy yard to the front steps. I knocked twice before I heard footsteps inside.

Duffy opened the door. His flannel shirt was unbuttoned and his suspenders hung lose at his hips.

"What are you doin here?" I asked.

"Spend a lot o' nights here," he said with his head hung down and his eyes lookin like a lost cow.

"That so?" I thought how funny it was that I'd been drawn to that place for no particular reason, like the way the bees know how to find each other through smell or just by thinkin.

"What are you doin out tonight? Awful dark out there. Come in." He moved aside and went in.

"I just wanted a little walk."

He motioned to a ripped-up chair. I sat down. The house was cold and nearly fallin apart. Sheets of wallpaper hung from the walls and strips of cardboard were taped over broken windows. The candle on a stand by an old cot was the only light.

"This place ain't much," he said as he sat down on the bed.

"What're you doin here then? Where's your wife?"

"Home, I suppose. Maybe up to Bangor with her folks. Don't see each other much these days."

"Ain't we a pair?" I leaned over and touched his hand. He put his other over mine.

"I seen your ma, you know," Duffy said. I pulled my hand back, feelin spooked.

"What are you talkin about?"

"A vision." He laughed and then explained it to me. "Or I just went plain crazy, but one night awhile back she come out to Stanley's Point. She smiled at me."

"You was dreamin."

"Somethin. But it was some real. I don't much like to stay out there now. I think your mama wanted me here."

"She liked you, I think. Hard to tell with her."

"She knew you were sweet on me," he said.

"I didn't even know back then, not for sure."

"She was tryin to tell me somethin. Wanted me to come back here. Home."

"I don't know. What about your family? You leavin them behind?"

"It don't work. I guess I ain't no better than Henry."

"Maybe it's just everybody gotta do what's right for them. Who knows?"

"Well, Coris knows where to find me. I just need a lot of time to myself. Maybe I'm alone too much. I'll still see her and my boys from time to time."

"Nice that we can talk again," I said as I looked down at my hands. "I missed havin someone to tell stuff to. I'm sorry about Gunnar and all. I know how it must've looked." I spoke so quiet I could hardly hear myself.

We sat in silence for some time. I don't know what he was thinkin about me, but I couldn't look up. The candle flickered on, jumpin our shadows around. The light seemed to hold both of us in its circle. The room was glowin honey-colored. We sat in the fans of our flickerin wings, the air heatin up. The tiny room held us tight and close. Time seemed to move slow. We didn't even have to speak to understand each other. I started to hear what he was thinkin, and he heard me.

He blew the candle out and I felt his hand take mine. He wanted me to stand up. I reached for his shoulders and he held me as our thoughts moved our feet around. He hummed some old tune we'd once danced to as kids. We thought out all of the things we hadn't said over the years, told each other all the stuff we'd stored up, told each other everythin without openin our mouths. It was all there, all night, takin us through our own dark places, along the roads we'd walked apart, and out into the sun where Mama's maidenpinks and hollyhocks brightened our little corner of winter.

Honey made from different kinds of blossoms often looks and tastes different.
—*from* THE WORLD BOOK ENCYCLOPEDIA,
c. 1955

CHAPTER THIRTY-TWO

Caleb

1956

I want to think that Duffy is the one, but is it Gunnar Sorensen? I wait in the kitchen for Ma to come out of the parlor. Edith goes to the bathroom for a bath and to dress. I have things to do to get ready for the service, but I ask Ma to sit with me.

"Caleb, I'm worn out. I can't say no more," Ma says as she sits down.

"You owe it to me. What did you do about Gunnar? How does it all tie into my story?" As I ask her this, I can't help but think of last night with Nora. Gunnar's shadow is long.

Ma sighs, looks behind her through the doorway to make sure Edith is out of sight. She takes my hand.

"I love you. I'm an old woman. I don't have much no more. Can't you leave me my secrets?"

"Not if they're mine to own as well. When this is over I want to go away. What reasons can you give me to come back here again?"

She puts her hands over her eyes. "Duffy wanted you to know everything. I guess I should give him this."

She puts her hand over mine again.

"You don't know what went on. That sister of yours, she's a broken woman. If I could've helped stop that mess I would have. I was too late."

"Too late? For what?"

"You was already on the way. No one to blame but myself. Edith walked right into her own Hell, all cause of me."

"Edith?"

"I knew something was wrong with her but I never imagined what it would be. She walked around this house like a dead person. She scared me to distraction."

"Edith, but how?"

PART SIX

The Massacre of the Males

*. . . the patience of the bees is not equal to that of men.
One morning the long-expected word of command goes
through the hive; and the peaceful workers turn into
judges and executioners.*

—*from* THE LIFE OF THE BEE
by Maurice Maeterlinck, c. 1901

*When the queen cells are sealed they are cut out of the
the parent colony and introduced into the other colonies
which have previously been deprived of their queens.*
—from FIRST LESSONS IN BEEKEEPING
by C. P. Dadant, c. 1957

CHAPTER THIRTY-THREE

Edith

1934

There are thirteen steps up to the second floor of the house. Edith
walks slowly, counting them as she goes, amazed that she has never
counted before. How could she have spent the past sixteen years
in this house and not known?

At the top of the stairs she stops and looks out the window.
Have the shingles on the roofs of the barn and chicken coops always been green? She tries to remember if Daddy ever reshingled
them in her lifetime. The window glass is dusty. At the bottom of
the sash she notices small handprints that show up in the moonlight. Hers? Her sister's or brother's? How long has it been since
the window was washed? Mama washes the downstairs windows
every spring, but never upstairs. The handprints could even be her
mother's. Hands so small that the palm is only the size of a silver
dollar.

Edith touches the handprint, then wets her fingers with her spit and washes it away, smears it into old grease and dust and spit. She puts her hand on her flat belly and feels the vibrations from her beating heart. Her heart won't stop thumping, thumping. She's given up running from its sound. Will she hear the other heartbeat soon? Will it be louder than her own?

Down the hall Edith notices the glass box that sits on a dark, spool-legged table. The box is not very big and has always been there. Inside there is a small dried bouquet of flowers nestled within a tuft of moss. Edith's mother told her once, when Edith was very small, not to touch it. The flowers had been picked in the gardens around the house, by Edith's grandmother. They had been treated with sugar and water. Dried forever, sealed, air-tight within the box that her grandfather made. Edith bends and looks closer to find the dried husk of the bee that sleeps forever under the faded petals of a pyrethrym. Edith supposes that her grandparents loved one another and this tribute to the combination of their passions was symbolic of their devotion to one another. She wonders if this bee was a queen, maybe their very first, the queen mother to all that live now in the hives.

She reaches for the doorknob to her room and then stops. Rose will be in there and she doesn't want to talk to Rose about why she has been out so late. She goes to her mother's door. It is closed. She opens it carefully, making only a slight creaking noise. The room is dark and Mama's bed is empty. Seeing the bed empty increases the speed of her heartbeat. Her mouth is dry. She smells Mama's lavender oil and feels the need to vomit. Her hand goes to her mouth. She rushes from the room and makes it to the toilet before the retching begins. But there is nothing to vomit. Her insides have been empty too long. Why nourish a body that is so obviously not worth the effort?

She runs the tap and splashes some cool water on her face. She heads toward her old bedroom where Daddy now sleeps. Is he in there or out somewhere? Off with Sven's father, drinking gut-rot, abandoning her once again? Even when he is standing beside her, she feels abandoned. His drunken eyes on her, seeing nothin that is Edith, his baby.

She doesn't open the door.

Walking past Mama's room again she pauses, thinking to close the door, but is drawn to the inside. Where is Mama tonight? Edith turns on the bedside light. The walls are papered with entwining amber flowers, stamens of gray, that were once probably white, bloom from the center of the flowers and topple under heavy drops of water. Once the paper must have been pretty, but it is faded, water-stained. There are rectangles and ovals showing a lighter shade of the paper, where Edith remembers framed photographs of her grandparents and other ancestors once hung. Their eyes were all flat, without sheen or depth, their expressions were angry, or shocked, or worst of all haunted. That is what she thought when she saw them, they are haunted. Mama took them down years ago, but Edith still sees them, glaring down at her.

She tries to remember if there were ever pictures of her mother as a girl. Could her mother have been a girl? Is that possible? Mama must have been born knowing all, born full-grown, capable, seeing what she wanted, reaching for it and grasping it. How could it be possible that Mama was a stumbling pretty girl? Edith tries hard to think, were there ever photographs of Mama? It seems there must have been because the harder she thinks, the more she forms in her head the image of Mama, chubby, dark-haired, sleeping among white pillows and blankets, dressed in a white frock of lace with her little fist curled to her cheek. A thumb in her pouting lips. And hands, hands of a woman, reaching to touch the child's head. And other hands, a man's and maybe her mother's sister. Just their hands, touching the sleeping child.

Edith touches her own face, surprised by how wet the tears have made her cheeks. She wipes them away and lies down on the bed. Turns off the light, tries to hear the voice of her child.

There is a strange duality in the character of the bee. In the heart of the hive all help and love each other. . . . Wound one of them, and a thousand will sacrifice themselves to avenge its injury.

—*from* THE LIFE OF THE BEE
by Maurice Maeterlinck, c. 1901

CHAPTER THIRTY-FOUR

Ginny

1934

The mornin after I'd spent the night with Duffy, I walked home real slow as the night was still bein pushed out of the sky by mornin. My legs felt weary, old, achy. I'd put on a few pounds over the years but it was the burdens I was carryin on my back that made me so tired, not my weight. All I wanted when I got home was a few quiet seconds with Teddy. Wanted to forget most things, like how Edith worried me and what to do with Henry. I went into a quiet house. I was afraid Edith might be up but there wasn't no one wanderin around. I sat down in the kitchen rocker and unlaced my boots.

There was Henry's coat still hangin on the peg on the cellar door; his boots, thick with dried mud lay on my kitchen floor. How I hoped he'd be gone. Hoped every day since he'd come home.

Every time I came through the door I wished those things would be gone. I listened to the faucet drip in the sink. Watched the sky lighten up as mornin come.

If the worse thing to happen to me that day was seein Henry's things around the house, or worryin about Edith's shaky mind, then I would've been all right. But more happened to me in the course of twenty-four hours than I thought anyone deserved.

I grabbed myself somethin to eat and went upstair to change my clothes and get ready to head down to the lunch counter. I also had ten gallons of honey that needed to be jarred up and labled for a big order. I knew I could get Walter to do most of the work, but I'd never been able to let go of my responsibilities so it weighed on my mind, wonderin how many things would go wrong with the order, as it often did.

I opened my bedroom door to find Edith asleep in my bed. She'd never come into my bed, even as a little girl when a thunderstorm or a nightmare would wake her up. She'd go to Henry for a hug, but never got in with us.

She was laying on her belly, her face turned my way. Her eyes were red and puffy and her hair fell over her cheeks, damp and lifeless. Her glasses were on the bed beside her. I couldn't remember what she'd looked like as a baby, or a little girl. I stood there listenin to her breath and wanted to lift her up, hold her, pull her to me and help her out of whatever it was that had sent her to my bed with tears on her face.

I pulled up a chair to the bed, not makin a sound, sat down and waited. Looking at her long legs and arms sprawled out there, I thought again of Duffy. He was tall and lanky as a young boy, and I remembered his mother too. The same brown hair, straight, with no chance of curlin it to soften her narrow, bony face. I didn't really know Duffy's mother all too well, only spoke to her a few times in passin. Never imagined I'd be seein her again, so many years after she'd died. But there she was in my girl.

Edith moaned and turned her head the other way, tucked her fists underneath her neck. I thought I'd better get ready for work so I went to my drawers and opened them quiet, pulled out some clean underthings, got my blue slacks and white blouse from the closet. I dressed and went to the bathroom to wash up. When I came back into my room Edith was sittin up, rubbin her face and pushin her hair back into a ponytail.

"You were sound asleep," I said. She jumped at my voice and looked like she'd been caught robbin me.

"Where were you?" she asked, puttin her glasses back on.

"You don't want to know. You been waitin for me?"

She stood up and started to walk toward the door, brushin by me.

"Hold on," I said as I took hold of her arm. "What was it you wanted to talk to me about?"

"What makes you think I wanted to talk to you?" She pulled away from me and folded her arms, pursed her lips, and scowled at me.

"Must be somethin on your mind. Why else would you have been sleepin in here?"

"I was just curious about where you were and how late you'd be. I didn't mean to fall asleep."

"I felt like climbin right in there next to you. Hold you like I had when I was still nursin you," I said as I turned away and grabbed my brush off my dresser. I couldn't look at her as I spoke. I was afraid of what her face might show.

She didn't know what to say to me. She sat back down on the bed and stared at the floor.

"You probably don't remember us two in bed when you was little," I lied to her. I didn't remember it either. If we'd ever cuddled up neither of us would have let ourselves think about it.

"No," she said. Her voice caught up in her throat. Somethin was botherin her, somethin big enough to make her come to me.

"I never told you this, but when you was a baby I dressed you up in blue clothes, boy's clothes, and took you to see my daddy. Told him you were a boy. He wanted a grandson so bad." I laughed and sat down beside her. I didn't tell her the real reason why I'd told Daddy she was a boy. Somewhere in my things, as well as in Percy Luther's office in Ellsworth, was a record of Daddy's will, leavin everythin to "my son."

"You really did that?" Edith's eyes opened wide.

"I was wicked, wasn't I?" I laughed again. It felt good to talk to her, share one of my secrets with her.

"You must have loved your Daddy to let him think I was a boy."

"Your grandfather and I had a strange relationship, to say the least. He could be awful mean. He drove my sisters away from here with his temper, but I could handle him."

"Do you ever hear from them?"

"Just from Dora. She's the one lives with my aunt Eula in Portland. A couple of old maids." I got up and looked for my shoes under the bed, found them, and sat in the chair while I laced up. Edith's eyes were still red and she looked like she was ready to cry again.

"You might think about your own sister. Someday you'll wish you had a sister to talk to. I lost my chances," I said.

Then she let the tears go, threw her glasses on the bed, covered her face. I went over to her and put my arm around her but she shrugged it off.

"Don't," she said.

"You gonna tell me what's botherin you?"

"Go away."

"If you want to know where I was, I'll tell you," I said. She looked up quick at me. "I was with Duffy. I love him."

"Why are you telling me this? I don't want to know."

"You've always wanted to know about him and about Gunnar. I'm gonna tell you. You're old enough. I've loved Duffy since I was ten years old. I should've married him but I thought your daddy was gonna change all my troubles, my money troubles. But let me tell you, Henry and me made each other miserable. I feel bad about it. I wish I could change it, but when I was sixteen I didn't have any idea about love, or marriage, or even having babies and that's why I guess you and me never been able to get along. I didn't know how to handle a kid, especially one as cranky as you were." Edith smiled when I said that, but then tried to hide it by frownin again. "Duffy and me have tried to build our lives without each other and we've hurt each other for years now. Tonight I had to see him after we had that fight earlier, and then with your daddy here, still drinkin and all, well, I had enough. Duffy's the only one I ever been able to turn to. If he and I were both free we'd probably marry. I don't mean to get you upset, but I wanted to tell you."

She turned away from me, put her hands over her face again. I sat still, waitin to see if she'd ask me anything. I waited for quite awhile, then stood up to leave. I figured I'd told her enough. I headed toward the door and then she cleared her throat.

"What about Gunnar?" she said real quiet.

"Gunnar? Well, that's harder to talk about." I sat back down on the bed. "Henry had left. We didn't have nothin. I had you kids to think about, and this farm. I always promised myself that I wouldn't lose it. I went to see Gunnar about borrowin some money. He set up our little arrangement. I didn't like it, and I've paid him back. I'm ashamed about it, but it got me the lunchroom, it kept food on the table, and you kids in clothes. I didn't have no one else to turn to." I patted her hand and was surprised to find her other hand on top of mine.

"Mama, I'm gonna have a baby," she said and started in cryin all over again. I pulled her to me.

"Oh, shit. You don't want to marry that boy do you?" I couldn't think of nothing worse than her havin a Sorensen for her husband. "Does he know?"

She shook her head.

"Look at me," I took hold of her chin, looked into her watery eyes. "What do you want to do?" I felt my blood pumping through me, my arms and legs felt like I'd been out dancin all night.

"I, I don't know." She sniffed and I handed her my handkerchief.

"You can't marry him. You're gonna go to school. You're too damned good for the likes of Sven Sorensen."

"Mama," she said and let out another rack of sobs. "Mama, it's not Sven's baby."

"What do you mean?" I held her shoulders away from me. "Who? Who else you been with?" I asked.

She shook her head, held her mouth closed, and cried on. After a second or two she jumped up.

"Where are you goin? You can't tell me somethin like this and then walk away. We've got to talk," I said as I followed her out into the hall. I couldn't figure who else she'd been with. Erik, Sven's brother? Then it hit me. A great, dark, mean old wind slapped me on the face, nearly threw me to the ground.

Gunnar's revenge, I thought.

"Edith, did Gunnar hurt you?"

She put her hands over her face and huddled into a corner.

"Did he? What'd he do?" I took hold of her shoulder, tried to turn her but she wouldn't budge.

"It was as much my fault as his," she whispered.

"What? How?" I asked.

"He said I was pretty. Pretty like you," she said real quiet and then let out more tears. Shook so I didn't think she'd ever stop. She cried into the corner, got down on her knees. I knelt down with her and rubbed her back, wishin I could kill the bastard. She drew her hand across her face, wiped her nose and stood back up. She turned to me and held up her hand, pointed to her daddy's door.

"I don't want him to hear," she said. "I need to sleep."

She left me standin in the hall as though I'd just been struck by lightnin. I couldn't move. My legs had lost all feelin.

I waited for the clouds to lift, the rains to stop, and the spinnin in my head to slow down. I went back to my room, set down for a minute and then wrote her a note. Told her we'd talk when I got home from work.

The day dragged on while I served up beef stew and dumplins. When I got home I had to help Walter with the honey order. He couldn't never get the labels on straight so I had to soak some of the jars and relabel them. Edith wasn't around and I couldn't think where she'd be. I was afraid she might've gone to the Sorensens'.

I thought hard, tried to make a plan out of her mess. Maybe she could go stay with her aunt Dora til the child was born and then find a nice home for it. I hated the thought of one of mine goin out into the world not knowin who they were, but Edith wasn't ready to be a mother, and too weak to take the abuse she'd get from the locals if she had a child out of wedlock. And then there was the Sorensens. They'd be after Edith and me to let them see the child. They'd be comin over to my place anytime they pleased. I could imagine Gunnar usin this baby as a way to get back at me somehow, promise to leave us alone only after I'd given him the hundred acres of my land that bordered his. I had to save the situation somehow. I owed somethin to my girl. To Duffy's girl.

I walked through the woods to Gunnar's place. I saw his boys outside, dressed in clean shirts, gettin into the truck. I waited for them to leave, then I went up the back door and peered in through the glass. I didn't see Noelle nowhere around. She'd been getting sicker each day, and was gonna have a baby, too. It would probably kill her, I thought. I'd heard she spent a lot of time in bed. Then I saw Gunnar come into the kitchen. I tapped lightly on the door. He opened it, lookin old and drunk. I told him I wanted him to come over, after dark, Henry wouldn't be home. He looked at me like I was crazy.

"I knew you'd come to miss me," he said with a grin. I didn't say nothin but thank you. Then I went back home and out to the beeyard. Duffy had built a nice tall fence around the place since I'd had trouble with bears. I got a hammer and a hand cultivator from the barn and went to work. I pried at the nails, loosenin some, and shook one side of the fence til it gave a little. I pulled one of the gate's hinges free and twisted the fence around til it looked like a bear had pushed right through it. Then I clawed at the wood with the cultivator. I gouged it up bad. I went in the house and took down Daddy's shotgun, loaded it, and went to sit in the bee-yard.

It must have been after nine o'clock fore I see old Gunnar walkin in the shadows around the house. He looked in the windows for me, not darin to go inside. We'd always met outdoor, or in the barn. I watched him go in the barn and then over to the chicken coops. Then he come my way, walking silently through the shadows of the trees.

He hadn't anymore than put his hand on the gate, when I pulled back the trigger. The shot was so loud I thought the ringing in my ears would never stop. I knew when the gun kicked that I'd soon have a big bruise swelling up on my shoulder.

Gunnar cried out and landed on the ground just outside the fence. I'd aimed and shot him right where I wanted to. I'd blown his kneecap to pieces.

Son of a bitch.

I went into the house. The girls weren't makin a sound, so I guessed they'd slept through it all. I put the gun back and went up the road to Gossler's, to tell what had happened. They all knew how the bears came around, and I put on a good show. They could tell I was sorry for what I'd done.

"Oh, Ginny, how horrible. Abel, call the constable. We ought to go out to the farm, see how he's doing," Maddie said, setting me down in a chair and handing me a bottle of root beer.

"I don't think he's dead," I said. "But it looks like I mighta tore up his leg some. I was sure it was that bear. If I'd hit him where I planned to, right through his heart, I'd've killed him for sure. I don't know what Gunnar was doin at my place, just peekin in windows is all I can figure."

"We'll take care of it, you just calm down. It ain't your fault," Abel said.

And they did, took care of gettin help, and sippin my root

beer with Maddie. The doctor fixed up Gunnar in my kitchen and I walked back to the house with Maddie. The girls were up and I told them what happened. Edith kept lookin at me, then took off upstairs. Abel cleaned out the back of his truck so he could run Gunnar home. When the bastard come to, I was standin over him.

"Next time I'll aim a little higher. Don't never mess with my girl again." I whispered in his ear.

He never could walk right again and every time I saw him hobbling through town, I'd just turn the other way.

And then the worst thing I could imagine happened to me. That was a night of surprises. I wouldn't expect anyone to forgive me for what come next. I washed up and went upstair. I decided to look in on Teddy before I turned in. I opened his door slow, so not to wake him. His room was lit only by the outside light, but I could see clearly that he wasn't in his bed.

First I run to Edith's room and woke her.

"You ain't seen Teddy have you? He's not in his bed," I asked, pulling on her arm so she'd sit up. She rubbed her eyes, buckled up her eyebrows, and shook her head.

"No, I thought he was in bed," she said.

"He ain't, and your daddy still isn't home. Have any idea where *he is*?"

"Daddy went fishing. In the middle of the afternoon. He would've brought Teddy home by now."

"Brought him home? You mean he took him with him?"

"Yes. Lois had to leave early. Daddy's good with Teddy."

I ran out of her room and down the stairs. Henry's boots were gone and so was his fishin rod. The truck was still in the dirveway, so they must've gone on foot, I thought. I lit a lantern and went down toward the swamp beyond the gardens. My heart jumped as I thought up all kinds of awful things that could have happened to them two. If Henry was drunk, no tellin what had gone on. Had my boy drowned? Or was he lost in the dark in the woods, cryin his eyes out?

I followed the trail through the high grass and the cattails along the soggy edges of the swamp. There was a sliver of moon in the purple sky, so I found my way easy. I marched along the path, through the alders and then onto dry land among spruce trees and ledges til I come to Henry's fishin spot. I knew before I went around a stand of alders that they'd both be there, and they'd both be dead. My heart thumped and I could hardly bear to look, but I had to. I moved through the bushes slow, pushing branches aside.

First thing I saw was Henry, layin on his back, with an empty bottle of whisky beside him. He looked dead.

Then I saw Teddy.

At first I thought my boy was dead too. He'd been roped to a tree, it looked like some of my clothesline, wrapped around and around the boy's belly and chest as he sat on the cold ground. His head was lollin to one side. He was covered in blood. His eyes were closed.

"Teddy! Teddy!" I yelled as I ran to him. I could smell shit and piss and the heavy scent of swamp mud. There was blood on his clothes and on his face, in his hair. I lifted up his head and he opened his eyes just a little. I hugged him and craddled him to me. I thought for sure he was near death, knew he wouldn't make it til I could get him home.

I turned to Henry who hadn't stirred. I bent down and shook his shoulders. He didn't wake up. But he was breathin, slow and deep. I stood up, yellin out his name, and then I kicked him in the ribs. Again and again, til my toes throbbed with pain. I know I wasn't thinkin right, and may God forgive me, but what come next changed everything about me.

I'd wanted to kill Gunnar only hours before, and I'd thought that rage was as much as I would ever know. But it wasn't. All I could think about as I stood there was that baby of mine tied to a tree, stinkin in his own shit, cut up, alone and cold.

I gripped the empty whisky bottle tight, lifted it, and struck

Henry in the head. As it shattered, cutting his temple and scalp, he opened his eyes for one split second. He knew who it was, he knew the face of the grim reaper. Maybe he'd recognized her from the beginning of our time together. Teddy spoke up and I jumped.

"Daddy say. I stay still. Don't move," Teddy said. I turned with the broken bottle neck in my hand.

"What?"

"Daddy tie me. I was bad. Mud all over."

I went over to Teddy and struggled with the ropes, got him untied. He'd cut his hands on glass, who knew how long he'd been there, but he didn't seem to be hurt too badly. He'd smeared the blood all over him so it looked worse than I'd first thought. He stood up, a bit clumsy at first. I noticed how bad my hands were shakin.

"Daddy sleep," he said.

I looked back at Henry and watched as trickles of blood came out his ear and the corner of his mouth.

"Yeah, Daddy sleep," I said and took Teddy's hand and went along the path home.

I washed Teddy up, put clean night clothes on him, and fed him. Edith came into the bathroom and asked what had happened. I told her that Henry had left Teddy out in the woods, that Henry had gone off somewhere, and I didn't give a damn where. After I knew he was asleep I went outside, plannin to go back to where I'd left Henry, but it was fogged over and too dark to see, and I couldn't seem to remember where the path was. Or if there was one at all. I couldn't remember much of what I did after that either, except, that later that night, I found myself sittin in my chair by the hives listenin to softness, to the low hum of the restin bees.

Sometime after two or three in the mornin I made my way to bed, but never slept. Funny I didn't think about what I'd done to Henry, all I could think about was what to do about Edith. Edith and this child she was carryin.

When sunlight come, I went down to the kitchen and started up something to eat. Edith come down first and we had a chance to talk.

"You must need somethin to eat," I said to her as I started to heat up some cornbread and put on a skillet of sausages. I looked at Edith sittin at the table starin at the floor. I noticed the cut on my hand.

"Your daddy's gone," I said, not facin her.

"What?"

"We had it out. I told him he couldn't stay here. I found a liquor bottle. I told him he wasn't gonna drink in my house. After what he did to Teddy, he was feelin pretty worthless. I doubt we'll see him again." My hands trembled again and I burnt my thumb on the skillet. I put it in my mouth.

Edith folded her arms on the table and lay down her head. She didn't cry, just watched out the window while I cooked.

She ate in silence. I fixed a plate of food for the other two and listened to Rose chatter about some dress she'd seen in a catalog, she wanted me to make one like it. Teddy was happy and I doubt he remembered much about the night before. I sat with them for awhile and then went up to Henry's room and packed his few things in a paper bag and stripped the sheets off the bed. I took everything downstair and put it in the back shed. I figured in the mornin I'd burn his clothes in the stoves at work.

Edith had washed her plate and was sittin in the front parlor.

"You can't keep mopin around. We'll think of somethin," I said.

"I don't want to think," she said.

"When you start to show I'll take you to my sister's. You can stay there. There's agencies that handle these things."

"I'm going to bed," she said as she walked past me and up the stairs. I waited til eleven o'clock before I slipped on my heavy sweater and walked down the lane to the village. I had to tell Duffy what I'd done. It dawned on me as I walked along in the quiet that Edith's baby was not only my grandchild but Duffy's as well.

When I got to the shack I didn't even have to knock. Duffy had heard my steps in the gravel. He opened the door and then I fell into his arms.

"Duffy, I've done somethin awful," I said as he kissed the top of my head.

Should disaster befall the little republic; should the hive or the comb collapse, should they suffer from famine, from cold or disease, and perish by the thousands, it will still be almost invariably found that the queen will be safe and alive, beneath the corpses of her faithful daughters.

—*from* THE LIFE OF THE BEE
by Maurice Maeterlinck, c. 1901

CHAPTER THIRTY-FIVE

Ginny

1934–35

When I told him, he handed me a glass of whisky and said, "I want you to git in the bed beside me." He undressed me and we got under the covers. I cried and then lay still while he kissed me the way I liked. We made love and my cryin stopped. I didn't think about Henry then.

I woke up before Duff did. The sun was barely up over the trees. In that yellowy-orange light I felt like I did when he was first mine, when I was still a girl and not yet married to Henry. Yet, beneath his boyish smile and smooth face, I imagined the lines of of our hard road ahead, our unplanned map that had scored itself on our skin. But love erases wrinkles and scars. I heard thrashers in the yard and the last of the hermit thrushes still singin out their tune through their magic flutes.

"What about Henry?" Duffy said, breaking the peaceful day.

"We gotta go back to the swamp," I said.

We dressed without a word. I made some coffee and some eggs but couldn't eat. We went out the door and the mornin was as soft as music. He took my hand and we headed out to the farm.

"Over there." I pointed ahead on the trail, Henry's fishin spot along the brook. We walked up to him. Already there was flies and bugs crawlin over his blue face. Dried blood under his nose and upper lip, all brown.

"You go back up to the house," Duff said to me. "You don't need to see him again." But I stayed, this was my mess and I couldn't leave Duffy with it. Duffy handed me the shovel he'd brought. He turned Henry over, took hold of him by his upper arms and dragged him through the grass. I wanted the poor bastard dead a lot of times over the years but now I felt bad for him. I moved along with Duffy and Henry down the banks of the brook, through the water, til we come to the marshes.

"How far you goin?" I asked. "Let me help, Duffy." He said "No" and went on alone through the mud, then through the ferns and grasses and cattails. I let them disappear into the swamp.

Duffy come back to where I stood and took the shovel. He avoided lookin in my eyes.

"The sun's up. You go to work. Don't want no one wonderin where you are."

"I won't go," I said.

"You have to. People will wonder."

I turned toward the trail that led to the house. I heard him haulin Henry further out into the swamp, deep into the willows. The water and mud would've gone way over the tops of his high boots, he'd've been in mud up to his thighs.

Later, Duffy said he didn't know if he'd ever git his boots dry again.

I guess the plan formed in my head as I walked up to the house. Everyone around knew Henry had always been a drinker, and they'd witnessed how he'd gone off and left me with kids and no money before. So all I had to do was to tell them he'd taken off again.

But not til I told them I was expectin.

How would anyone know we hadn't been together? Lois knew Henry had his own room, but she couldn't be sure what went on in the dark hours of the night.

I walked to the house, washed up, dressed, and when Lois got there I told her I was pregnant.

"But . . ." she stammered.

"I know, he has his own room, but you don't expect a married couple to stay apart forever. Like a goddamned fool I let him in, and now this. As soon as I told the bastard he took off. Go upstair and look for yourself. He's packed up and left. Worthless piece of baggage." I slammed the breakfast dishes around and made it look like I'd had enough of men. Lois put her hand on my shoulder and tried to keep herself from cryin.

"Don't worry about me, Lois, I've got by before. I'll do it again." I put my hands on my belly and smiled, like it didn't bother me that I was havin another child.

I went upstair and woke Edith.

"You're goin to Dora's. I'll put you on the bus this afternoon. When the time comes, we're gonna say the baby is mine."

"Mama, how . . ." she rubbed her eyes and sat up in bed.

"Don't worry. I'll take care of everythin." I started throwing her things into the leather valise that I'd taken with me the one time I'd left the farm, to go to Henry's mother's. "No one will have any reason to believe this baby ain't your daddy's and mine."

"But your stomach . . ." she said.

"I've got enough cotton batten, or blankets, or somethin. And who'd dare touch *my* belly? They'd be afraid I'd bite their hands off."

"Sven will wonder where I've gone." She got up and started dressin.

"I'll tell Sven. I don't want you to have nothin more to do with him."

I knew Dora would take good care of her. Dora and my aunt Eula, who was now in her late eighties, lived like little church mice, or so I gathered from Dora's letters. They shared a little house outside of Portland. Eula had taken to Dora as though she were her own. They seemed to be devoted to each other. I knew Edith would like their quiet life.

I got to work, kept lookin out the window for Duffy. The first few customers that come in was from Steuben. I knew them well enough to start in on my no-good husband. They said if they saw him on the road to Ellsworth they'd pick him up and drag him home. I kept cookin for the others that come in, kept jawin about my troubles and by lunchtime, when Maddie Gossler come in, she'd already heard that Henry had taken off again. I patted my belly and said he'd left me with a little present though. Maddie, who always regarded me with a questionin eye, told me her prayers were with me.

After the lunch crowd left I was washin a chowder pot when Duffy walked through the door. No one was around. I went right up to him and took his hands.

"Where've you been? I've been worried sick."

"I come by earlier and the place was full of people. I didn't think we ought to be seen together. Let folks get used to him bein gone fore we look too chummy." He sat on a stool and pointed behind the counter. "You stay back there. Someone could walk in."

I did as he said. Poured him some coffee and tried to keep my hands busy scrubbin the pot.

"Abel Gossler told me Henry had left," Duffy said.

"You heard already? Don't take no time to spread things around in this pissed-up place."

"Nope. He won't be found. What about his things, his clothes?"

"He didn't come back with much. I brought them with me to work and burned them up in the stove."

"Poor sorry bastard, that's all I can say," he said.

"You blamin me? I didn't mean to do it. You'd've done the same thing if you'd've found him like that. All I could think was how he'd hurt my boy."

"Will Teddy say anything?"

"He don't understand. Henry was just someone that come into his life for a few weeks. By next month Teddy won't remember him." I rinsed out the pot and turned it over to dry.

"Duffy, Edith told me she's gonna have a baby. That god-damned Sorensen kid."

"Shit. Gunnar probably put him up to it. What's she gonna do?"

Before I answered I noticed the thick curls of mud under Duffy's fingernails. Mud from the swamp. My heart raced for a minute. I saw my hand going up in the air, with the whisky bottle. I heard the thud, the crack of glass, and maybe bone. I leaned against the counter and caught my breath.

"You alright?" Duffy asked.

"I can't forget it. But I can't believe it happened either."

"Don't let go, don't cry. Someone could come in here," Duffy said as he looked out the window over his shoulder.

"I'm gonna say the baby is mine. Mine and Henry's. Edith's gonna go with my sister Dora. When the time comes I'll go there. Say I went into labor on the trip, I'll come back with it. Gonna say Edith's in Castine at school."

"How are you gonna pull that off?'

"I can do it. I have to. I've already told Lois and Maddie that

I'm expectin. Half of Washington County knows by now." I took hold of Duffy's hand just to steady my nerves.

"So you'll have one more thing of Henry's," Duffy said, curlin his lip a bit. After what he'd done for me I figured I owed him the truth.

"It ain't like that. Henry ain't Edith's daddy. You must've known that. You remember the time we got carried away and went out to the barn, just fore you left for the war?"

"Course I do. You mean . . ." He looked hard at me and then his eyes teared up.

"She looks a little like your ma. Took me most of her life to look at her, to really see the resemblance." I wanted to cry. I wanted to get out of the restaurant and hold Duffy while I told him, but things had been movin too fast the past twenty-four hours and I had to hold on tight to keep from fallin off the vehicle that I was aboard.

"When she was little she got lost. Remember that? She come to my door. I could see somethin in her face, but I always thought you'd o' told me."

"Didn't let myself see it. I knew how much it would hurt us."

"So this baby, it's as much mine as yours."

"And this time I want one of my kids to have a daddy they can lean on from time to time."

He leaned over the counter and kissed me. He didn't even look to see if anyone had driven into the drive. We let our good sense slip away, if only for a second.

That afternoon I put Edith on the bus in Ellsworth. I told her I'd be sendin money, and when the time come I'd come to Portland to see her.

It was too late in the fall for her to start school in Castine but I told people that that's where she went. Only Maddie Gossler thought it odd that my girl was beginning school in October. I told her Edith hadn't made up her mind and when she did the school wanted her, cause her grades were so high. I'd packed her things, told her what I planned, and she went. She was too dazed to argue.

She had no more idea what it was to have a child than a man does. And so she left.

I spent months complainin about my swollen feet, my indigestion, my useless husband. People in the restraunt would come in and ask me how that thrashin, cantankerous baby was acting up.

"I've never had such an ornery child in me before," I'd say and laugh, or jiggle the round paddin on my belly and swear at it, say I was gonna find out where Henry had gone so I could ship the child to him. In the beginning of April, Abel Gossler come into the lunchroom and told me that my sister Dora had phoned the store and left a message for me to call back. We'd arranged it like that. It was my signal to head to Portland. I told people that Dora was sick and I had to go see her. Some warned me about the bus ride to Bangor and then the train, but I'd always been a sturdy woman. I told them if I had the baby on the train then it would just have to be patient til we got to Dora's. I'd thought of sayin I was goin to Castine to see Edith, but then I thought it best to keep her name out of things.

Duffy wanted to come with me, but I wouldn't let him. He said we could travel separately, he'd follow in another day or so, but I didn't want that. I'd be helpin Edith birth the child and I didn't need a nervous man standin outside the bedroom door wonderin what all the screamin was about.

We kissed good-bye at the bus stop, after he'd driven me to Ellsworth and I watched the tears, big as hail stones roll down his cheeks as the bus rode away.

Edith had changed. She was almost pretty. Her face had good color and her eyes shined for the first time in her life. We both let out a few tears when we come face to face and held onto each other harder than we'd ever done before, and harder than we ever would again. Her labor wasn't too bad. She didn't let out the cries like I'd always done, though I told her to scream to Kingdom Come.

When I first see the dark head of the child, I knew it was the healthiest child ever to be born into my family, and maybe Duffy's too.

I named him Caleb, smelled the sweet scent of birth on him, looked deep into his dark blue eyes hopin I'd never find a trace of a Sorensen in him.

As you grew your eyes changed from the blue to green, eyes like Duffy. The next few years of my life were good, happy, but moved too quick. Looking back it seems like there aren't enough happy memories to fill a teacup. But I guess the bad memories stay in a sharper focus. Sometimes I felt full on sweetness, then I'd think about that dead body in the swamp, and the bitterness would sneak into me like foulbrood attackin the hives.

The end of my short-lived life of happiness come when Teddy died. I had my Duffy with me now, and I had you, but Teddy was more to me than my child, more than somethin that needed me. It was only through his eyes I could see the good parts of me. He wouldn't never have recognized that streak of meanness in me that my other kids saw too clearly.

In his eyes I was beautiful, I was the honey.

I waltzed through your early childhood. People talked bout me and Duffy livin here and not bein married but it didn't bother us; we had you, I had my Teddy, and I was makin a good livin. But I swear the day you run down to the diner to say that Teddy was on the ground by the hives, I knew it was the end of me. I'd seen those little pills of his work when he got stung, so I'd always thought we were safe. Once I'd thought of torchin the hives, gettin rid of them all, but still it was no guarantee he wouldn't get stung by a wild bee. I know it was the spirit of Henry that lived in the bee that finally did Teddy in. Henry wanted to take Teddy from me just to see me suffer.

That day you found Teddy dead in the beeyard, I felt everything in me freeze cold. Cold and hard. How could I ever look at myself again, when all there was was ugliness?

I went into the swamp after dark that night. I took a shovel and a lantern and looked for where Duffy had hid Henry. I drove the spade into the muck a few times, hitting roots and stones and then somethin soft, punky. I thought I'd found him. I dug through that black mud and came up with shreds of shirtsleeves and busted eyeglasses, but I couldn't keep the water from fillin in the holes. I had it in my head to see Henry's skull, see the crack I'd put there years before.

I stopped diggin, kicked at the dark water, cried, and went to sit by Teddy's grave. Each day after that I felt like I was walkin faster and faster down a quiet hallway of an old house where no one lived. I looked into each room, out each window and see only snow fallin with no sound. Just shadows and the dark, or a blindin white. Couldn't see nothin. You was only seven, and broke up bout your brother's death, but I couldn't find one soft place in me that could make me put out my hand to you. I was so cold and brittle I thought someone might just snap off my arm if I let them touch me.

Duffy always knew me, could understand better than most. He took his time with me, helped me if he could, stood by me when I lost the restaurant after the war, and stood by to help raise you, to give you the things that I'd let spill from me down into Teddy's grave.

Poor ol' Duff. He loved my pies and my gravys, all the things his doctor told him he shouldn't eat. Last thing he had fore he got so sick was one of my chocolate cream pies. Probably his doc blames me for his heart givin out.

I think of all I've taken, all I've squandered over the years, and know that at least I was blessed with gifts from all the men in my life. Duff give you to me. Henry give me Teddy. And my daddy give me the bees.

It may be that these things are all in vain; and that our own spiral of light, no less than that of the bees, has been kindled for no other purpose save that of amusing the darkness.

—*from* THE LIFE OF THE BEE
by Maurice Maeterlinck, c. 1901

CHAPTER THIRTY-SIX

Caleb

1956

These were not the words I'd hoped to hear. The woman upstairs dressing herself for Duffy's funeral is my true mother. My father is not the man I wanted to be my father. I hate Gunnar Sorensen, and I hate this woman who sits across the table from me. My grandmother. I want to squash her like we do the old queens when we steal them from the hives. When they have become useless we replace them. Yet I can do nothing to replace her. I can't change who she is, who any of them are, who I am.

"You all right?" she asks.

I look at her. I am frozen. I can think of nothing to say that will erase the hurt, erase her and all she's done to me. Like always, she has taken from me once again. Taken the possibility that I was the one child she wanted to have because I was the result of her

David C. Fickett

love for Duffy. I don't know if I can forgive either of them. My grandmother and my grandfather.

I stand up. I have to leave. Today.

"Wait, Caleb. Don't go," she says. But she is gone to me. In front of me is only a charred crust of a carcass. Clearly I can see the dark, burned, and shriveled muscle that was her heart.

I turn and move toward the door. Briefly I think of the things of mine that I wish to take with me, but they are all somehow connected to her, to this terrible place where I've been their fool.

"I've always loved you," she stands and comes toward me. "Really, I have. I know I don't know how to show it." She touches my shirt sleeve and I pull away. "It was hard convincin' people you was mine, but I did it, cause I wanted you. Edith was too young. Duffy and I wanted you, our own flesh and blood." She sits back down and cries, covering her face. "I love you," she mumbles into her hands.

Love. The word accosts me like a vulgarity, profane and frightening. I quickly open the back door and stumble down the steps. I can think of only causing her pain, of destroying all the things she cares about, her bees, her hens, her tiny castle of weathered shingle with its overgrown fields. But to destroy them would show her that I care too much.

I run to the truck, get in, and start the engine. I will never come back.

The day is sunny with a few light clouds. Indian summer. The warm breeze comes in the truck windows. I see the flaming leaves scorched against the bright blue of the sky. I drive to Gossler's and buy some beer, then head out again, past Duffy's old repair shop, past McGrath's, once my mother's Queen Bee. I head along Route One, racing down the blacktop as if in its unfurled miles ahead I will find a peace. I swill down the first beer.

I drive off into the woods on a side road, then toward Smith Pond. I remember last summer when, at the Blueberry Festival, I had my finger on the trigger of a rifle, ready to kill my own brother. Now, I wish I had. I wish I'd spit in Gunnar's face when he came

310

around the house, demanding to know when Duffy's funeral was, demanding that he should attend. I think about Olaf's quiet tears that night I slept in his bed, another one of Gunnar's victims. Of all of them, Olaf is the only one worth saving.

My family.

My blood.

And then I think of Nora. I must take her from them.

I walk around the shoreline of the pond, drinking, tossing the empties into the water. I lose track of time. I sit against a stump, lean into it, watching the last few bugs of the season flit above the green surface of the pond. I close my eyes.

It must be nearly noon when I wake. I open another beer, my fifth. I fight the need to be with Duffy. But I can't abandon him, even as angry as I am. I get up and pace back and forth around the truck, then kick the door of it as hard as I can, denting it deeply. I get in and drive back onto the main road. I don't head toward home. I know where I have to go.

When I reach the lane that leads to Gunnar's house, I step on the gas and spin up the gravel. I drive faster and faster until I am barreling toward the house. Gunnar is asleep on the porch, in a hammock. He lifts his head as I near and jumps up, hobbles along toward the door, but he doesn't get there in time. His eyes are wide and full of fear. Just as I ram into the post that supports the porch roof, I push the brake to the floor, and the engine dies. The post comes apart, splitting like a pencil, broken in half, and the corner of the roof slowly collapses, fragmenting the beams into swordlike splinters. It tips down toward me, stopping before it hits the hood of the truck.

"What the fuck are you doin'?" Gunnar yells at me.

I get out of the truck and stagger a bit up the steps. I pull back my arm too quickly for him to react. I slam into his face with all the strength I can find. He falls back into a jumble of rusted machine parts and a galvanized pail behind him. I open the screen door and start to go through when Sven comes running down the stairs and stops me with his big meaty hand. He pushes me back. I hit the porch floor on my ass. I stand up quick. I look at Gunnar's bleeding face, his broken nose.

"Jesus Christ," Sven says. "What's this asshole doin'?" He pushes his hand at me again, slamming it into my chest. Gunnar puts his hand on Sven's leg.

"Leave him be," the old man stammers.

"What?" Sven asks, clearly amazed that his father would let someone go who had just hit him.

I hit Sven hard with both hands and push him clear of the doorway. I go inside, slamming the door behind me. Nora is standing in the doorway between the parlor and kitchen. She is wiping her hands on her apron.

"Caleb," she says.

"Get your clothes. You're not staying here," I say. I take hold of her and want to cry. I know if I say one more word I will. My insides are becoming only liquid, jellylike, my skin is the only thing holding me from spilling over Nora's washed floor.

"What are you talking about?" she asks.

"Take her, get the hell out," Gunnar calls from the screen door. Sven is standing behind him, ready to spring into action if his father lets him.

Nora runs upstairs. I feel like I'm going to pass out. I back into a chair and sit down. The tattered upholstery smells of dog, mildew, and ash. I lean my elbows on my knees and cover my face with my hands.

"Go into town, go anywhere," I hear Gunnar say to Sven. Sven swears at his father and then I hear his truck's engine start up. I keep my eyes closed as the screen door slams and Gunnar hobbles across the parlor floor and into the kitchen. I hear running water in the sink and then he moans a few times.

"Didn't think you had the strength in you, to break my fuckin' nose," he says. I look up at him. He's standing at the sink. Even in the short distance between the parlor and the kitchen he appears to me small, shrunken. I never noticed how, as I grew, he became smaller. In the light of my mother's confession, he has become even more insignificant to me than he ever was before. I put my head down again, cradling it in my hands.

I pray that Nora will hurry and I can leave this house for good. As I wait, though, I hear him moving around in the kitchen and then water running again. I look at the floor in front of me and can see his shoes. He's standing there watching me.

"Here boy. Have a drink," he says.

I look up. His face is frightening. Toothless, only red, wet gums. Black hollow holes where eyes should be. Grizzly and pitiful. How could Edith have lived on after he loomed over her, hurting her, forcing her, crumbling her fragile shell, entering her, taking any hopes she may have had with him as he left her crushed and confused? How did she keep from killing him?

"Come on boy, you look like you could use a drink. It's my whisky. You'd like it." He grins at me as he speaks. Of course he's always known I was his. Somewhere along the way he must have seen something in me that was a part of him. Maybe it happened long before that day at the festival when he looked at me in that odd way and Ma noticed too. That day all he may have seen was the anger that proved to him I was his. I will never know. I cannot speak to him.

Nora comes down the stairs with a worn suitcase and a paper bag. I ignore the old man, wondering if I want Nora so badly because she is a valuable possession of his, something of worth that I can take from him. I stand to take the case from her. She looks at Gunnar waiting for him to say or do something but he turns with the whisky in his hands, tips back his head, and drains the glass, then he goes into the kitchen. I take Nora's arm and we walk out of the house.

As I back up the truck, the roof collapses more, until one whole half of it is down, barring the doorway. I turn around and head down the lane to the road.

I realize as Nora and I drive down Route One, that it is time for the funeral. Has Walter found some men to carry the coffin down to the gravesite? Is Ma waiting for me to come back home? Has Ma closed the lid?

I feel wild, out of control. I've no idea what to do next. What is around each corner in the road?

"Caleb, slow down," Nora says as she takes hold of my arm.

I look at her and know that she is seeing much deeper into me than I could ever see. I need to press my head to her breasts, hear her heart and her soothing words.

"Caleb, stop the truck. I won't go anywhere with you if you drive like this." She folds her arms over her chest.

I pull over to the side of the road and stop the truck.

"I need to get out of here. Out of Josiahville," I say. Tears are coming down my face.

She looks at me a long time. She wipes the tears off my cheeks. Then she pulls me down to where I want to be. She is warm. Her heart is racing.

"You can't go anywhere. Today is Duffy's funeral. I want you to go back."

"But I can't. You don't understand."

"I think I understand. What with living with Gunnar and some of the mistakes I've made in the past, I've seen a lot. I've always been around people who don't know that they can make their own choices. I've never had any, not really. I came from dirt and never knew anything else. Until you." She kisses the top of my head. "Whatever has happened to make you so mad at Gunnar, and ready to leave your family, isn't worth running. You'll feel horrible if you don't say good-bye to Duffy."

"How would you know?" I sit up and stare at her.

"I've seen you with Duffy, down at Gossler's and I've heard Gunnar and his sons talking. I know Duffy is like a father to you."

"But he isn't my father," I say and turn my head away from her.

"I know. I've heard Gunnar talking to Erik and Sven."

There are no longer sounds of birds or passing traffic. I hear only the soft hush of the sea, like the inside a shell. I don't remember hearing these things as clearly before.

She is holding me and saying "Shshshshs . . ."

Then I kiss her.

"Aren't you worried about what they'll do to you?" Nora asks. "Gunnar's boys have mean tempers."

"They won't come near us," I say and feel the fury rising in me, almost hoping they will come and try to take her. I want to feel their fists. I turn quickly to Nora and say, "Don't you want to get out of that place? Out of this pathetic town?" I nearly shout. Nora looks surprised. I've kept my temper quiet for too many years like a sleeping lion, and though now I want to roar at the world, I know I won't. I possess the self-control that my half-brothers lack. I won't follow their example again, like I did when I drove into Gunnar's house. I hit the steering wheel over and over until my hands sting.

"Caleb, stop. Stop that," Nora says, taking hold of both my wrists.

"I'm sorry." I look out at the rusty-colored blueberry fields, stretching for at least three acres ahead of us, disappearing over a hill that sets neatly against a cloudless blue sky. It is only that shade of blue in the fall. I start up the engine, turn the truck around, and we drive in silence for awhile.

I drive past the lane to the house. The funeral must be starting, but I can't face Edith and Ma, not right now. I turn in at Duffy's old repair shop and park, turn off the engine. As I sit in the truck, I know Nora is looking at me. I begin to cry. I can't stop myself. My shoulders shake, the sobs rip from my throat. Nora pulls me to her.

And I am caught between the unbearable pain of my mother's deceptions, and the need to be in her arms. The memories that I find frightening to look at, cast their long shadows over me.

I can see a hazy, sunny day when mist rises over the hay fields, a humid fog rolls along toward the tall spruces, giving my world a filmy, translucent sheet to peer through. I am thirteen. I sit on a stump some distance from the house watching as Ma, faded by the haze, hangs clothes out on the line, knowing that the fog will burn off before noon. My jeans, my shirts, her aprons, Duffy's overalls, white, white sheets. This memory is one that surfaces now because of this anger. It tries to cast new light on the pain.

But I can't turn from this moving picture in my head, no matter how frightening it is.

One of the last border collies we ever owned is there with Ma, lying at her feet in the tall grass. He used to follow her everywhere during her day, would sleep on a braided rug in her and Duffy's room, would amble to the mailbox with her, and died at her feet, simply slipping away without a sound, and Ma's strong hand was on his back as she stroked the thing into a peaceful death.

Within this perfect hazy day I feel peace. Duffy works for awhile, tinkering on the tiller in the sun, in front of the barn. He stops and leans against the red shingled barn, on his stool, and smokes. I've no idea what they have between them. I am only a child. Love is taken for granted in childhood. Taken for granted when it is always there, though at times unrecognizable.

Their love was something that had weaved itself into days like those. Some days were good, and yes, I have to admit, even as time went on without Teddy. Ma's grief was rooted to many things, things I never knew, but possibly Teddy's death gave her pain the fodder needed to rise above the soil and grow. Her black moods are things that only now are being given names in textbooks, ailments that are serious and considered by doctors to be treatable. Not that long ago, moods, depressions, anxieties, were thought of as weaknesses, laziness, or liquor induced. But Ma is far from weak, far from lazy, and rarely ever takes a drink.

I remember that particular day only because, as a child of thirteen, I'd become aware of time moving by, and I'd made a mental note to stop and watch what was before me. There were other days like that, ones I've let myself push to the back of my head for fear of finding them too close to the surface of my skin. I've wanted to find fault in Ma and in Duffy. I've wanted to be angry at two people who shouldn't be blamed. They've done their best. Have gone through more than I can imagine to get to the place that is my home. Her story had definitely left its mark on me, but also it has explained so many things about her and about our small universe, our dark and warm hive.

As we drive down the lane toward the house, Nora holds my hand and smiles at me. I don't know how to get through the next few hours but her hands will help me. I don't really know this woman but feel as though in time I can know her. I can love her. And I need to love someone. I know my motives for taking her away from Gunnar have been irrational, selfish, and so obvious to me, I wonder is it obvious to her that I need to have her now? No matter, we will learn about each other, she will adapt to me like a new queen to its hive.

Ma is on the porch in her black dress. Edith supports Ma as they walk down the steps. She looks toward me and waits til I park the truck. It's me she wants to hold her arm as we follow the worn grass to the small group of mourners. I'm not ready to be so close to my mother. It is Nora's arm that I hold. Abel Gossler stands near the casket, playing "Come Homeward Angel" on his violin.

As evening comes I go back to the gravesite. I stand next to the fresh earth. He's down there, never to be seen again, yet his face is so clearly etched into my eyelids, I only have to close them to see him. His easy, confident strength, always taking time for me, like when I needed to learn the game of baseball. He encouraged me to continue practicing when I knew I was horrible.

Without hearing her, I know Ma is standing on the porch in

the dark, Nora is there beside her, standing back a little, hesitant to be there, next to the old queen.

I think of Ma and Duffy. All they must have been to each other, all of their hurt, their suffering, their selfishness. They may have been a near-perfect balance of love and hate, bad and good. I kneel down and look at the earth, trying to hear his voice. The voice that has kept me looking forward into my future and helped me, piece by piece, bit by bit, to build the foundation of my own kingdom. There was no other power like his love.

It is only with his love that I may find the strength to love her.